W9-BKW-707

Praise for the novels of Rosalind Noonan

TAKE ANOTHER LOOK

"Noonan grips readers in this suspenseful novel . . .
worth picking up." —*RT Book Reviews*

AND THEN SHE WAS GONE

"A story of optimism and encouragement, despite the
heart-wrenching subject matter." —*Chatelaine*

ALL SHE EVER WANTED

"Noonan has a knack for page-turners and doesn't
disappoint . . . a readable tale." —*Publishers Weekly*

THE DAUGHTER SHE USED TO BE

"An engrossing family saga and a suspenseful legal thriller.
Noonan covers a lot of narrative ground, with a large cast of
characters whose situations involve morally complex issues,
as well as knotty family dynamics. This novel would fuel
some great book-club discussions." —*Shelf Awareness*

IN A HEARTBEAT

"Complex, intriguing characters and an intensely emotional
plot make *In a Heartbeat* compelling." —*RT Book Reviews*

Please turn the page for more praise for Rosalind Noonan!

ONE SEPTEMBER MORNING

"Written with great insight into military families and the constant struggle between supporting the troops but not the war, Noonan delivers a fast-paced, character-driven tale with a touch of mystery." —*Publishers Weekly*

"Noonan creates a unique thriller that is anti–Iraq War and pro-soldier, a novel that focuses on the toll war takes on returning soldiers and civilians whose loved ones won't be coming home." —*Booklist*

"Reminiscent of Jodi Picoult's kind of tale . . . it's a keeper!" —Lisa Jackson, *New York Times*–bestselling author

PRETTY,
NASTY,
LOVELY

Books by Rosalind Noonan

ONE SEPTEMBER MORNING

IN A HEARTBEAT

THE DAUGHTER SHE USED TO BE

ALL SHE EVER WANTED

AND THEN SHE WAS GONE

TAKE ANOTHER LOOK

DOMESTIC SECRETS

PRETTY, NASTY, LOVELY

SINISTER
(with Lisa Jackson and Nancy Bush)

OMINOUS
(with Lisa Jackson and Nancy Bush)

Published by Kensington Publishing Corporation

PRETTY, NASTY, LOVELY

ROSALIND NOONAN

KENSINGTON BOOKS
www.kensingtonbooks.com

KENSINGTON BOOKS are published by

Kensington Publishing Corp.
119 West 40th Street
New York, NY 10018

All Kensington titles, imprints, and distributed lines are available at special quantity discounts for bulk purchases for sales promotion, premiums, fund-raising, educational, or institutional use.

Special book excerpts or customized printings can also be created to fit specific needs. For details, write or phone the office of the Kensington Sales Manager: Kensington Publishing Corp., 119 West 40th Street, New York, NY 10018. Attn. Sales Department. Phone: 1-800-221-2647.

Kensington and the K logo Reg. U.S. Pat. & TM Off.

eISBN-13: 978-1-4967-0803-8
eISBN-10: 1-4967-0803-2
First Kensington Electronic Edition: September 2017

ISBN-13: 978-1-4967-0802-1
ISBN-10: 1-4967-0802-4
First Kensington Trade Paperback Printing: September 2017

10 9 8 7 6 5 4 3 2 1

Printed in the United States of America

With Alpha love and affection
for my sorority sisters
from our small village at Wagner College
to the international community
of philanthropists

CHAPTER 1

It was over.

It had been a hellish night of blood and pain, but at last, it was done.

With hands clammy from sweat, I reached for the door to the basement lounge known as the "babe cave" and pushed in. In the eerie glow of orange jack-o'-lanterns and Halloween lights, suspicion filled the air as the small group of Theta Pi sisters stopped talking. The Rose Council had assembled, and all eyes were on me.

"You scared the shit out of me." Courtney flopped back against the couch, her hair pale against the brown leather as she adjusted the silver cone cups of her "Material Girl" costume. "For a second I thought you were the cops."

"Don't be paranoid," Tori snapped at her, combing through one of her blue-and-white pom-poms. She had spent the evening dressed as a Dallas Cowboys cheerleader, and it was hard to believe that her hot pants, tiny vest, and boots were still snow white considering the level of partying that must have gone down in the meeting room. "The police are never going to hear about this. Emma will make sure of that." She folded her arms imperiously. "Right, Emma?"

Tori's words were thick with accusation.

I nodded, struggling to swallow the bitter regret that clung to the back of my tongue. My eyes burned and every muscle in my body ached. How had I fallen into this? My evening plans for a costume party with dance music, pumpkin shooters, and drinking games had given way to a night of screaming and cursing, crying, and . . . and all that blood. I hadn't expected that.

"I have to go back to my room." What time was it? In the red haze of agony, I'd lost track of everything. The muted light peeking through the edges of the curtains on the small windows told me it was morning, and I knew I had a quiz and an assignment due, if I even made it to class. Right now even my most difficult sophomore classes seemed like trite indulgences compared to the trauma of the night.

But we had survived, my sisters and I. Every bone in my body ached and my muscles were screaming, but I had made it through the night. Now my body desperately craved sleep and solitude. "I'll see you guys later."

"Emma, wait." Tori was suddenly at my side, guiding me back into the room. "Come. Sit."

They sat me on a folding chair used for meetings, the bony chair strategically placed in front of the flat-screen TV. The hot seat. Although the sun had risen outside, the curtains were closed, and the only light came from Halloween decorations and candles.

Ritual candles, I realized. Who had gotten these out? The glow of votive candles cast peculiar shadows on the girls' faces as they, the Rose Council of Theta Pi, sat facing me. Someone handed me a white taper.

The candle of truth.

My throat felt raw and dry as I squinted through the flickering candlelight, trying to find the door behind the pretty faces marred by scowls. Although Lydia's vampire-dark hair fell over her eyes, I could feel the hot mess of emotion there. That girl was on fire. Or maybe the image of fire came from the red satin cape she wore—my Red Riding Hood costume. Had she stolen it, or had she asked to borrow it during the chaos of the night?

I couldn't remember.

Tori's beautiful mouth was a fierce slash of disapproval as she set her shimmering pom-poms in her lap. Courtney echoed the stern look just as she mimicked everything Tori did, same leg crossed, hands on hips, shoulders raised in that camera-ready pose.

And Violet, looking delicate and leggy in a fringed, beaded flapper costume, showered me with thick pity. "Bless your heart, but you're a mess." Hers was the voice of our rituals: soft, with a Southern lilt and firm backbone that shut down argument. "First of all, no one can ever know about this. Now we're all going to swear an oath of silence. Swear on our loyalty and love to the sisters of Theta Pi."

We all pledged secrecy, but I was the one holding the candle of truth. The vow would burn deep. "Can I go now?" I felt like a heap of sodden laundry, wrung out and abandoned when the owner found that all the dorm dryers were full. I was so exhausted I was beyond caring about the festivities that I'd missed tonight. "I'm so tired."

"Don't you think we're tired, too?" There was condemnation in Lydia's voice, stern and imperious, as she flipped up the red hood of the cape and scowled at me.

I wished I could simply rise from the center of the circle and slip out. Vanish in a curl of smoke beneath the door frame. Escape seemed so simple, but appearances were deceiving. Reality was twisted and thorny and complicated, and it kept me in that chair.

Now I belonged in this ring of fire. I had pledged this sorority, vowing to remain loyal and true forever. As the song said, *I'm Theta born. Theta bred. And when I die, I'll be Theta dead.*

Death seemed like a restful option.

"I really have to go." I handed the candle to Courtney, who blew it out and plunked it on the table without hesitation.

"Poor baby," Tori cooed, with half-closed eyes that twinkled with blue glitter shadow. She looked way too good to have stayed up all night long. Had she sneaked off for a nap in the middle of everything? "You need rest. But before you go to beddy-bye, tell us, what did you do with . . . *it*."

I squinted. "What are you talking about?"

"You know." Courtney leaned closer, wincing. "The body."

Those two words stole away my last ounce of energy and hope. This night had been the worst of my life, and it refused to end. "I didn't . . ." I shook my head, not wanting to think about it anymore. "I left her there." I pointed toward the room where I'd left the body wrapped in towels and tucked into a laundry basket, as if she were asleep. She had seemed too peaceful to move.

"Wait." Courtney's mouth dropped open. "You left it in the suite? That's disgusting!"

Violet was shaking her head and Tori was getting all puffed up with indignation. "That cannot happen," Tori said. "What if Ol' Jan sees?"

"She's not going in there." Our housemother wasn't in the habit of barging into girls' rooms.

Violet stared as if seeing me for the first time. "Bless your heart, I don't think you get the enormity of the situation. Look at me, Emma. Sweet pea, you've got to get rid of it."

A wave of emotion crashed over me and I had to bite my lower lip to hold back the tears that formed when I thought of the baby—so tiny, with velvet mini-fingers—wrapped up in fluffy towels like Itsy, the doll I used to bathe when I was seven. "I couldn't move her. She seemed so peaceful."

"Oh, no. No, no. We will *not* have that *thing* found in Theta House." Suddenly, Tori stood beside me, hustling me to my feet. "You need to get it out of here. Pronto."

"I can't." I knew the baby couldn't stay here, but I couldn't bring myself to touch her again. "I can't do this. Get someone else."

"Like who?" Lydia chimed in, her dark gaze fixing on me like a leech. "Who wants to get stuck with that?"

I stared back at them, wanting to shrink away and disappear. After all I'd been through, how could they expect me to handle this horrible task? "Why are you ganging up on me?"

Violet gave a whimper of a sigh as she adjusted the skinny strings of her spangled dress. "Bless your heart. We're just trying to help you."

"You're not thinking clearly," Tori said.

That part was true. I was a hot mess.

Tori forged on. "We have bent over backward to help you. We're like all 'Go, Emma!'" she said, jiggling one pom-pom in the air. "But we can only do so much, and what would be the point of us jumping in to finish off what you started? You created this mess for yourself, and it's your responsibility to clean it up. Get that body out of here. Now. Put it in a shopping bag or hide it in your laundry bag and toss it in a hole. Bury it deep or throw it in the ravine. I don't care, as long as you get it out of here."

It was a *her*. Didn't they get that? And she was a living being. Well, she had been living a few minutes ago.

I was crying now. Silent tears, though I could feel my mouth crumpling in that pathetic frown that, Violet insisted, caused creases. "I can't do this," I murmured. "I can't."

"You can," Tori said steadily, "and you will."

"I can't even . . ." I shuddered, hot and cold and dizzy at the same time. "Why do I have to do this?"

"Silly boo." Tori granted me a condescending smile, her teeth super white against her tanned skin. She leaned so close I could feel the heat from her body. "You know this is the consequence of your actions. This is what happens when you kill your baby."

CHAPTER 2

Eyes shut, Rory MacFarlane let his mind rise above the earth as he lingered in a meditative, foggy state. Slightly groggy, intensely happy. He could feel that the back of his jeans was getting wet. Cold, too. November chill, not snow chill. But that didn't matter in the cerebral, honeyed glaze that bathed his soul.

If anything, the sensation amplified the sensory experience. Cold and hot, dark and light, yin and yang. Opposites and contrasts layered upon each other, swirling in one universe.

He smiled. At least his upper body was comfortable and dry in his Omni-Heat jacket, his head topped by a wool beanie. But his fingers rooted in something cold and damp.

Grass. Grass? Ha ha, not that kind. Real grass on the ground.

Slogging through the mist in his mind, he opened his eyes and realized he was lying on a patch of damp grass. Spread-eagle. Somewhere on campus.

"What the hell?"

"I know. Really skank." Adam was hunkered down beside him, arms slung around his knees, all loose limbed and sleepy eyed. No sign of the joint they'd smoked, but Adam was too cautious to leave any evidence in sight. He was premed, needed to keep a clean record. Even in Oregon, where weed was legal, you could get jammed up for life if you were under twenty-one.

"I'm all wet." Mustering the energy before it rolled away, Rory pushed himself up from the earth and slouched forward. He recognized the flat grassy knoll, park benches, and statue of Benjamin Merriwether at the edge of the clearing. Top of the World. People came to this campus hilltop to play Frisbee, picnic, stargaze, and smoke. "Did I fall asleep?"

"I don't know. Did you?" Adam had a habit of repeating things when he was totally baked.

Rory dug in his pocket to make sure his cell phone was there. Yeah. The time glowed in bold white numbers against the dark screen saver of Rory's graphic art: 1:43 a.m. But then it had been late when they'd headed out of the fraternity lounge, looking for fresh air and a break from the drone of normal. They were into the November crunch, the last gasp of the term before Thanksgiving sent them into preparation for finals. Rory had been studying for an economics test, trying to digest Keynesianism and macroeconomics while his brothers watched a late-night talk show, battled in a video game, and played cards. That was the curse of growing up in a large family: Rory needed ambient noise to feel at home. He studied best when a wall of sound freed his mind from present surroundings, but after a few hours, no matter what the content, the brain shut down.

He'd hit saturation when Adam cut out of the card game, looking for someone to kick it with. They had left Greek Row and headed across the bridge, away from the security guards who occasionally patrolled the residential areas at night. Although it had rained earlier, the sky was dark and clear now, a black ceiling over the silent campus. They had passed a stoned-looking couple and a family of deer that had stared at them from the bushes near Chambers Hall. The guys had walked right past and climbed the hill.

Now Rory was good and buzzed and tired, ready to crash. His mind was crammed with all the information it could take. He needed sleep, then coffee, then an hour and a half to spit out everything he'd devoured on the weekly economics quiz.

"You ready?" Rory stood up, swiping at the seat of his jeans.

"Yeah. Let's head back." Adam drew himself up slowly and

took a few careful steps across the lawn. He moved in slow motion; Rory probably did, too, but there was no way to see himself. Sometimes when he was high he imagined himself hovering above it all, watching his body move and cataloging the words that came out of his mouth, as if they snapped into written dialogue bubbles in the air. Yeah, that was cool.

They crossed the lawn, pausing at the edge of the hilltop to take in the towers and lights of the north campus that filled the panorama below.

"Top of the World. You see that?" Rory said. "We're lucky."

On their left were the majestic peaks of Chambers Hall, and straight ahead were the rectangular towers of the North Campus Bridge, an ugly suspension bridge that served the campus well. Across the darkened ravine were the houses of Greek Row, the Craftsman-style structures from the old Merriwether estate. Beyond that were modern, square boxes of glass—university buildings that dotted the distant hillside. The darkness between buildings consisted of green things—boxwood hedges, jasmine bushes, tall cedars, and Douglas fir trees, some of them hundreds of years old.

The Merriwether campus was a balance of nature and architecture that seemed museum-like to Rory at times. His friends from home couldn't believe it when he posted photos on Instagram. It was so picture-perfect he half expected a camera dolly to swoop down on the old mansions on Greek Row or the bridge over the falls or the windows of the old buildings sparkling like diamonds in the sunset.

"Amazing," Rory said aloud.

"What?"

"Where we live, dude. It's a beautiful patch of the planet."

"That it is."

Right now the campus was still and dark, like a model train village with the low-wattage lights twinkling. Even in the vise grip of pressure, Rory could still recognize the natural beauty that surrounded him. He wasn't one of those ungrateful morons who trashed the place and then flunked out mid-semester.

Something sounded from the direction of the ravine, like the harsh cry of a crow.

"What was that?" Adam's eyes grew round.

"Someone on the bridge?" Focus narrowing, he squinted toward the flicker, an object moving in front of one of the bridge lights.

A large bird? Something flapping near the deck of the bridge.

No, not a bird. A person.

The breath left Rory's lungs as the small commands were barked in the air. A girl was mad at someone. Who? No one answered. The only voice was hers, lashing the air. Was she talking on a cell phone? "You promised. You *promised*." The words traveled through the emptiness over the ravine, as if amplified by the surface of the water.

"Did you hear that?" Adam asked.

Rory lifted one hand to shut his friend up, and Adam hunched his shoulders as they listened. She was raging now. Growling. She was pissed, but her words were muddled.

Adam's face went pale. "Is she going to jump?"

"She's probably thinking about it." A sudden rush of adrenaline told him this was the real deal. Shit. Alarm shivered up his spine, but it would be hard to shake the buzz.

"We need to stop her," Adam said, voicing the obvious.

Rory stared hard, wishing he could close the distance between himself and the distraught girl. He wanted to fly through the night like some superhero, be on the bridge now, hold her back. Sure, he could run to her, but that would take precious minutes, far from an instant intervention.

Something moved again on the deck of the bridge. A large bird flapping its wings in front of the dull amber light.

"She's pacing," Rory observed. "She's on the edge." Stalling? A rumbling of hope in Rory's gut urged him forward. Maybe he could get to her, talk with her. "But I don't hear her crying anymore."

"Is that a good sign?" Adam asked. "Do you think she—"

Rory was already running, tearing down the hill, legs pumping like pistons as though someone's life depended on him to rescue them. With each breathless stride he pushed himself harder.

Get there. Get there. Get there.

He raced ahead frantically, knowing that, by all standards of logic, it was probably too late. Too late, but he had to try.

CHAPTER 3

On our campus, when the lights of emergency vehicles flashed over the landscape from the access road leading down to the ravine, it meant only one thing.

"Another suicide." Angela Newton squeezed the straps of her backpack as dismay shadowed her beautiful light-brown face. "There's an ambulance down there now, and look at all the searchers. You were right. They think someone jumped."

Earlier, as we'd walked to our Monday morning class, we'd seen some orange traffic cones and yellow caution tape roping off a small section of railing at the center of the bridge. Angela had thought maybe they were going to do repairs, but that sick feeling in my stomach didn't ease as I spied the sheriff's SUV near the bridge and a second police vehicle on the access road to the ravine. Cops did not come out for bridge repairs.

While we'd been in class, the small police presence had blossomed into a full-blown crime scene with flashing lights, rescue crews, and spectators. Now I knew my instincts had been dead on. Someone had jumped from the cordoned-off spot on the bridge.

We stopped at a juncture in the footpath to stare at the panorama. Students stood three deep on the North Campus Bridge, while college staff, cops, and paramedics lined the street. Across the ravine, on the flattest treeless portion of the riverside drive, two media vans sat with their antennae projecting up toward the sky. This portion of the picturesque river canyon that crisscrossed our campus—a tear in the land filled with rock, trees, and a few spectacular waterfalls—was now overrun with invaders, rescue workers in shrill orange vests who dotted the landscape.

This was not going to end well; it never did.

I glanced behind me, wishing I could return to the nineteenth-century cafés of Manet or the amazing dotted landscapes of Seurat. Someone else's life, some other time and place. But no. The lift I'd gotten from viewing slides of colorful impressionist paintings in art class began to drain away, giving way to the chilly November morning. A shudder rippled through me. When I'd awakened that morning my most pressing issue had been trying to avoid my former boyfriend at an upcoming party that his frat was throwing. That seemed so junior high compared to this.

"How do you think they found out this time?" Angela asked.

"Usually someone sees something in the river." The splash of bright color in the river that turned out to be a jacket. The doughy raft of a floating body. "Unless the jumper leaves something behind on the bridge. The guy that jumped from the Stone Bridge left a pile of neatly folded clothes on the bridge wall." I would never forget the photos of his clothes folded beside a coiled belt and running shoes lined up like two sleeping cats on the bridge. Like a monument to everyday life. Maybe it was freaky, but I had studied those things in newspapers and online articles. Images and details. I needed to know the truth, the awful facts, before I could let it go.

I thought of the police tape on the bridge this morning. "The jumper probably left something behind on the bridge. That's probably why it was marked off this morning."

"That's right. Maybe it was a suicide note." Angela coiled a braid around two fingers. "Most of them leave a suicide note, right?"

"Notes are found in only a small percentage of suicides. Something like one out of six." She was asking me because I was a nursing major and my sisters thought I was their resident expert on all things medical and psychological. While I was getting pretty good at articulating muscles in the cadavers we dissected in the lab, my knowledge of suicide came from my own research. I'd been somewhat obsessed since the crash that killed my mother and sister. "The cops didn't find notes for the three suicides on campus this year," I added.

"That seems so sad," Angela said forlornly. "To kill yourself and not leave behind a hint of what was bothering you."

"It's always sad," I said as we stared down at the rescue workers. A slight man wearing an orange vest and skullcap was raking through the tall weeds in the riverbed with a heavy white object like a giant comb attached to two ropes. What would he find there? A wallet? Some discarded condoms and cigarette butts? Or worse. I imagined the giant comb making a dull thudding sound as it hooked on a body. "I can't watch this."

"Oh my God." Angela grabbed at the sleeve of my denim jacket. "Those are divers in the river. They must have seen something. Oh, for sure there's a body in the water. I can't deal with this shit." She let out a breath. "Do you think it's the real deal?"

"Looks like it," I said, feeling myself withdraw from the cool November morning.

That familiar defense system rose within me as I braced myself for the inevitable bad news and sorrow that would sweep through the campus. Steel doors slammed shut as the cold front settled in my heart. The news would be tolerated in public, tamped down until a later time when I could panic in private.

"Why does this keep happening here?" Angela asked. "This is how many this year?"

"This will be the sixth since January. The thirteenth in two years."

"Unlucky thirteen." Angela tugged on her braids again. "We're living in Suicide Central."

"Not according to statistics, though it feels that way." I turned away from the river, trying to regain equilibrium by staring at the staunch concrete towers of Chambers Hall. I had read that the number of suicides at Merriwether was on par with other universities of its size with approximately 12,000 students. The thing that made it so obvious on our campus was the method, using one of the five bridges to launch into the afterlife. When someone jumped from a bridge, their death was more of a spectacle than someone who overdosed or slashed their wrists on another campus.

"When I toured this campus with my parents, we thought the river running through it was spectacular, like some western resort," Angela said. "We didn't know about the suicide problem. I guess that's a good thing. My parents probably would have sent me somewhere else. That would have sucked."

"I can't imagine being here without you, boo."

Angela was probably my best friend in Theta Pi. There'd been an instant bond during rush, helped along by the fact that neither of us were really classic fits for sorority or Merriwether culture and we both desperately wanted to fit in. Unlike the average upper-middle-class Merriwether student, I was the daughter of a poor musician, working my butt off in the nursing program, making ends meet with a scholarship and the savings of two jobs I'd held down during a gap year. After losing my only sister and moving a lot in high school, I wanted a place I could call home for four years.

Angela had been drawn here by her boyfriend, Darnell, a center on the basketball team, after she realized that her "mixed race" status brought her a chilly reception at most of the colleges on her wish list. Even here at Merriwether, a female student had sized her up at orientation and asked, "What are you, exactly?" And Angela had answered, "Um, a person?" Half Iranian and half African American, she had a dark, exotic mystery about her that made some people stare in curiosity. I thought it was kind of cool to turn heads, but sometimes she got annoyed and sneered the gawkers away.

We were staring into the gorge, where two boats were churning through the water and a group of the searchers had been signaled to come over to the riverside. If they found something,

I didn't want to be around to watch. Vivid images like that were hard for me to shake; I knew that much about myself.

"Looks serious down there." I turned away. "I can't. I don't want to be part of the sick audience." I kept my gaze straight ahead on the bridge brimming with people who'd come out to watch the recovery effort. We had just left our Visual Arts class—an early-morning hassle, but an easy A if you made it to class—and the best way back to Theta House was over the North Bridge. "Look at the crowd. Think we can push past those rubberneckers? I need to get home and grab my Psych notebook."

"They'll let us through. They'd better, 'cause I gotta pee in the worst way." Angela grabbed my upper arm and guided me forward. "Let's do this with Theta Pi charm and grace."

We walked up the approach, passing a sign that read THERE IS HOPE, MAKE THE CALL. A number for free counseling was listed, but we had learned that there were serious consequences to reaching out to campus counselors. Proof that nothing in life was really free.

Angela and I stayed close and tried not to engage the watchers crowding the rail in their fleece jackets, hoodies, or quilted vests. I held my breath, trying to stay away from the drama of the scene, but there was no avoiding their comments on the activity below, which seemed to pick up as we reached the middle of the bridge.

"Did you see that? All that long hair. It's a girl." The male voice could have been calling a basketball game.

"Could be a dude with long hair."

"No dude wears that shade of pink. What's it called? Magenta?"

"Crawl out of your cave, man. I'm a dude and I love pink."

"You're full of it."

So they thought it was a girl wearing pink? I shivered, hoping I didn't know her. Even the suicide of a total stranger was going to be upsetting; I knew the ripple effects of a tragedy, the mothers, fathers, sisters, and friends who ached in grief as they fumbled through a world of loss. I'd been twelve when my mom and sister, Delilah, had been killed in a car crash that left me unscathed; I understood how the tragedy of a few seconds could impact the rest of your life.

"Oh my God. The divers are pulling up a body. Look! Over there."

Exactly what I did not need to see.

Beside me, Angela squeezed my arm. "I just wanna cry," she whispered so that only I could hear.

"I know. Just keep moving."

My own instructions slipped away the minute we saw them facing the river, the Greek letters Theta Pi embossed on the back of a few jackets. From the long hair sweeping over their shoulders it was hard to identify individual sisters at first, but I recognized the two blondes. Our president Tori Winchester stood at the railing in her swaggering pose, hand on one hip, while Courtney hovered nearby, shifting from foot to foot. As always, Tori was model perfect, her bomber jacket pulled tight above the swell of her rump shown off in tight blue jeans over shit-kicking western boots. Two other dark-haired sisters stood close, hugging each other, but I didn't recognize them from behind.

"There's our girls," Angela said, slowing down and calling to them.

The minute they turned toward us, I could tell something was very wrong. Everyone had been crying, eyes watery, noses pink. Even Courtney, one of the toughest nuts to crack, was crying. The dark-haired girls, Mia and Megan, seemed to be holding each other up, one sob away from total collapse. Only Tori remained calm and distant, though she was squinting at us fiercely, as if bracing herself against a storm that couldn't be avoided.

"What's going on?" I asked.

"The body." Tori gestured over her shoulder. "The cops think it's Lydia."

Lydia? The slow-talking, self-absorbed rock of a girl seemed like the last person who would jump.

Angela held up her hands in disbelief. "Are you shitting me?"

"She was gone this morning when I woke up." Courtney swiped at her red nose with one sleeve. "I thought that maybe, finally, she had snapped out of her thing and gone to class. But when I called her cell, a man answered. It was a cop. He said they found her phone on the bridge last night, and..." Her voice broke as a tear rolled down her cheek.

"But it could be a mistake," I said. "Maybe she left her phone on the bridge and—"

"Denial runs deep," Tori said coldly. She never hesitated to interrupt. "Some guys saw her. They saw her jump."

"What?" Angela sounded skeptical. "Why didn't they stop her?"

"They tried. Said they couldn't get to her in time." Tori cocked her head to one side, her thick, pouting lips worthy of an advertisement for BOTOX. "It's so sad."

Tori didn't seem sad at all, but she knew it was the right thing to say. There is a word for people who don't feel empathy for others, and in the year I'd known Tori, I'd come to see her as the face you should find next to a textbook definition of *sociopath*. A harmless one, but still, not nice.

"Who were the guys?" I asked. "Do we know them?"

"Two Omega Phis," Courtney said. "Rory MacFarlane, and that Adam kid with the glasses."

Of course she remembered Rory's full name. He was one of those good-looking slacker guys who made you feel like his best friend when you talked to him. His near miss for a medal in snowboarding at the last Winter Olympics made him something of a celebrity on campus.

"Rory MacFarlane," I said. "Lydia would have loved to see him rushing to rescue her."

I closed my eyes against the image of a solitary figure on the bridge, an indigo sky behind her as she leaned forward and fell to the earth in a graceful swan dive. Or had it been awkward and ugly? Her arms flailing, legs kicking to try and stop the inevitable.

A knot was growing in my throat, threatening to choke me. *Don't panic now. Take deep breaths. Stay on solid ground.* I imagined a brick inside me, solid and heavy as Tori's heart. I was not going to fall apart here. I was going to be strong. A brick.

"I still can't believe it," Angela said.

"Shit happens," Tori said softly, as if soothing a child. "Mrs. J is down there with the rescue team."

"Identifying the body," Megan said breathlessly. "Poor Lydia."

Tears glistened in Mia's eyes as Megan supported her with one arm. "We couldn't see her face, but her black hair was all stringy when they pulled her out of the water, and—and—"

"Shut up! Just . . . stop," I said, cutting off the description, which was already bringing up a graphic image I didn't want in my head.

"We offer the family members a look at their loved ones before burial," the funeral director said. "Sometimes it helps with the grieving process."

"I think we should," Dad said.

No, no, no.

But he pushed, and I caught a glimpse of my mother that overshadowed my memories of her life. When it came time to view my sister, I left the room.

This time I wouldn't have to look.

Still, trauma flared, a wound quickly reopened. How easy it was to go there again. I tamped down the tremors of panic, struggling to keep my breath even, trying to rein in my accelerating pulse.

"We didn't come here to gawk," Angela said pointedly. "We had a class in Chambers Hall."

"She looked so bloated. Like maybe she binged on Ben and Jerry's and nachos." Megan's face puckered. "Lydia would hate having people see her that way, and look at all the guys who are watching. She'd be so mortified."

We gave a sideways glance at the students on the bridge—mostly guys, but some girls, too. They were in that odd state of wonder that overcomes people at accident scenes. Any minute now people would start talking about their individual connections to Lydia, pooling tips about what they knew of her.

At last, Lydia was getting the attention she'd always craved.

I had known Lydia Drakos for more than a year, having met her when I was a freshman rushee and she a junior. Despite some personal interactions, Lydia was still a cardboard-cutout character to me—a Barbie doll in search of her Ken. She was all smug smile and milky white skin, a flirtatious girl who had plenty of dates but no long-term boyfriends. Occasionally, she had mooned over a childhood sweetheart and a frat guy who broke her heart last year, but I think she had impossibly high standards that no human being could fulfill. And the stories... Lydia was full of them. Stories of boarding school, of the proper way she had been raised by nannies and kindly aunts, of the shipping business that had made her grandfather a billionaire, of the family-owned island off the coast of Greece where she basked in luxury every summer. How she loved her nannies but regretted the way her parents foisted her off so they could host amazing parties and sail on their yacht. Maybe I doubted her because she never invited anyone to go along to Greece the way Tori invited the Rose Council girls to her parents' house in Cabo or as Tamara had hosted the entire sorority at her family's lakeside mansion in Coeur d'Alene. Or maybe it was because this granddaughter of a Greek tycoon had the wardrobe of a runaway nun, tending toward black and navy T-shirts and cable-knit sweaters. Some of her recent actions had cast serious doubt on her claim of family wealth, though I couldn't be completely sure. You could spend three days straight with her and still not understand what made her shadowed heart tick. Lydia and I were bound to sisterhood and secrecy, but I had felt more like her slave than her friend.

Angela nudged my arm, jarring me back to the moment. "I gotta go. I'm gonna burst."

I was equally desperate to escape. The flashing lights of emergency vehicles, the ogling crowd, the workers scuttling in the gorge below us to remove human remains ... the whole sickening process knocked the wind out of me. Once you've been on the receiving end of a trauma, the curiosity and excitement of accident scenes give way to panic.

"We'll see you guys back at Theta House," I said, stepping away from the group.

"Seriously? You're leaving?" Courtney called after us. "They might want you to help identify her."

I knew from experience that they would call in the family for that task. Pretending that I didn't hear her, I lifted my hand in a wave as we headed off.

"I feel sick, but I'm not gonna lie. I wasn't a fan of Lydia Drakos," Angela said as we made our way down the stairs at the end of the bridge. "But I don't wish that on anybody."

"We should have known. We should have stopped her." *I should have stopped her.* I had witnessed Lydia's unraveling when she'd pulled me closer these last few weeks. Not close like a friend. I had been hooked, netted, and dragged along in Lydia's boat.

"It's not that simple, Em." Angela's voice was sympathetic. "We're sisters, not keepers. You know the Theta Pi creed: Freedom to Unify."

"Still, I've got the guilts. My heart hurts."

"There's gonna be a lot of that going around." Angela grabbed at a handful of dark braids and twirled them around one finger. I recognized the nervous gesture. She didn't usually mess with her hair once it was done. It was currently wound into dozens of braids, swept back with a fake braided hairband that looked totally real. She had amazing hair, but as her roommate I had seen firsthand how much time she put into getting it just right. Our recruitment chair, Violet Sweetwater, the hair and fashion cop of Theta Pi, should have been pleased, but she never gave Angela the credit she deserved. Vi was always sending out e-mails about how it's forbidden to wear open-toed shoes if you need a pedicure, how bra straps should never show, how anyone caught biting their nails would be given extra cleanup duty at the house.

Although I rarely polished my toenails and frequently bit

my fingernails, I somehow flew under Violet's radar. With ordinary brown hair, shoulders that were too broad, and a chest that was too flat, I think my averageness helped me to roam with the pack, unnoticed. Or maybe my eyes made up for those other deficits. Electric-blue eyes. People are charmed by blue eyes, as if something magical were going on behind them, and I wasn't going to be the one to debunk the myth.

We rounded the stone posts at the bottom of the stairs and headed down the river path leading to west campus. The twin gables of Theta House beckoned from between tall fir trees framing the Tudor-style house that had been home to our sorority for more than sixty years. Ours was the closest residence to the Stone Bridge.

I stared at the paving-stone path. "She would have walked this way to the bridge."

"Late last night, or early this morning, so no one would see her."

"No one to stop her." I imagined a figure huddled in a cotton-candy-pink robe on the rail of the bridge. "They found something pink in the water. It's that damned robe she never took off."

"What do you want to bet she walked out of the house in that thing? Walked straight to the bridge in her pajamas and jumped."

"In a total daze."

"Do you think she was on drugs?"

"Not Lydia." Depression seemed far more potent than any drug.

Angela shrugged. "Well, if that's really Lydia down there, get ready for a shit show of fake tears and stories that cover up the fact that she was a mean, bossy bitch. I almost stopped pledging because of her. She was the one who tortured our pledge class every time National turned their heads." National was the name for Theta Pi headquarters in Des Moines, where dues were collected, standards were enforced, and networking activities were staged. "Honestly?" Angela added. "Nobody liked Lydia."

"I know, but still . . ." Everything Angela said was true, but it was small stuff compared to Lydia dying. "All her annoying qualities don't add up to this. We should have stopped her."

"She wasn't our friend."

"She was our sister," I said, "and we knew she was in a bad place in the past few weeks. Sleeping all the time and sitting in the dark. Always in that robe." A chill traveled through me.

"That fucking pink robe." Angela let out a huff of air. "At first, I was a little glad to see that the mighty Lydia had fallen, but she was such a pathetic mess, and pity just made me hate her more. She was a wreck, but what were we supposed to do?"

The obvious answer would have been to get her help, but reaching out for crisis intervention on the Merriwether campus was no longer an option. After the rash of suicides in the spring, the administration had changed the policies in the student clinic. Under the guise of "early suicide intervention," the counselors now treated every panic attack and bout of depression like full-blown mental illness. Show up at the center with the smallest concern and they'd strap you to a gurney, cart you out in an ambulance, and badger you to sign papers of withdrawal from the university as they wheeled you out.

This had happened to one of our sisters, a freshman from the spring pledge class who had been in the Merriwether honors program. A smart, fragile girl with blond curls, sweet as a baby chick, Lexi had gone into the clinic to talk about her exam anxiety and she had never returned. As soon as the counselor got a whiff of suicide, Lexi was carted off to a loony bin. After taking her finals online in the psych ward at Portland General, she had been forced to withdraw from the school.

It turned out she signed a form when she was freaking out in the counseling center, signed it without realizing what it said. She'd been kicked out, just like that.

And she wasn't the only one. My friends and I had heard about girls in other sororities, kids in other classes who had gotten the boot once they went to the counseling center for help. The process was always the same. Someone would go in to talk about stress or anxiety, they would mention suicide or the desire to cut, and just like that their counseling session turned into a deportation. Within an hour they were strapped onto stretchers and sent to the psych ward in Portland.

Although the university was insisting that their more "stringent policies" were saving lives, some of us realized that Merriwether was dumping at-risk kids to save their stats and look better on paper. It was totally fucked up, but when the student council asked the administration about it, they said they weren't allowed to discuss students' medical profiles.

Having watched Lexi disappear, the girls of Theta Pi were wary. So when Lydia had begun to unravel earlier this month, we knew she couldn't go to the student clinic. But we didn't know where else to take her.

So she stayed in Theta House. She stayed in that fuzzy pink robe and spent most of her time in the suite she shared with Courtney.

Until last night.

The windows of Theta House reflected the silver sky, giving a pallid look to the old mansion. It was the first time in my year and a half on campus that I'd sensed a gray gloom hanging over the old house.

I pressed a hot hand to one icy cheek. My body temperature was all out of whack. "I feel like nothing is ever going to be right again."

"We'll get through this," Angela said. "But right now I'm pissed at Lydia."

CHAPTER 4

Unbuttoning her raincoat, Dr. Sydney Cho approached the mullioned windows of the old admin building, keeping a respectful distance from the university president, who unnerved her under the best of circumstances, and the board member who always seemed to be a breath away from asking her out. The president's office afforded a fine view of the usually breathtaking ravine below. The two men watched the police activity intently, as if overseeing a surgical procedure. Although the details of the search in the gorge were blurred, Sydney focused on the flashing light of the ambulance as it made its way up the access road of the ravine, carrying the body off to the medical examiner. An autopsy was a standard procedure for a suspected suicide. A procedure Sydney now knew all too well.

She wanted to be down there on the scene, not just to escort the police but to provide a presence, to let the students know that the administrators weren't hiding in their ivory towers in the wake of tragedy. When she had taken this job, she'd vowed to make her office accessible to students, and that meant being out on campus. But when the president of the university summoned her to his office, she got there, quickly.

"The housemother, Jan Johnson, has identified the body as one of her residents, Lydia Drakos, and that matches the cell phone left on the bridge," Sydney said as she slipped off her raincoat. It was warm in here, and she would have liked to remove her blazer, too, but wanted to maintain a professional appearance, as well as a sense of boundary for Wendell. "Of course, we've notified the family, and I'll continue to work with the police."

Dr. Martin Salerno spoke in hushed gray tones that were far more menacing than any parent's stern reproach. "It's unacceptable. A disgrace for the university, another black mark on our record. And God knows, our *U.S. World and News Report* rating is going to be shot to hell." With his spidery gray brows and gritty voice, Salerno always reminded her of a cold-blooded creature that had slithered out of the old crypt under Chambers Hall.

"Fortunately, we score so well in other categories, our overall rating won't be affected," Sydney said, not as an excuse but as a way to temper the situation. Her boss tended toward doomsday scenarios.

"Merriwether's reputation for excellence won't be harmed by something like this," Harry Wendell agreed, giving her a smile of support. His pale blue eyes might have been attractive if they weren't always staring at Sydney's chest. As if she were teasing him with her blazer, scarf, and buttoned-up blouse. Or perhaps he was simply enticed by the mystery of wondering what was inside the package. In the few months since her appointment, Sydney had been able to rely on Wendell for support, even if it was for all the wrong reasons. "Let's not overexaggerate the consequences, Martin. Don't make this a thing."

"Hyperbole is not my *thing*," Salerno said in a blistering, low voice.

"I didn't say that, Martin, but there's a way to navigate this judiciously." Wendell held up one hand defensively. "Let's not make a scandal where none exists."

"Believe me, I would love to let this go." Salerno tucked his chin, as if he were a turtle retracting his leathery head into his shell. "But I get flak from our alumni every day. Famous graduates. Politicians and CEOs. Playwrights and doctors. They all want to know what we're doing to address the problem. I have responded that we hired you—" He wheeled around, latching his gaze on to Sydney. "A young person who appeals to our youth, a dean with a plan to remove suicide liabilities from the campus. I keep blowing your horn, Dean Cho, but quite frankly, I'm running out of hot air."

The image of old man Salerno pumped up like a Thanksgiving parade float made for an awkward moment, and she turned away from the window to hide a smirk. "We have a plan in place," she said, "but the culture of a campus does not change overnight. It will take time for troubled students to find their way to counseling, and we haven't completed the curriculum for our stress-management program." The new program, a requirement for next year's incoming freshmen, would address stress, depression, and anxiety and offer advice on coping strategies.

"When will that curriculum be ready?" asked Salerno.

"It should be ready for review soon. We'll have a final version completed before next fall's orientation session."

Salerno grunted. "Doesn't help us now."

"These things take time," Wendell said. "We invested in this strategy knowing that it was long-term."

"While I can peddle that off to the alumni, the local media will counter with the obvious. What have we done to help students like the one who just jumped? Doesn't every life matter?"

"Every life is vital. Of course each person matters." Sydney knew that more than anyone here, but this was no time to spill her story. "I share your frustration, Dr. Salerno." She kept her voice level as she thought of the recovery effort she'd witnessed in the ravine. "A young girl jumped to her death last night. I wish there was something we could have done to prevent that. I really do. But isn't that the nature of a free society? Respecting our students' freedom is of utmost importance." Where was this coming from? She wasn't usually quick on her feet, though she'd expected Salerno's sour attitude. She had learned through the grapevine that he had tried to stop the board from hiring her, but had been overruled because the trustees wanted to demonstrate that they were addressing the suicide crisis. She had gotten past him before. It was time to move past her fear of the gray curmudgeon and maintain focus on her mission.

Saving kids.

That was at the heart of this job, the reason that she had stepped back from the career in hospital administration she'd been aiming for and had agreed to serve in the university. It was all about saving lives. While the university was currently more concerned about reducing liability and negative media attention, Sydney believed that, with the right approach, she could accomplish both tasks.

"Most university students are too young and naïve to appreciate a concept like freedom," Salerno rambled on. "They think it affords them a free ticket to hedonism without consequence. Alcohol and marijuana, video games and sex, skateboards that mark up our curbs and stairs, and cell phone addictions."

"That's a bit harsh, Dr. Salerno," Sydney said, standing her ground. "Though, in some cases, it's true. But it's our job to open their eyes to the various interpretations and possibilities of freedom. And it wouldn't hurt to teach them how to harness and master the use of vices and technologies."

"Touché," Wendell said with a spirited smile.

Really? Wendell might have stepped out of an Oscar Wilde play. Well, at least he was on her side.

Sydney turned back to the window and noticed that the ambulance was gone. "I need to get back out there. The police will be finishing up at the crime scene and looking to interview students."

Salerno scowled. "Our security chief can handle that."

"Security forces and police can be intimidating, even for the innocent. I want to make sure our students are treated respect-fully."

"Excellent point." Wendell's furry brows moved like spider legs as he squinted at her. "We're finished here, aren't we, Martin?"

"Fine. Go." Like a disappointed father, Salerno dismissed her.

CHAPTER 5

Trying to maintain some semblance of normal, I plodded off to my Psychology class, usually the high point of my Mondays, and found a seat in the anonymity of the large amphitheater. Today the professor came to the front of the desk and removed her glasses. Alice Habib usually had a brusque demeanor, though I had seen her rein it in once when she had talked about her Syrian heritage and the difficulties of maintaining an "unpopular" culture in America. Her penetrating dark eyes and stern retorts kept the class in line. But today, her face had softened with the weight of sorrow.

"It's good to see you all." Dr. Habib pulled her nubby blazer closed over her ample form. "Before we begin, let's talk about the tragedy that happened on our campus last night. An apparent suicide, they're saying, but that doesn't make it any easier to rationalize."

I was glad that she was addressing the crisis, and grateful for the respectful silence in the class. I didn't want to talk about Lydia, but it was important that we acknowledge what had happened.

Habib leaned against the desk. "Can anyone offer insights on why we have so many suicides here at Merriwether?"

A girl in the front raised her hand. "The pressure. Our grading system is harsh."

Dr. Habib nodded and called on another student.

"Merriwether attracts a lot of achievers," said a kid in a black hoodie. "Perfectionists. When something goes wrong, they have no coping skills."

Other students mentioned depression, the competitive culture of college, the failure of society to recognize mental illness, and the alienation many students felt when they went away to college.

"These are all potential factors, but what makes our campus different from others?" Habib asked.

Although I had planned to keep quiet, I raised my hand. "It's the gorge. The bridges." I kept my eyes on the desk at the front of the room, knowing that emotion would surface too quickly if I looked directly at Dr. Habib's sympathetic face. "They offer an easy means of death. Most people don't realize that it's not so easy to find a way to kill yourself. Drugs might be hard to find, and not so reliable. Using a gun or falling from a tall height, those methods are generally effective."

"Yes."

I could feel Dr. Habib's approval.

"The beautiful gorge that runs through our campus also offers a rather effective way for a person to kill himself," she said. "And you may be surprised to learn that, in your age group, fifteen to thirty-four, suicide is the second leading cause of death for Americans." Habib picked up her glasses from the desk and tapped them against one palm. "For people your age, guns are the weapon of choice for suicide. In the psychiatric community we believe that the availability of firearms makes them a popular method. And then there are older methods—hanging, drugs, fast cars. But here at Merriwether, we have the bridges. Fairly effective, and very public."

"So wait." A tall, broad-shouldered guy in a team tracksuit raised his hand. "If suicide is so common for people our age, why don't we hear about it happening at other colleges?"

"It's happening, but it's behind closed doors, or off campus. And if you attended Harvard or the University of Chicago, I think we would be having a similar conversation. But I don't mean to diminish the tragedy of suicide. For the people who are left behind, grief can be overwhelming. Unfortunately, we don't have the time to do an entire lesson on coping with suicide, but I prepared a handout for you to take home."

A few hands shot up as she started passing out stacks of the handout. "I see hands. The answer is no, this will not be on the test. But take the time to read through it. I think you'll find it helpful. If not, come see me during office hours."

I took a sheet and passed the stack on. The handout focused on healing from suicide grief, and gave a list and explanations of the emotions triggered by suicide. Shock and anger. Guilt, confusion, and despair. And feelings of rejection.

Yeah. This would probably be helpful after dark, when everyone was asleep and grim thoughts overwhelmed me. I tucked it into the back of my notebook and tried to let myself be distracted by Dr. Habib's lecture.

When I left Psych I made a point of walking south, all the way down to the Main Street Bridge, a larger crossing that most people took when they were driving into town. With the fumes and periodic rumble of cars, very few students chose to walk this way, but I didn't feel ready to cross the North Campus Bridge on my own. Not just yet.

As cars roared past I kept to the far side of the walking path, took out my phone, and connected to social media, hungry to know more about what had happened to Lydia. The local news had a tiny blurb about a suicide, but I had an inside source. Rory MacFarlane, the Olympic snowboarder, had seen it happen. He wasn't a personal friend, but I figured I could find him on Facebook.

And there he was—green eyes, brown hair shaved close on the sides and piled thick on top, and a smile that suggested that everything would be totally fine. I dinged him a message, telling him that I was a friend of Lydia's and hoped he would meet with me. I was working at the library that day from two to six.

By the time I got back to Theta House lunch would be over, and although I was a little too sick to be hungry, I knew I would get sicker if I didn't eat anything. I had passed the tall flower arrangement on the front table and the gallery of photos on the foyer wall and was heading toward the kitchen when I was summoned by a handful of girls in the parlor, huddled around someone's laptop.

"Emma! Oh my God, I can't believe you went to class with all this happening." Isabel Delgado, one of my suite mates, popped up and wrapped her arms around me.

"You know me. Grade grubber." I hugged her back, noticing the fine edges of her bones in my embrace. A petite girl, she struggled to keep food down and always worried about gaining too much weight. After a crisis last year she had gotten her eating disorder under control and finished the year with a healthy glow and a burst of energy. I hoped that she wasn't slipping back into it again.

"Come. Sit." Isabel hustled me into her chair. "Suki found the TV news press conference about Lydia. I guess they did it later this morning. It's short, but you have to see it."

"Hold on!" Suki held up a hand as she leaned over the computer, cueing it up. Meanwhile, the handful of Theta Pis slumped low in the furniture, each girl staring at the screen of her cell phone.

"Are you guys skipping your classes today?" I asked.

Two of the girls nodded morosely.

"We're too sick about Lydia," Chloe said, nuzzling into the arm of the sofa.

"I have Mondays off," Jemma said, "but I feel awful, too."

I nodded, half wishing I could join them and lounge away my stress. But that was not me. Grades mattered; my future depended on my success here.

"Here it is." Suki clicked the video open and stepped away.

A female reporter with short, spiky hair used a somber voice to announce that there had been a tragic death on the Merriwether campus, another apparent suicide.

They cut to a press conference, on the steps of one of the campus buildings, where the police chief, Phil Blue, stood. A lot of students were anti-anything-authority, but most people liked Chief Blue, a tattooed descendant of the Chinook Indians. The guy was in a band in his spare time. Definitely cool.

"At approximately two a.m. Merriwether student Lydia Drakos jumped from the North Campus Bridge. Ms. Drakos was twenty-one. She died from injuries sustained in the fall. At this time the incident is still under investigation. An autopsy is pending, but we believe it was a suicide, not a suspicious death."

My lips tensed when they cut from Chief Blue to Merriwether's head of student health, Dean Sydney Cho. I despised everything about that woman, from her stylish asymmetrical A-line hairstyle to her soft, approachable demeanor. That voice could melt butter, but I knew better. Dean Cho was a monster. I wondered if she knew that, in a roundabout way, she was responsible for Lydia's death. Not that it would matter to her.

She made some watery statement about sorrow and sympathy and best efforts.

"Whatever," I said aloud as the segment ended.

"It's too awful," Chloe moaned. "Poor Lydia."

Jemma patted her arm, though I wasn't sure either girl had ever exchanged words with Lydia. Not that I had a right to question anyone's grief, but I didn't have much patience for anyone who sat around moaning.

"I think I'm still in shock," I said mildly, "but I need to keep on moving." I turned to Isabel. "Did you get lunch?"

"I can't eat."

"Come to the kitchen with me. I need some yogurt or something."

With a toss of her hair she joined me, and I felt glad to get away from the slugs in the parlor.

In the kitchen I sliced up an apple and grabbed two yogurts from the fridge as Isabel told me how many of the sisters had been crying all morning. Glad I missed that. "Oh, and there's an emergency house meeting this evening. It's mandatory."

"I saw Mrs. J's e-mail when I was walking back from class. Here." I handed her a yogurt. "It's fat free, sugar free, and sixteen grams of protein. We both need it now."

She frowned down at the cup, but I felt relief when she dipped the spoon in and took a bite. Protein and calcium. Yeah, baby.

"Are you going to class tonight?" I asked.

"I can't miss the meeting here, and my head's not in schoolwork now. I feel so bad for Lydia, the loneliness she must have felt. It makes me worry about the people I love. You never know what's in someone's head, Emma."

As we were talking the side door opened and Defiance, Isabel's roommate, trudged up to the island and paused. "Do you feel that?"

I squinted at her, not sure what she meant, though I admired her lace-up boots, obviously new. She wore them with tights, a pleated black-and-white miniskirt, and a black leather jacket with lots of zippers. Defiance had the ability to make combat boots look elegant, and guys loved her look. She spent a lot of time fending them off.

"What are we supposed to feel?" Isabel asked as she scraped up another spoonful of yogurt.

"Lydia's spirit." Defiance gripped the straps of her backpack and closed her eyes. "I feel her here, lingering. She's not at rest."

"Seriously?" Isabel tossed her spoon into the sink, scowling as it clattered against the stainless steel. "That is too creepy, D. You just can't say stuff like that without scaring the crap out of people."

"Please." Defiance opened her eyes, black as coal and thickly outlined with smoky liner. She had a dark, exotic beauty, a rare black rose, a crown of black tourmaline. "Don't shoot the messenger. I'm just telling you what I know is true. I've always been able to feel this stuff. Both my grandmothers say I have the gift." Defiance credited her Roma background for making her an expert on all things supernatural, saying that psychic abilities ran in her family. I wasn't into magical thinking, but I didn't mind her stories and rituals, like when she poured salt and saffron into the four corners of our suite to absorb the negative energy of previous residents. The place felt cleansed when she vacuumed it all up two days later. Or when she warned us that storms—atmospheric *and* proverbial—were coming because there was a halo around the moon. Did I believe Lydia's spirit was lurking in the walls? No. But the idea rattled Isabel, who was a much more sensitive, gentle soul.

"The only spirit I believe in is the one in the Holy Trinity," Isabel said. She had plucked the empty yogurt container from the sink and was now rinsing it thoroughly. "But you know how ghost stories and superstitions upset me." We knew. And if she scrubbed that plastic any harder, the PCBs would be airborne.

Defiance stared at Isabel. "If you don't believe the spirits are there, then why do you fear them?"

"Listen to yourself." Isabel chucked the plastic container into the recycling bin and reached for a paper towel. "You have no idea how creepy you sound. If those sisters in the parlor get wind of this, they are going to drop a complaint into the chapter relations box."

"Don't worry about me." Defiance folded her arms with a sigh. "I can defend myself from the snob contingent."

In my time as a sister of Theta Pi, no one had ever been brought before chapter relations, but in less than three months on campus Defiance had probably come close. As a transfer student, she had been guaranteed a spot in the sorority, even if it wasn't the best cultural fit, and that didn't make our executive board happy. After D's first visit here at the end of last semester, Tori and Courtney had made some snide comments, calling her a gypsy and joking that she'd be skewering pigs in their suite if they roomed with her. I had told them to watch it and offered to have Defiance move into our suite. I knew that Angela and Isabel would be happy to have a fourth, and they were. At the time, I hadn't realized how "in the box" our sorority was.

"D, it is a little creepy," I agreed.

"Is it my fault that Lydia is stuck here? I'm sure she wants to go." Defiance's dark eyes rolled up to the ceiling. "Don't you?"

Isabel's mouth dropped open and I had to bite back a smile. "Come on, Isabel," I said, "try not to let it get under your skin. We're all kind of freaked right now. Just take a deep breath."

"I can breathe just fine." Hands on hips, Isabel faced Defiance. "But I don't know how I'm going to sleep in the same room with you, if you're conjuring spirits and talking to the dead."

"I don't mean to frighten you," Defiance said. "Would you rather I don't tell you what I know? I'll say nothing. Is that what you want?"

"You put these images in my head. Sad ghosts, and poor Lydia stuck in limbo." Tears sprang from Isabel's eyes. "I don't want to be here anymore. I want to go home and hide in my bed. And never come out." She sobbed into her hands.

I patted her shoulder as Defiance and I exchanged a look of concern. Defiance was stubborn, but she didn't mean to be cruel, and we both knew that "home" might seem safe to Isabel, but after an initial welcome her mother would dissect her appearance and criticize her weight and send her back into an anorexic hibernation.

"You know, I wish I had a home to go to," I said in an attempt to distract her. "My father moved in with a friend in Portland, and there's no room for me. He already told me he won't be around for Thanksgiving."

Isabel swiped away her tears. "I'm sorry, Emma. What will you do? Will you go visit your brother?"

"I don't think so. We're not close, and I barely know his wife."

"Then you need to come with me," Defiance said. "If you don't mind helping out in the restaurant on Thanksgiving. We always have a feast the day after."

"That sounds great." A big, noisy family was my dream come true. "But you'd better check with your parents."

"They'll say yes, of course. It's no trouble."

I nodded, glad the diversion had worked and the conversation had shifted away from Isabel threatening to leave school. Now she was talking about the paper she had due right before Thanksgiving break, while Defiance rooted around in the fridge for sandwich fixings and I finished off the apple. On the surface, it was like any other day.

Except that our Theta Pi sister had killed herself.

As I rearranged my backpack and set out to the library, I went through the list of questions that swelled in my mind. Like Defiance, I was haunted by Lydia, only for me it wasn't a spirit invasion but an obsession with how and why it had happened. I needed details, some clues, so that I could imagine the entire scenario and then let it rest.

How had she gotten to the bridge?

Had she been alone?

Why didn't she wake up one of the girls? In a house this size, there was usually someone around.

Had she been in a panic, or in that calm trance that had overcome her recently?

I hurried off to the library. As I passed a line of maple trees on fire with autumn reds and golds, my sick mind tried to reenact her death in my head. But some things didn't make sense. Her first trip out of the house in a week or more, and she had traipsed to the bridge in her pajamas.

It pissed me off that none of us knew how bad it was for her, but everyone gets trapped in their own body.

Forty girls living in a house together, each one caught up with fending for herself.

I pushed a cart of books up the aisle and ducked into a shadowed corner, tracking down the exact number and letter to replace a copy of *Guns, Germs, and Steel*. It had been a quiet afternoon, allowing me time for schoolwork, but as my brain felt like putty I'd resorted to shelving books.

"Are you Emma?"

I turned toward the voice and took a breath. He was like a mirage of energy and straight, strong lines. A beanie sat on the back of his head—not my thing, but he wore it well—and the thick tufts of hair that framed his eyes looked wild and smooth at the same time. "Rory. Thanks for coming. I've got a million questions."

"I probably can't answer them but, yeah." His gaze fell. "I can't get her out of my mind. It's like the scene keeps replaying in my head." He looked behind him to see if anyone was nearby, and then stepped into the shadows, closer to me. "I talked to the police for, like, hours, and they asked me the same questions over and over again. You'd think it would feel good to recount it all, like, to get it out of your system? But it doesn't. Nothing about it feels good."

"Except that you were there."

"Didn't make any difference." He dug his fingers into the hair over his forehead, and then let his hand drop. "Adam and I spotted her on the bridge from the Top of the World. We saw her pacing, and then I think she climbed over the edge. I called to her, trying to get her attention as I ran toward the bridge, but I don't think she heard us. It was like she was in her own world."

So he had tried to stop her. "Did you see anyone with her?"

"I think she was alone. At first I thought someone was with her. She was yelling at someone, but there was no answer. Maybe she was on her phone."

"Yeah." My lower lip puckered at the thought of the lone figure of Lydia standing on the cold, dark bridge in her pink robe. "So there was no one else around?"

"There was one other person leaving the walkway."

My heart sank. He'd seen someone else?

"I caught a quick glimpse of him disappearing down the far stairs as I raced onto the bridge." He squinted as if trying to see the memory. "But it happened in a flash. All I saw was someone in a dark hoodie with Greek letters on the back. Two Greek letters, but I couldn't see what they were. It happened so fast."

"Was the hoodie person leaving Lydia, or just crossing the bridge?" I asked.

"I don't know. As I said, I didn't even know anyone else was there until I got onto the bridge. But if Hoodie was with Lydia, I didn't hear any interaction between them. The talk was one-sided."

"I wonder who that was. Could it have been a Theta Pi sister?"

Rory shrugged. "I just know that all the time Adam and I stayed with the police, no one else came forward."

It was possible that someone walking alone didn't even see Lydia as he or she passed by. "What was Lydia like? I mean, did she seem scared, or was she determined?"

Distress shadowed his face as he swallowed hard.

"I'm sorry to probe, but . . ."

"I get it," he said. "She was your friend."

Not entirely true, but this wasn't the time to correct him.

"At first she was pissed. Yelling out, 'You promised!' That's what got our attention at first. Then she kept saying how sorry she was. Like she was apologizing to someone."

Apologizing . . . I don't think I'd ever heard Lydia say she was sorry. She'd been too confident and entitled to admit a mistake. "So she might have been talking to someone else?"

"I don't know." He shrugged. "It happened so fast. We looked out and saw someone moving in front of the bridge light. At one point I thought it was a large bird flapping its wings. That's stupid, I know. Birds aren't out at night, and it was, like, two in the morning."

"It's not stupid. It must have freaked you out, seeing her on the other side of the rail."

"When I got to the approach of the bridge, I saw her go over the edge," he said. "I stepped up to the rail and saw her drop down, free-falling."

"Did she scream?"

He shook his head. "She was quiet on the way down. Peaceful. That part happened so fast. It took just a few seconds. It's weird because, in my memory, it was all in slow motion."

I nodded as the car accident came back to me, those stretched-out seconds of sliding motion swinging toward destruction. "There's a time warp when something awful happens. It seems to stretch out in your mind, but everything happens in the blink of an eye."

He squinted as our eyes met. "Exactly. But I keep replaying it in my head, thinking that everything would have been different if we were on that bridge five minutes earlier. If we'd just noticed her earlier or if I'd run faster, maybe she'd be here now."

"It's not your fault," I said. "I know it'll take a while for you to really get that, but you're not responsible for what happened." He was a good guy. Even the way he talked about Lydia, he made it clear that her life mattered. Unlike the gawkers at the bridge, he understood that a light had gone out last night, and that was the real tragedy. "Did you know her?"

"I met her once, but my friend Charlie knew her. He went to a frat formal with her last year. He's pretty freaked out."

I didn't know this Charlie, but he was probably among the one-date-wonders Lydia had always managed to find for important events. "Lydia was so into those formals. As Theta Pis we have to attend a few a year, but Lydia never missed one."

He shook his head. "I've been to one in my three years here."

"Doesn't Omega Phi have a rule about that?"

He shrugged. "They haven't kicked me out yet."

I liked his unfazed attitude. "I'd talk with you some more, but I have to go." I nodded at the large moon of a clock that hung on the second-floor balcony. "My shift ended five minutes ago, and I have a meeting at Theta House."

"You'd better get going." He gave the book cart a push back toward the main desk.

"I can do that."

"I don't mind. Who reads all this stuff anyway?"

"Umm, students?"

"Not what I meant. I read everything online. Books make me nervous."

"Then I really appreciate you coming into this scary place. But really, thanks."

He nodded. "And you'll hit me up when you know the details about a service for Lydia? I told Charlie I would go with him."

"I'll let you know."

He turned toward the door, then looked back. "Hey, Emma, do you have a cell phone?"

"Sure." It was an odd question, but I handed it to him, figuring he needed to make a call. Instead, he tapped the keys. "Just adding my number to your contact list. Easier to reach me that way."

As he handed the phone back to me I bowed my head to hide my smile. It was wrong to think that Rory and I had something in common beyond Lydia, and I had a whole new set of worries now, knowing that someone had been seen on the bridge near Lydia. Coincidence? The sick feeling in my gut told me no.

CHAPTER 6

With his heels propped on his scarred desk and a stack of Comp 120 essays in his lap, Dr. Scott Finnegan was working his way toward a pint at Scully's Tavern. If he plowed through four more essays and then grabbed a beer and a burger at Scully's, that would have him arriving at home with an hour or so to endure Eileen's wrath for being a terrible father, an inconsiderate partner, and an overall loser. He was wondering if he had the stamina to finish off all the essays tonight when the e-mails chimed in. He didn't really care to open them. Anything that came in after six was fair game for the next morning. But he was already distracted, so he figured what the hell.

The two e-mails came from the university's director of student health, Dr. Sydney Cho. The first was a generic e-mail sent to all staff to confirm another death on campus, a female student who had apparently jumped from the North Campus Bridge in the early hours of the morning.

Another suicide.

Another confirmation that Merriwether University was an incubator of stress. Finn wished these kids could see beyond the horizon and recognize that there was a hell of a lot more to life than getting a college education, but he knew this generation juggled a hornet's nest of newfangled issues: broken families, rising substance abuse, the increasing financial burden of a college education, and flimsy family bonds due to time-consuming extracurricular activity, to name a few.

The second e-mail was more specific, though still lacking the warmth of a personal message.

> You are receiving this e-mail because the recently deceased Lydia Drakos was a student in one or more of your classes. The Pioneer Falls Police are investigating her death and have requested any information you might have regarding this student's profile. Please respond with a progress report and any pertinent observations.

Dean Cho was really digging herself in with this one. Did a request from the police trump FERPA, the Family Educational Rights and Privacy Act of 1974, which protected the privacy of a student's records? Finn wasn't sure, but if he had any information on this student, he wasn't going to give it up in an e-mail, and Sydney Cho should realize that. The thirtyish wunderkind was already showing her lack of experience.

And even if he did have information on this young woman, was it fair to put her under the microscope, toss her personal information onto the table so that the police could probe and prod the remnants of her psyche now that she was gone? He understood the need to establish that the dead student hadn't been a victim of homicide, but it seemed wrong to scrutinize the victim. It was just wrong.

He clicked through his rosters until he found Lydia's name in one of his Comp classes. His grade sheet showed two incompletes and a C on her first paper. Ouch. At the bottom he had written a note to himself about giving her an extension on the third paper.

So he'd spoken with her. He rested his forehead against one palm, trying to remember. Dark hair. Polite but flirty in that aristocratic way. Lydia Drakos. He'd been kind to her, thank

God. Patient but firm, allowing extra time as long as she got the work done. Which was probably nearly impossible if the girl had been choked by depression.

As he skimmed over the only paper Lydia Drakos had submitted electronically—a mediocre effort with a rushed conclusion—the realization that the administration was looking to write this student off inflamed his fury. This wasn't just about ruling out foul play. They cared not for the life lost or the grieving family and friends; the school's reputation, its ranking in magazines and guidebooks, and its endowment were the priorities here. Damn the admin, obsessed with fiscal gain and reputation at the expense of the students.

Those student protestors had been right.

He was tempted to give the story to the editors of the student newspaper, who had condemned Cho when she'd failed to revamp the harsh policies of the campus counseling center. He was itching to fan the flames of rebellion, but he couldn't divulge the details of Lydia Drakos's student records.

He would have to settle for a more private duel. Scrolling through the university directory, he found the number and placed the call. At this time of night, he expected to get her voice mail. He was wrong.

"This is Dean Cho."

"Time to step away from your desk. Stop hiding behind e-mails," he said. "We need to meet, face-to-face."

"Who is this?"

"Scott Finnegan. I was Lydia Drakos's English teacher."

"If you have information for me, you're better off e-mailing it. That way we both have a record."

"Not gonna happen. When can we meet?"

"I'd prefer e-mail. I've had to cancel tomorrow's appointments to escort the police on campus. They're still investigating."

"Are they with you now?"

"Well . . . no."

"Sit tight. I'll be there in ten."

CHAPTER 7

"Ladies, I'll be brief. Thanks for being here." Our house manager, Jan Johnson, forced a smile that revealed her slightly crooked teeth. Her demeanor was cheerful, her silver hair pulled back in a loose bun as usual, but I noticed that her hands trembled a bit, and that scared me. Mrs. J was our rock. If she was shaken, there was no hope for the rest of us.

"I know you had classes and other commitments. I appreciate your being flexible, but it's important to have you all here to support each other and share this information."

The room was silent, most of us still inhabiting a bubble of shock that coated everything with a surreal glaze. Most reactions to the news had little to do with feelings for Lydia. There'd been tears, yes, but the displays of emotion reminded me of what you'd see at the end of a heartbreaking film. That cathartic cry that made you feel so much better when you took a deep breath and walked out of the theater. There was also the creep factor of the idea of suicide, and already I sensed most of the sisters separating themselves from Lydia, a mystery in life and in death.

"By way of warning, I just wanted to let you know that Lydia's mother will be here tomorrow or the next day. Mrs. Drakos. She's driving out to . . . pick up Lydia's things."

Driving out? From the Greek islands in the Mediterranean?

It appeared that we'd caught Lydia in a lie, but this was no time to question Mrs. J, who was already rattled.

"Lydia was an only child, so this will be particularly hard on her parents," Mrs. J said, as if thinking aloud.

As if a person were dispensable when she had siblings. I imagined Mrs. J calling my father and saying, "Emma's dead, but it's not such a grave loss for you as I hear she has an older brother to take her place in your heart."

"I'm afraid Mrs. Drakos will be a little lost when she gets here," Mrs. J continued. "Sorting through her daughter's possessions. What a terrible thing. I'm counting on you to pay your respects when she's here and help her in any way you can."

My resolute shell began to crack at the thought of a parent having to come and claim the unwanted physical evidence of their child's life. What would Mrs. Drakos do with Lydia's jeans, sneakers, and dresses? Cable-knit sweaters, nightgowns, and underwear that no other living soul would want. Personal items that were important just a day ago, now fairly useless. A life reduced to piles of trash that you can't bear to part with.

I had done much of the sorting through my sister's possessions after the crash. The dried corsage from senior prom. Tickets from a performance of *Les Miserables*. Lip glosses and palettes of eye shadow. Mud-caked garden shoes and spangled heels that had barely been worn.

Thank God my aunt Rose had been there to handle my mother's belongings. A person accumulates items that are loaded with meaning and useless to anyone else. Small, pretty trinkets, favorite sweaters, photos and shoes; a closet full of possessions that contained mountains of memory. It was one of those horrible things about death that no one talks about: dealing with the remnants a person leaves behind.

"Let's talk about the police investigation," Mrs. J went on. "Some of you spoke with Detective Taylor this afternoon, and I want to say I'm proud of the way you girls handled yourselves. Over the next week or so the police will be investigating Lydia's death to make sure it was a suicide. They'll be here in the house, and they'll want to interview many of you, but I will be with them whenever they're on the premises. At this time they don't think any of us are at risk. I guess that means, so far, the evidence points to a suicide. In any case, I know you'll cooperate fully, and if anyone has information regarding Lydia's death, you can call Detective Taylor directly. I'll leave this stack of business cards on the front desk."

My gaze skittered quickly over my sisters' faces, trying to sense whether anyone would take the bait, but no one seemed at all interested. Although we'd probably never know for sure, the consensus at Theta House was that Lydia had jumped of her own volition, driven by a secret that would die with her.

"Beyond that, I just want to say that Lydia was . . ." Mrs. J's eyes filled. I'd never seen her cry before, and the sight of steady, solid Mrs. J crumbling inside struck me hard. We'd be sunk if Mrs. J fell apart. I was relieved when, a moment later, she pulled it together. Swiping at the tears with the back of her hand, she let out a breath and forced another smile. "She was a good egg. Kind and dependable."

I bit my lower lip as I noticed Isabel rolling her eyes. That was not the Lydia we knew.

"At times she could be stubborn and intractable. . . ."

That was the girl we'd butted heads with.

"But I like to think that she pushed because she believed so much in the values of Theta Pi and the support of her sisters."

Highly unlikely, but way to cover, Mrs. J.

"I've been talking with Dean Cho about grief counseling, and they're going to set something up for you girls, as well as other students on campus."

"Wait." Tori raised a hand. "Hold on, Mrs. J. Do you mean with the counselors at the student health center?"

Mrs. J squinted at her, ever serious. "That's right."

Tori shook her head imperiously. "That's not going to happen. Sorry to disappoint, Mrs. J, but you know how they've been pouncing on students lately."

"But, Tori, this is different. Dean Cho promised that there would be no strings attached for students seeking support."

"Yeah. We've heard that before." Tori held one hand out, gesturing to the room full of girls like the queen of the homecoming parade. "Thetas? We can take care of our own house, right? We have the Rose Council and the Chapter Relations Committee if you need anything. Our doors are always open."

Some girls nodded, and the general feeling of agreement filled the room.

"That's admirable," Mrs. J said, "but be aware that other help is out there. And you can always come to me. I'm not a professional counselor, but I'm a pretty good listener."

But not a friend, I thought as I ran a fingernail along the seam of my jeans. Mrs. J was a master problem solver when it came to fixing a leaky sink, getting a sick girl to urgent care, or coordinating the cleaning staff. But in less tangible matters, she didn't seem to have the patience to weigh issues properly. Which was okay, because none of the Thetas was going to cry on her shoulder.

As Mrs. J rattled on, my gaze floated over the pretty faces of the sisters gathered there, many of them glazed with boredom. I had hoped for more of a feeling of solidarity in this meeting, our first time together since we'd lost Lydia, but mostly it seemed to be business as usual.

This time last year, it would have been so different. Letting my focus go fuzzy on the string of pink heart-shaped lights, I fell into the memory of those days. The way things used to be—the functionality of Theta Pi just last year when I had pledged. My "Theta big sister," Kate, had been president, and I'd been so focused on her group of seniors that Lydia's crew had been more like background noise. People had left their bedroom doors open and conversations spilled out to the hall. The senior girls insisted we join them for meals, and they let us stay over in their rooms before we were able to move into Theta House. There were spontaneous dance parties and all-night Monopoly games. Study buddies and secret sisters who wrote you encouraging notes during the term.

Things had been so different back then. Not that I didn't still love my sisters. They were family, and I knew some of us would be close for the rest of our lives. But that first semester of freshman year . . . those were good times.

CHAPTER 8

Emma's Freshman Year
Halloween

The air in the frat house was popping and buzzing, warm and fuzzy and friendly as I swayed on the dance floor with my two best friends, Angela and Isabel. With pledging done and midterms behind us, we had come to the Delta Tau party to let loose, celebrate Halloween, and test our new confidence on campus as sisters of Theta Pi.

"Are we having fun yet?" I shouted over the music, and my friends roared in response.

"I love this song!" Isabel yelled, dancing around me.

"Yeah!" Angela whooped and waved down a bare-chested prisoner dragging a ball and chain and carrying a tray of test tubes.

"I've got fireballs and pumpkin shots," he explained as Angela reached for the tray.

"No, no, not those," I said, pulling Angela away.

"Thanks, anyway!" Isabel smiled sweetly as the prisoner dude shrugged and moved on.

"But they looked so festive," Angela said, falling back into my arms. "Especially the orange ones. Happy Halloween!"

She was pretty wasted from the apple-juice-and-rum mix that had been circulating at the pre-party back at Theta House. "Apple yums!" Isabel had called them. We had powered down a few "yums," then filled flasks with rum and Coke to take *with us, as no one wanted to take the chance of getting roofied or going over the edge with something like grain alcohol.*

"Drink from the flask, girl!" I said. "We're not going to let anyone take you down!"

"Theta Pi forever!" Angela shouted, straightening up to pump a fist in the air.

"Forever!" we chanted.

Our costumes bobbed as we danced and laughed together. In our search for a theme costume for our threesome we'd found way too many costumes that exploited women. A cleavage-hugging leather bustier and tiny rag skirt for the pirate wench, red fishnet stockings for the sexy nurse, a bare midriff top with fringe for the "Indian Princess."

"Really?" Isabel had winced. "Who comes up with this shit?"

In a total reversal, we had decided to be "Rock, Paper, and Scissors" with large cardboard costumes dangling from our necks over black tights and tees. We thought they were sexy enough without shouting, "Use me!"

As the song ended, I saw a few of our sisters waving from the side of the dance floor, where a sliding door was open to a patio and the cool October night.

"There's Kate!" I said, guiding my friends over to my Theta Pi big sister, who was hanging out with other senior girls. Kate Sun and her friends were dressed as superheroes, and as we approached she put her hands on her hips to part her cape, revealing her red, white, and blue leotard. Her dark hair was curled at the ends and pulled back with a gold crown with a red star at its center.

"Wonder Woman, have you come to save us from evil?" Isabel asked.

"You three seem to be fending off the villains pretty well," Kate said as she gave us all hugs. "I mean, who can beat a united Rock, Paper, Scissors?"

Although everyone loved Kate, as her little sis, I felt a special bond. She was a "live in the moment" girl who worked hard to bring out the best in the people around her. Angela had pledged Theta Pi because she liked the loving tone Kate set as *the sorority's leader. "That and the fact that they'd chosen an Asian-American girl to be president," Angela had told me. "I figured that if they could go there, they could accept someone like me."*

"Have y'all met any of the Delta Taus?" asked Belle, whose long red hair covered the shoulders and back of her Supergirl costume. "Some of them are really nice guys."

"They're kind of like us when it comes to recruiting," said Tara. At least, I thought that was Tara under the Batgirl mask. "No assholes allowed."

We all laughed, partly because it was the truth. Theta Pi was a middle-of-the-road sorority in many ways. Girls weren't chosen based on looks, academic success, family ties, or wealth. We weren't all type-A leaders, but we weren't wussies, either. So what was the common thread? I had joined because I saw compassion in these girls.

"We've just been dancing and chillin'," Angela said, throwing an arm around Isabel and leaning heavily into her. Isabel stooped under the weight.

"Come out on the patio with us," Kate said, supporting Angela from the other side. "We'll introduce you to the guys we know."

Moving as a group, we went out back. Braced by the cool air, we snapped out of the fuzz a little and joined in with a bunch of guys who were telling stories and passing a bong. The details from there are kind of fuzzy for me, but I remember laughing and feeling uninhibited enough to tell my own stories.

That night, my friends and I met guys who became our boyfriends. I fell in with Sam Mattern from the first flash of his blue eyes, and we sealed the deal when he loaned me his jacket in exchange for a drink from my flask. We joked about how sharing a flask was like swapping spit, and the next likely step was making out on a chaise at the edge of the patio. I was just drunk enough to not care when his hands began to roam over my shirt, and my response went quickly from permission to participation as his fingertips created a fire inside me.

*   *   *

Isabel split from Gabe pretty quickly, Angela is still seeing Darnell, and me? Well, I managed to hang on to Sam for a few months under the impression that if we stayed together long enough, Sam would mature out of that stupid boy brain that told him he was too young to be tied to one girl. A false impression. I didn't know that some guys never mature out of the asshole phase. In retrospect, I wish I'd let him go long before that.

CHAPTER 9

Mrs. J was still droning on at the front of the room. "I don't know what else to say."

Please, not one more word. I needed the lecture to end.

"All right, ladies. I guess I'll pass the meeting on to you, Tori." Mrs. J moved off toward the doorway as our chapter president rose from one of the white leather sofas.

All attention shifted desperately to Tori. Honestly, she was like eye candy as she moved to the speaker's spot in front of the fireplace with the long-legged grace of a gazelle. Tori Winchester was probably the most strikingly beautiful Theta Pi girl. With a thin, finely boned face, gilded gold hair, and a kickass body, Tori had model potential, while the rest of us were average chicks with a determination to make the most of our looks and personality.

"Ladies, my heart is aching, and I know yours are, too." Tori pressed a manicured palm to her breast, and I noticed that the black-and-white nail art matched the black embroidered pattern on her white shirt. Perfectly.

I picked at a loose cuticle on my thumb, and then quickly buried my hand between my thigh and the sofa. I could lose Rose Points for these crappy fingernails, but no one was watching me. All eyes were on Tori. The sisters didn't seem too broken up over Lydia, but they were definitely interested in hearing what one of Lydia's best friends had to say.

"Lydia was our sister and friend, a bestie to many of us. There's so much to say, but at the same time, the words get caught in my throat." A glimmer of emotion squeezed her voice as the room grew silent. In that moment, I believed that Tori actually liked Lydia. The air was thick with love as Tori spoke about what Theta Pi had meant to Lydia. Although most of us didn't know Lydia well, Tori plucked the strings of the chord that bound us together, and one by one my sisters began to cry. Not so much for Lydia, but for the sisterhood. Contagious tears.

I held it together, watching. Tori knew how to work an audience, grabbing you by the collar so you couldn't look away. The girl had a gift.

Tori finished with a message of hope, her eyes sparkling as she went on to say how Lydia would want us to carry on and do the speed-dating pancake social as planned.

"Pancakes?" I muttered, looking at my friends for a reality check. Angela rolled her eyes, but Isabel and Defiance were under Tori's spell. As if anyone was going to be in the mood for midnight pancakes or rapid hookups after this.

"Hold on a sec." I waved a hand and pushed off the sofa. Granted, I was only a sophomore, but I was a year or two older than most other girls in my grade, and I wasn't afraid to speak up. "Shouldn't we postpone the pancake social? It seems wrong to sponsor something so festive so soon."

Tori fixed her eyes on me cautiously, as if sizing me up for a wrestling match. "We could cancel it, but then everyone on campus would think we're unreliable."

"And it's a campus tradition," Courtney added. "Besides, if we don't do it, some other sorority will steal our idea."

"Y'all need to look at the sunny side. Lydia loved the pancake social. Think of it as a tribute," Violet said.

The thought of flipping pancakes and rapping with drunk guys made me nauseous. I wanted to shut the thing down. Now. "Can we take a vote about postponing it? Just for a week or two." I surveyed the room and was happy to see nods of encouragement.

"No, we cannot take a vote," Tori said indignantly. "Voting takes place only during general meetings. This"—she extended her pointer fingers like an airline attendant—"is an emergency session. It's not the proper time to conduct business. Sorry, Emma."

Her fake sincerity made me all the more determined to nix the pancake thing. Later, behind the scenes. I dropped back onto the sofa, plotting another strike.

Violet stood up next, a gloomy expression on her face as she fluffed her loose red curls over her shoulders. Violet was the second of "Charlie's Angels," the secret name we had for the top three leaders of Theta Pi. Now that Lydia, our own uncool Lucy Liu, was gone, we would need to drop it.

"I talked to National, and they were just devastated. They're sending us little black mourning ribbons to wear under our Theta pins," Violet announced. "And there's a special ritual to do in Lydia's memory, but they said we should wait a week until . . . till . . ." Her voice quavered and dropped off. "After the hurt settles down a bit."

Tori patted Violet's shoulder and took the floor again, reminding people of their committee assignments for the pancake social. Business as usual. While I understood the wisdom of moving on after a crisis, this seemed a little too slick and fast, but the meeting was not open for comments or suggestions, and there was really no time. Some of the girls had evening classes, and Mrs. J had emphasized that there would be no excusals due to Lydia's death. Harsh, but we all knew we could weasel a day or two out of a professor if we needed it.

As I headed toward the back stairs with my friends, Mrs. J called to me.

"Do you have a minute?" She pressed back a strand of silver hair and it immediately fell back in her face. The aging hippie look had appeal.

"Sure," I said politely, though I wanted to bolt. I couldn't imagine that this involved anything good. Sisters peeled off around me as they headed out of the meeting room.

"I wanted to give you a heads-up about the police."

Her words had the impact of a bucket of ice water. "What about the police?" I asked in a feeble voice.

"They wanted to talk with you this afternoon when they checked out Lydia's room, but you weren't here. I checked your schedule, saw that you were in class. Detective Taylor said she'll be back tonight or tomorrow, but you might hear from her. I gave her your cell number."

I shook my head. "Why does she want to talk to me?"

"Apparently, you're mentioned in Lydia's journal, and they're interviewing everyone close to her. Don't be nervous. This is standard procedure when someone commits suicide. They talk to family and friends, look for reasons why it happened."

"But why me?"

"You seem surprised, but I told the detective how you two spent time together of late. You girls think I don't notice, but I saw you sitting with her, listening to her. In some of these last days, I think you were one of her few connections to the outside world."

"Me?" She was making too much of something simple and stupid. "We weren't close."

"But you were there for her, and that was big of you, Emma. I knew you were connecting, and I knew Lydia was depressed. I wish I'd known the extent of her crisis, but then I'm not a health care professional. Still, I'm kicking myself now."

"I know what you mean, but . . ." I had to tread carefully. "Lydia had tons of support. But I guess no one can really know what's going on in someone else's mind."

"You're right. Wise for your years. It's just that . . . I've never lost one of my girls before and . . ." Her voice was hoarse now, and I stared down at the floor, respectful of her personal space as she pulled herself together.

The awkward moment seemed to span an hour, but when it passed I told her I would be sure to talk with the detective. "Although I don't have any special insights," I insisted.

"You're too modest. You meant more to Lydia than you realized."

Thanks, but no thanks, I thought as I extracted myself. As I took to the stairs I felt the new weight of worry over the police pressuring me, as well as the question of the journal. What had Lydia written about me? Had she been idiot enough to scribble down the secrets we had shared? Or was it just a perfunctory mention of my name? Maybe I was overreacting. She might have written about half the sisters of Theta Pi.

But during the meeting, Mrs. J hadn't pulled anyone else aside.

Just me.

CHAPTER 10

On the way from his office to the admin building, Finn was fighting images of the dead girl in his mind when he encountered a collection of students quietly working on one of the lawns on Greek Row. Only a week into November, it was early to be stringing Christmas lights, but that was exactly what they were doing, stringing white lights around the Theta Pi sign on the front lawn. As one of the girls stepped back from the sign, he noticed a few bouquets of flowers and votive candles placed around the base of the sign. Oh. A memorial.

"What's going on?" he asked two guys in flannel and down vests, who stood watching from the edge of the road.

"It's a memorial for the girl who jumped," said the tall beanpole of a guy. "What was her name?"

"Lydia Drakos," the other guy answered, shifting from foot to foot. "She was a Theta Pi."

"It's sad," Finn said with a nod toward the flowers and candles. "Did you know her?"

"We were just walking by," the tall guy admitted.

As Finn moved on he recalled Lydia mentioning something about a sorority when she'd asked for an extension. Something about pledge week or rushing or some Greek function—all a load of crap when it came to excuses, but he liked to give his students some play. No use making college deadlines tighter than deadlines in the real world, which, in his experience, usually had some latitude. There was enough pressure in the world without ramping up fake stress.

Up ahead, the North Campus Bridge reached across the ravine, its steel posts forming defiant Xs against the pewter night sky. He slowed at the staircase leading up to the bridge, then pushed ahead. As the roadbed came into view, he saw police tape at the center of the walkway, and a campus security guard strolling past it. A handful of pedestrians crossed, heads down against the wind, pausing briefly to view the site.

Nothing to see, as a cop might say. Just yellow tape rattling in the wind. Still, there was an eeriness in the air, an emptiness, as if a vacuum lingered at the center of the bridge. Finn knew he was probably projecting, trying to assign a loss and sadness to a death ritual that was cold and without meaning.

Suicide.

He'd danced with that one more than once. Posttraumatic stress could lead a person to dark places.

Finn slowed his pace as he came up on the campus guard assigned to the bridge. "How's it going?" Finn asked casually.

The guard nodded. He had craggy skin, sunken eyes, and an outlaw mustache. Probably in his sixties, most likely a retired cop. Finn valued experience.

"Are you here through the night?" Finn asked.

"Until after sunrise." The man gave a sad look at the yellow tape. "But I don't know how long they'll keep someone on duty here at night. Not in the budget."

"True," Finn said, and he knew some of the students would be resistant to having a police presence on the bridges. "Well. Stay warm."

The guard nodded, already shifting his attention to a trio of young women coming from the east side, the spires of Chambers Hall lit against a gloomy sky. Beneath the cliff-side building, the gorge was a black hole, dark fingers of shadow. Nothing to appreciate by night, but come the sunrise, the view below would be nothing short of spectacular.

Walking on, Finn considered the dilemma of the bridges and

gorges. He knew the cops would have shut down the bridge during the investigation if they could, but the closure would have crippled the north end of the campus, where the campus had spread across the river into the town of Pioneer Falls. Dormitories, classrooms, sports complexes and stadiums, and food courts peppered both sides of the gorge. Merriwether was a campus of bridges.

There was no denying that the rocky, varied landscape drew students from across the country, but the stunning gorges were a mixed blessing. The natural marvel of waterfalls and creeks carving their way through ancient rock offered beauty as well as a simple means of suicide.

The admin building was a squat Tudor-style structure, far more impressive from the outside, as its hallways were warrens and the rooms inside were too small and dark to hold classes. His key card allowed him access to the front door. From there it wasn't difficult to find Dean Cho's office—the only open door with a rectangle of amber light in a glum second-floor hallway.

"Looks like you're the only one working late," he called, mostly to give her some warning of his approach. When he swung into the open doorway, she was at her desk typing.

"I like the quiet," she said. "It's the best way to get things done." She clicked the mouse, and then turned toward him.

Although he had met her before at a campus meet and greet, the light back then hadn't been nearly so flattering. In the warm glow of the desk lamp, her smooth skin and finely angled cheekbones lent her a movie star grace in that high contrast way of old black-and-white movies. With dark hair cut so that it angled in at her jawline and almond-shaped eyes, she possessed lovely features that couldn't be disguised by dark-framed glasses and an oversized cardigan. "I'm Sydney Cho."

"Scott Finnegan." He reached out and they shook. Damn, she had a strong grip. "We met before. I was the professor who requested that you review the policies of the university counseling center."

"One of those," she said, gesturing for him to sit. "Had I known, I would have locked my door."

Was that a joke? With her robotic delivery, he wasn't sure. He took a seat.

"So, Dr. Finnegan, did you bring me Lydia Drakos's grade reports?"

"I did not. Doesn't Ms. Drakos have a right to privacy after death?"

"Not if that death is under investigation. This is for her own good."

"It's a little late for that," he said.

"I meant—"

"I know, the cops have to verify that it was suicide, but are the circumstances suspicious? Do they suspect homicide?"

"Not that I've heard. Her diaries were disjointed, and the girl hadn't left the house for more than a week. There were signs of clinical depression, but that's not for me to determine. The police won't rule on the death until they have evidence and interviews in hand, and that includes Lydia's grades and student profile." Her hands seemed delicate next to the bulky sleeves of her sweater as she crossed her arms on the desk. "Did you know Lydia Drakos?"

"Not well. We had a chat about grades. She was falling behind, late on two essays, and she'd gotten a C minus on the first paper."

"And we're talking about a required Comp class. What was a senior doing in a core curriculum class?"

"I have a few seniors in my classes. Some of them have failed it before. Others leave Comp until the end, especially the left-brain kids. The engineers and premed students. Did Lydia take Comp before?"

"She did, in her freshman year. She withdrew with a D. But that's the only blip on her record, until now. She has a D and a C in her other classes this term, and she had already dropped Astronomy. The term wasn't going well for her."

"What kind of grades did she get in the past?" he asked.

PRETTY, NASTY, LOVELY 63

"That's the thing." She scrolled through a document; Lydia's transcript, he assumed. "We're looking at a senior with a three-point-one average. Aside from her D in Comp, Lydia was a solid B student, a sociology major, so writing a few essays in a Comp class should have been a breeze." Cho removed her glasses and glanced up, contemplating Finn. "She was struggling, but it may not have had anything to do with academics. Clinical depression? Mental illness? Financial issues, or relationship issues? There are a multitude of stressors tugging on our students."

Cho's voice was still monotone, but she was concerned—far more sympathetic than he had expected.

"So you do realize the pressures these kids face," he said.

"Of course I do. It's my job to understand what these students need and to advocate for them."

"Then why are you letting those quacks at the counseling center crush them?"

The moment Finn said it, he knew he'd pushed too far too fast. The flicker of humanity left her eyes, replaced by a chilly veneer.

"I mean," he pressed on, "if you're mandated to look out for our students, why is it that the university's reputation is prioritized over the individual students who legitimately need help?"

Something blazed in Cho's eyes before she iced over again. "You can't possibly understand my mandates, the protocol and safeguards I'm trying to put in place to save these students' lives."

"Save them, or your job? Isn't this more a matter of weeding out any kid who admits to suffering from depression, kids who experience bouts of hopelessness, as any thinking adult would? These kids go to the counseling center to work through anxiety, and leave the place strapped to a stretcher. You dismiss them from the university!" He delivered the last barb in the booming voice he saved for punctuating his lectures, often for entertainment value, but it didn't affect Cho's pert demeanor.

"We cannot have suicidal students on this campus when every half mile there's a bridge that offers them an easy out—a way to jump to their death before they have the time to think it through. It's a fact that suicides are more frequent when the opportunity is there. The bridges are a built-in suicide venue on our campus. There's nothing I can do about that, but the clinic, that I can control."

"By sending every student out on a stretcher, dumping them in the psych ward?"

"Not every student. Don't make me out to be the villain here, Dr. Finnegan. I'm not killing anyone. I'm saving lives."

"I beg to differ, Dean Cho. First, there's the fate of the kids you badgered into signing medical withdrawals. Have you tracked their progress since they were dumped?"

"We have no way of monitoring a student once they exit the university."

"Right. And then there are the hundreds of kids out there who need help but find that they've been cut off. Unless of course they want a vacation from classes. A permanent one. Which, for most of our high-achieving students, is a form of death."

"You have a dramatic flair, Dr. Finnegan. I see why you pursued language arts over science."

He recognized the thinly veiled insult. "Just because I'm passionate about the topic doesn't diminish the underlying truth."

"That is your opinion, Dr. Finnegan, and I don't have time for further discussion." She rose from her desk, clearly indicating that the meeting was over. "Please e-mail me Lydia's records this evening. I want to turn everything over to the police first thing in the morning so that they can close the case."

"Over and done, so that everyone can move on," he said, rising slowly. He was a head taller than Cho, and yet she commanded the room. He'd read that she'd played college basketball, and he could imagine that. A wiry, fiery point guard could run circles around dead wood on the court.

"Exactly."

He moved toward the door, then turned back, scratching his head. "Just saying? I'm not moving on."

"Excuse me?"

"I won't let this matter drop. Our students deserve better." He zipped his down vest halfway up and held out his arms. "Take a good look, Dean Cho. I'm going to be your worst nightmare."

CHAPTER 11

I was glad to escape upstairs to the suite I shared with Angela, Isabel, and Defiance. Inside these walls, we could live without filters, share our feelings, and let comments fly. My suite mates were the very best part of Theta Pi; they were the sisters I imagined when I set my sights on Merriwether and Greek life, delaying my freshman year to work my buns off and save money for the extracurricular part of college life that was important to me.

Say what you will about Greek life—the concept of buying friends, rewarding conformity, and creating an exclusive club. While those things may be true for some people, for me the attraction to joining a sorority was the need to be among sisters—friends who were of like mind, girls who laughed at the same jokes but celebrated the differences among us. I had found that with my friends in Theta Pi. There was a level of trust binding all the sisters together—sort of like a big extended family, where you might not know your Kentucky cousin well, but you enjoy her when you see her. Yes, some of the senior sisters on the Rose Council were pushy and demanding, but I understood that they had a job to do, and they needed our full cooperation to get it done.

My father, a fan of rebels from Jack Kerouac to Jerry Garcia, had clearly voiced his disapproval of sorority life. Anything that smacked of conformity or institutionalism clashed with his self-imposed bohemian lifestyle. He'd even suggested that I was latching on to sorority life to replace the sister I'd lost. That had hurt, mostly because I'd realized he was right. I missed Delilah. "Are we having fun yet?" she used to say, usually sarcastically, but I took it to mean that good times were on the horizon. After Delilah was gone, I carried her mantra with me, pushed to the back corners of my mind for later. Delay gratification. Nothing was going to be fun while I was the daughter of a broke slacker musician. But someday . . . someday.

I sorely missed my mom, too. She'd been the caretaker in our family, and as a kid I hadn't realized that it was her job as a surgical nurse that usually paid for rent and groceries. Her crazy twelve-hour shifts hadn't stopped her from baking cookies or throwing us all in the car and driving to the coast on a summer day. It wasn't until after she was gone that I realized how much I'd relied on her, how I'd taken for granted that my mom would always be there for me. My view of her had been so narrow; I had only seen her for the way she built my world. My mom, never Brenda Danelski.

For a while after the accident, it had helped to have my brother around, but Joe was seven years older than me, and as I finished my freshman year of high school he graduated from college and headed up to Seattle to take a job with Boeing and move in with his girlfriend. I'd been the sole female and the only child at home for the past six years, and though I'd had friends, relationships had been severed every time we moved. It had been hard to hold on to them after we moved to Eugene at the start of senior year. That had been a rough year until I bonded with Jordan, a brilliant, adorable outcast like me, who ended up taking me to prom. He got me. "Are we having fun yet?" became our inside joke. His parents loved me. I think they thought I could persuade him to be straight. Jordy and I were still friends, but time and distance had pulled us apart.

That left me with my father. Gary Danelski, known in the biz as G-Dan, was a jazz musician, semi-famous for one recording that had made him a name and some money when it crossed over to the pop charts. Now and then he got money in the mail for that song, but mostly he paid the bills with gigs at bars and festivals and outdoor fairs. After years of moving from town to town, living on egg-drop ramen noodles and waiting for cash gigs to buy groceries, it was clear I couldn't count on Dad for fiscal stability, much less college. Long before I'd turned eighteen, I'd been on my own financial track. I geared up to be a nursing major, knowing it would guarantee me a job, and I took a gap year to earn money to supplement my scholarship funds. I held down two jobs that year, and my father treated me like a friendly boarder who occasionally left Chinese take-out in the fridge.

Besides the anti-authority thing, my father hated the idea of throwing money into sorority membership and activities. "I'm paying for it myself," I had told him when he'd objected to me pledging in freshman year. "I took a gap year and worked my butt off and saved every penny. Can you just leave it alone? Can't you just let me be happy with this?"

Dad just waved me off and muttered something about it being a different era. At least he hadn't brought it up since then. He had even attended last year's father-daughter dance, and, true to form, he'd been unimpressed by the wealth and fame that surrounded him. Dad had talked sports with Isabel's father, a professional basketball star, and he'd gotten a gig out of Angela's parents, who hired entertainers for corporate events in Silicon Valley where Angela's mom was a dot-com genius. Sometimes, my dad could rise to the occasion. Was I embarrassed to have the only father with no sports coat and a scraggly ponytail halfway down his back? A little. But at least he'd made an effort. Since then my father let me do my own thing while he downscaled to a trailer and traveled around for gigs.

It made me feel a little better that I wasn't the only one who had a rocky relationship with my father. Defiance was always navigating ways to avoid her parents' demand that she give up school and let them fix her up in an arranged marriage, as some Roma families still did. Isabel had a polite, distant relationship with her famous father, but she sensed the resentment from his new wife and her kids. Angela knew that her average grades would always make her seem like a failure to her overachieving parents. So nobody's life was perfect.

Now as I moved through the halls and stairways of Theta House, I realized that everything looked the same—the swell of carpeting over the stairs, the worn doorknobs and moldings touched by countless hands every day—but the house felt different. A veil of mourning had fallen over all of us, manifesting itself in the typical range from denial to rage. As one of the most pragmatic, level sisters of Theta Pi, I didn't go in for ghost tales, but even I felt the residue of Lydia's presence in these halls, as if her depression lingered in the air, the scent of disappointment and sorrow.

Avoiding some sisters who were hugging in the hall and sobbing about Lydia, I stepped into the suite and closed the door behind me. "I'm glad that's over," I said, kicking my Ugg slippers into the entry closet.

Angela was with her guy on the couch, and Isabel and Defiance sat on the window seat with the glass pane cracked open to suck away the smell of weed. With all kinds of digestive issues, Isabel had a medical marijuana card that allowed her to smoke, and fortunately for us, she was generous with her medicine. Personally, I preferred to drink my way to nirvana, but after a rough freshman year Isabel's stomach wouldn't allow her even a sip of alcohol.

"What did Jan want?" Angela asked as she snuggled into the crook of Darnell's arm. Even seated, he was about a head taller than her, but he was a gentle giant, laid-back when he wasn't getting aggressive on the basketball court.

"She said the police were looking for me." I dropped into an upholstered chair. "Apparently, Lydia wrote about me in her journal, and they think I might know something about why she killed herself."

"Shit!" Defiance said, looking up at me through a cloud of vapor.

"I know." I gathered my hair back. "I didn't do anything wrong, but the cops can be scary."

Isabel blew a breath toward the open window. "It's so mean that the police have to come around when everyone is already feeling down. What do they want from you?"

"They need to make sure that Lydia wasn't murdered," I said. "And if she killed herself, they'd like to know the reason why." I didn't think the police had a chance in hell of finding out why Lydia jumped from the bridge, but I understood why they had to try.

"Does anyone *ever* know the reason why someone commits suicide?" Angela asked.

Darnell stroked the braids on her shoulder. "That's deep, babe."

"We know she was depressed." Isabel sat cross-legged on the window seat, picking at the seam in her leggings. "But I never thought this would happen. What was her deal? Was it about a guy?"

"Did she ever have a real boyfriend?" Angela asked. "Honestly, I thought maybe she didn't like boys so much."

"You talked to her, Emma," Isabel said. "Did she ever say anything?"

"Lydia loved the notion of having a boyfriend. She was focused on guys. The way she always wanted events where you had to bring a date?"

"Hold on here. Listen to the person who could see inside her heart." Defiance insisted that she had the ability to read a person's thoughts. I didn't necessarily believe her, but she was definitely a good judge of character. She pulled her hands inside the cuffs of her sweater. "Lydia was always wanting a boy by her side, but she rarely got too close. Never more than two dates."

"Except for that boy from high school." Angela snapped her fingers, trying to remember. "What was his name? Nick.

Any person who talks that much about a guy clearly hasn't hooked him."

"She talked a lot about Nick," I said. "And sometimes she mentioned one other guy from last year." I was hesitant to say his name, not sure how much Lydia's connection to this dude was public knowledge.

"That's right." Angela snapped her fingers. "The senator's son. Graham Hayden." Graham was well known on campus because of his father and his star status on the soccer team. "Lydia was all upset when they broke up last winter, but really? They were dating, like, ten minutes."

"She liked Graham, but I think Nick was the love of her life," Isabel said wistfully.

Defiance folded her arms. "Is there any such thing?" Her most recent boyfriend was a lacrosse player from Alpha Sigma Chi who had impressed us all by showering Defiance with flowers until we learned that he expected sexual favors for each and every long-stemmed rose. "So pedantic. It just gets tired," Defiance had told us.

"That's because you haven't fallen in love yet." Isabel folded her legs into the lotus position and pressed her palms together in the center of her chest. "Be patient, little Defiance, and things will come together for you."

"Do you think anyone has told Nick?" I asked, recalling the stories Lydia had told of her parents' disapproval of the young man who had worked in the gardens of their estate. Lydia's parents had thought that a simple gardener was not an appropriate match for their daughter, and so she'd had to sneak around to see him.

"Good question," Angela said. "He might still think she's alive. Like maybe he's waiting for her to answer his texts and he thinks she's pissed at him."

"That would be so sad!" Isabel's lower lip jutted out in a pout.

Although Isabel tended toward the dramatic, this was a tragic possibility. "And what was Mrs. J saying about Lydia's parents driving out?" I said. "They're on the other side of the effing planet."

"That would be quite a drive from Greece," Defiance agreed as she tapped her phone. "Coming by duck boat."

"That was old Jan getting choked up," Angela said. "Sometimes she gets the details wrong, even when she's not rattled."

"Look at that. We've made it to Snapchat." Defiance lifted her phone up to reveal a photo of the Theta Pi sign in front of our house, with a sad face emoji and the caption "Feeling Sad. RIP Lydia Drakos."

"They're building a memorial out front?" I rolled out of the chair and went to the window.

A small crowd was forming, congregating around the sign. "They're turning the sign into a memorial," I said.

We huddled at the window, curtains behind our heads to block out the glare. On the lawn below, students were gathering, some stacking floral bouquets, others sitting at the base of the lawn with lit candles. Someone had strung white Christmas lights over the Theta Pi sign in front of the house, and the lights twinkled over a spreading mass of flowers, candles, and posters heaped near the sign.

"Who are those people?" Defiance asked, as we knew this hadn't been organized by our sisters. "Did any of them know Lydia?"

"Probably not," I said. "Death can bring strangers out of the shadows." I remembered the handful of neighbors and church members who had come forward after Mom and Delilah were killed. One of the nurses Mom worked with had delivered a sweet eulogy, and our neighbor Joy started bringing us dinner every day—soup casseroles and Crock-Pot corny wiener chowder—until Dad called her off. I had loved her lemon chicken soup, but Dad had struggled with Joy's chattiness.

"Ugh!" Angela groaned. "It makes the yard look like a cemetery. We live in a freaking cemetery."

"You don't see lights like that in cemeteries," Defiance argued.

Isabel cupped her hands over her eyes and leaned against the glass. "I like the lights. They're festive. Like we're celebrating Lydia's life."

"Really? I wish they'd just take their shit and go," Angela said. "Take it to the bridge. Put the memorial there."

"But that's where Lydia died," Darnell said quietly. A rare comment. "The bridge symbolizes her death. The Theta Pi sign? That's her life. It's cool."

Angela let out a sigh. "I guess you're right."

I turned away from the window and grabbed a warm fleece jacket. "I'm all in. There are a lot of people out there. Let's make it into a candlelight vigil."

Isabel was tentative. "But we don't have permission."

"We can't wait," Defiance said. "We know the university will never permit it."

"They won't allow anything that draws attention to another suicide on campus," I said. "But I don't care. I mean, what's the worst they can do? Send a security guard to shut it down?"

"You go, girl." Angela plunked on her fedora and wound a navy scarf around her neck. "You coming with us, homie?"

Darnell shrugged. "I guess."

"This is going to make Violet crack." Defiance was beside me in the closet, picking through the rack for a woolen pea coat. "NAY-shun-all didn't tell us we could have a candlelight VEE-jall," she said in a sugary voice.

That made us all laugh, and for a moment I realized there was hope. There would be life after Lydia.

Within an hour, all of my sisters were out on the lawn, singing songs and holding candles to the gray sky. Violet had surprised us by unlocking the sorority ritual cabinet and bringing out a box of white candles to pass out to people who joined in.

Had any of these guys and girls singing and swaying in the dark known Lydia? I scanned the starry field, flames casting glimmers of warmth on their faces. Glasses, hoodies, beards, and tender eyes. Most of them had probably never noticed the girl in the drab, oversized sweater. But that was okay, right?

We all have to die alone. But it's good to have a crowd at the after party.

CHAPTER 12

"And then I told her I was going to give her the fight of her life until she did something to help the students." Although Finn was a few pints in, he felt the edge of his earlier battle returning as he brought Jazz up-to-date. "After that I stormed out. It was a fucking momentous exit, man."

"Really?" Jazz seemed unimpressed. "Sounds kind of overdone."

"It was a significant blow to administrative policy," Finn insisted. "I rattled the cages."

"Sounds to me like you were a bit of a dick."

Jazz's disapproval was a thorn in Finn's side. Jasper Patterson grew up in Willowbrook, a Los Angeles neighborhood where nearly half the residents didn't finish high school. That Jazz had gone on to finish his doctorate and land a teaching job in Oregon was a testament to his work ethic and blind faith. Jazz knew both sides of the street. If Jazz's bullshit monitor was getting a reading, Finn had to respect it.

Still . . . he could ask questions. "I'm a dick?" Finn asked. "I'm a dick when Merriwether's policies send these kids plummeting to their deaths?"

"Damn, Finn. You could radicalize a turnip, but it won't make anyone want to eat it."

"What the hell are you talking about?"

Jazz wiped the condensation on his beer glass with his

thumb. "Look, you're upset. A student died today. But give Sydney Cho some respect, too. Don't you think she's upset about a kid dying?"

"Not that I noticed."

"People don't always reveal their grief. If you ask me, you need to dial down the anger. You know that old nugget about catching more flies with honey than vinegar? I'm just saying, you'll make more progress as a nice guy than a dick."

"I'm a nice guy. At least with the students." He shook his head, thinking back to Lydia. "Maybe not nice enough. I should have reached out to Lydia Drakos. Kids like that, they're the ones we're fighting for."

"You can't blame yourself for her suicide. You weren't her only teacher. You were nice to her. You weren't her biggest problem. You said she was struggling to pass all her classes."

"But I met with her. I should have seen the signs."

"What? Depression? Anxiety? Alienation? You're not a shrink, Finn. This one is not your fault. Don't take it personally."

Finn took a swig of beer, a bitter sting on the back of his tongue. "I can't sit back and do nothing when I have the power to save a life." He looked at Jazz, his angular brown face punctuated by bold black glasses. "You have the power, too. Get in on this and talk to Dean Cho. Let your voice be heard."

"I'm like Batman," Jazz said. "I don't come out until people really need me."

"These kids need you now, man. The local papers are calling this autumn Suicide Fall. Work with me on this. If we can get a few professors on board, the administration will have to hear us out. There's power in numbers."

"Aw, man, it's too risky for both of us. That's a mission for the fat cats with tenure who have some weight to throw around. Or better yet, get the students on board. This is their community; it's their time to engage and become activists."

"Come on, Batman." Finn leaned over the table, nearly spilling his beer in the process. "You can't count on the others to save Gotham City." The last word came out on a sliding slur, and Finn wondered if he'd had too much to drink. Probably so.

"Finn, come on. You and I are hired guns. I'll do what I can to help the students, but I can't stick my neck out to buck an administration policy right now. And you'd be wise to hold back, too."

"I can't hold back. I never could." Finn stared down at his empty glass. "Restraint was never my strong suit."

"It's cool to have passion, but you need to watch your back, too." Jazz looked at the curling piece of paper with the bill. "Are we done here? This is bad form, man. Drinking on a Monday night. Nowhere to go but down."

"We're done." The alcohol had kicked in, dulling Finn's senses, muddying the edges of his vision. He put a twenty on the table, grabbed the backpack with his laptop, and paused. Closing time. This was the dark time of the day, when he had to face the biggest mistake of his life.

Jazz took a last swig of his beer, and then reached into his wallet for a few dollar bills. "You sacking on my couch tonight?"

"I should go back to the house." Finn lifted his cell phone and read from his text messages. "Eileen told me if I wasn't home by midnight not to bother coming home. EVER."

"Well, there you go. She set you free."

"Yeah. I wish it worked that way. Not a fine use of sarcasm." Finn yawned. "*Should* I go home?"

"You have no desire to be there. Hence the three or four beers, prolonging the inevitable."

"True." Finn pulled his jacket on, then paused. "I keep thinking it's going to get better. That I'll bond with him and suddenly she won't seem so abrasive. That a relationship will develop."

"That's optimistic."

"It's possible, right?"

"My opinion? Hell no. But if we take on that topic right now, we'll be here through finals week." Jazz's hand fell onto Finn's shoulder. "Let's get out of here."

They walked down the main street of Pioneer Falls, the cool darkness filling in for the lack of conversation. Across from Scully's the windows of the coffee shop were dark, though Finn knew the lights would be on in a few hours as the baristas started a few pots brewing and loaded the cases with pastries. Finn was still a patron, although the café had been the original scene of the crime, the place where Eileen had badgered him over drinking his coffee black, her form of flirting, and damned if he hadn't bought her a latte, grateful for the company. Hard to remember, but he had been attracted to her back then, only two years ago. So much had happened in the intervening months, the original meeting seemed like ancient history.

They passed Oogey's, the 24/7 diner that offered everything from vegan Thai tofu rice to Southern fried chicken. Despite the late hour, a dozen or so students and locals sat at tables and booths. Eileen had ruined that place for him, too, always complaining about something to the students waiting tables.

Nothing on Main Street was safe from Eileen's taint of criticism. The IHOP, the Shell station, the Safeway . . . each business they passed had been dissed by Eileen Culligan. Had she always been so sour? It was hard to remember a time when he'd been attracted to her, when her voice hadn't seemed shrill and full of criticism.

The scenario resembled a poorly done film noir with Eileen playing the femme fatale. It was embarrassing, the way that he'd been duped. Eileen hadn't been a student—Finn had always vowed he wouldn't fall for that—but she'd been employed in the university admissions office, allowing her free tuition. She was five years younger than Finn, a "pioneer," as the locals called themselves. He'd recognized ambition in her and had mistakenly thought she'd had her sights set on education. Instead, Eileen had chosen a simpler, more tangible goal: to become the wife of Scott Finnegan.

No intellectual discussions or galas at the university museum for Eileen. She wanted a house with a white picket fence. A set of china. Kitchen appliances and juicers. Linens from

Ralph Lauren and curtains from effing Martha Stewart's Collection. And now a minivan. One child, and she needed to buy a minivan for a mere thirty grand that neither of them had.

As he walked alongside his friend, Finn cursed himself for letting control of his own life slip through his fingers. He'd been an idiot to get involved with Eileen. A moron not to break it off earlier. A fool to let her move in and take over his home.

How green he'd been when they'd first met. He'd been vulnerable—an emotional wreck from an injury sustained just ten days into a tour in Afghanistan. He'd been so focused on healing what was left of his leg and learning to walk with his prosthesis that there'd been no time to deal with the psychological damage. His family and doctors and therapists had warned him to take it slow, but he'd wanted to get back into the race, pull ahead at full speed. He'd needed to prove that he hadn't lost an important part of himself on that roadside near the Pakistani border.

So when he'd met a leggy blonde who wouldn't stop interrupting him as he tried to write a course syllabus, Finn had sensed his luck changing for the better.

"I'm a forever kind of girl," she'd told him early on. "Don't mess with my heart." That was how Eileen spoke, in platitudes worthy of a sixties hit song.

"Don't worry. I'm not a surgeon," he'd teased, trying to temper her fortitude.

That had been the tone of the relationship: He'd tried to keep things light, while she pushed ahead. She'd wanted to move into his place, get married, start a family, but every time she'd pushed for more of a commitment, Finn had stood his ground. While he enjoyed seeing Eileen from time to time, he didn't see that their relationship had a future. He made no promises and tried to keep things casual. No strings attached.

Which had worked for him, until Eileen had gotten pregnant.

When he'd gently suggested that she end the pregnancy, she'd called him a baby killer.

The negotiations had gone downhill from there.

"So you're coming to my place?" Jazz called, interrupting Finn's bitter reverie.

"Hell yeah." Finn tripped over a curb, but caught himself. "You're stuck with me, Jazz. A broken soldier, drinking your coffee and taking up space on your couch."

"I'm fine with it, man."

"But it's not okay. Not all the time. I need to fix this." Somehow it was easier to throw out the personal details this way, walking into the dark future, face to the cool wind. And it didn't hurt that he was slightly drunk.

"It's not like you haven't tried," Jazz said.

"Tried and failed. Jazz, I want my house back."

"And you've asked her to leave?"

"Begged her, more than once. She can move back with her parents. Her mother's crazy about Wiley, and they have the room."

"But she won't go?"

"Says she values her independence. Translation, dependence on me."

"So . . . can you stop paying the rent? Find another place."

"Not quite so simple. My name's on the lease, and that would jam me up for finding another rental in town. And then there's the threat."

"The threat? From Eileen."

"Exactly. She'll drag my ass into court for child support, and report me to the university."

"Report you for what? She wasn't a student, and you weren't her boss. Is she saying that it was rape?"

"She'd be willing to fabricate a story to get her way."

"That's a crock of shit."

"A domestic Crock-Pot of shit."

"Have you told her she'd be breaking the law? That it's blackmail and she'd be lying under oath?"

"She just spins it into some sentimental crap. Says I'll learn to love her, that we were meant to be together. That soul mate shit."

"Do you think that's going to happen?"

"The more I'm around her, the more she grates on my nerves. I make an attempt for the kid. Maybe I could tolerate it awhile, for Wiley."

"That's not a good reason. Stick around now and you'll screw up three lives. You need to get the hell out so both of you can move on."

"I wish it were that easy."

"You're the one making it hard."

"It's the kid. It feels wrong to bail on him." Finn was about to say more, but he kept his mouth shut as he followed Jazz up the cobbled driveway to the cottage. Finn didn't want to dredge up his absentee father, who hooked up with a woman when Finn was in fifth grade and ended up divorcing his mother. It wasn't the loss of his father that hurt Finn as much as the fact that Mitch Finnegan had joined Helen's family, playing father to her two girls and moving them all to California when he got a job offer there.

Jazz fished his keys out of his pocket and held the gate open for Finn. "Plenty of men bail on their kids, and those kids survive. Some of them thrive. The term 'nuclear family' was coined by some white guy from Yale who wanted to maintain the status quo. A family unit does not need an alpha male. Not a requirement."

"I know, I know, but I don't want to be the one who bails."

"Are you even listening to me?" Jazz shook his head as he unlocked the door and turned on the light. "I don't know why we're even having this conversation after a night of drinking. You won't remember anything in the morning."

"I'll engrave it on my brain," Finn promised as he took a seat on the increasingly familiar couch. "Tell me."

"God's honest truth? Eileen manipulated you from day one, and she's still trying to steer the boat. The only thing that's going to develop is animosity, which, from my experience, doesn't take much work when someone traps you like that. The kid—he's an innocent in all of this—but that doesn't mean you'll ever feel an attachment. Maybe you'll both get lucky, but chances are, it's not going to happen. You and Eileen will torture each other until you can't stand it anymore. One of you will duck out—probably you. You'll be stuck with child support, but if you can extract yourself, maybe you can walk away with your balls intact."

Finn dropped his face into his hands. "I have no balls."

"If that were the case, you wouldn't have a son, which seems to be at the core of your dilemma." Jazz tossed him a pillow and blanket from the closet. "But all kidding aside, it's time to man up. There're plenty of people out there with worse problems than you and they keep on keeping on. Talk to a therapist or a lawyer or an accountant. Do what you need to do to get free."

Freedom seemed like an impossible notion. For now, Finn would start with sleep.

CHAPTER 13

That night I woke up in our suite with my anatomy textbook open in my lap. With a groan I stretched my legs over the arm of the little sofa and tried to untangle the throw around my waist. The love seat was okay for studying, but not for sleeping.

Planning to go to bed, I plodded to the doorway of my room and paused at the sound of Angela's breathing. There was something unnerving about having a body in the bed across from mine; I had tried to fall asleep in there hours ago, but I kept worrying that I might wake up to find her stiff and cold and reeking like the cadavers in anatomy lab. Irrational, I know, but when you're in that phase of twilight sleep, the mind wanders to some strange corners.

Just then Angela sniffed and turned on her side, startling me. I froze, holding my breath.

This was ridiculous.

I backed out, quietly closing the door behind me. Outside at the memorial, Courtney had told us that she had moved in with Aubrey and Violet, unable to sleep in the suite she'd shared with Lydia. "And I'm never going back," Courtney had said in a quavering voice.

"But that's a prime suite," Angela had said. "You can't just leave it empty."

"Then you move in," Courtney had said with all the petulance of a two-year-old.

With the blanket slung over my shoulders, I grabbed my notebook and cell phone and headed into the hall. I wasn't going near Lydia's old suite, and the study rooms were too stiff, with only a desk and chair in each little closet. Instead, I plodded downstairs to the parlor, determined to stretch out on one of the largest couches we had in Theta House. It was a wide-open area, but Lydia had figured out that we had a wide view of the foyer and stairs if we nestled in the corner of the two couches, and the control freak inside her wanted to monitor who came and went. I turned the floor lamp to its dimmest setting and settled into the pool of pale light. Watching over everything, I felt safe and in control again.

It didn't even bother me that this was the place Lydia and I used to sit for our late-night chats. She would be down here waiting out a bout of insomnia, and I usually slipped down to recover from a panic attack that shot me out of a sound sleep and into a sweaty hysteria.

We had talked for hours with Lydia doing the navigating. She had this way of veering off my questions and venturing into long elaborate tales about the antics of the pet cats in her family. When I asked her about a professor who was being gruff with her, she answered with a story about a family friend who had squeezed her chest tightly at a family picnic when she was seven. When I mentioned a job opening at the library, she told me about her first lemonade stand and her family's strong work ethic. And if I asked her about the latest guy she was accompanying to a football game or a dance or a party, she inevitably spiraled back to a story about her childhood sweetheart, Nick.

"God, Lydia." It was still hard to believe she'd killed herself. "And you left a mess behind." It worried me that the cops wanted to see me. What did they think I had done?

I turned the page and started drilling myself on the bones in the human hand—distal, middle, and proximal phalanges, then metacarpals were the bones in the fingers and . . . As I stared at the drawing, the bones of the hand suddenly resembled an exotic palm tree, the small nuggets of bone at the base of the fingers resembling coconuts nestled in the tree.

I must have fallen asleep again. The next thing I remembered was a shift in the air, as if something were moving near me. I opened my eyes and found my face nuzzled into the velvety side of the throw. I recognized that I was sleeping in the parlor and knew that someone was walking in the hall. Was it morning?

Shifting slightly, I peered over toward the hallway. One of the sisters was facing away from me, moving toward the stairs.

"Hey," I murmured.

She didn't answer. From the black Theta Pi hoodie and tights, there was no telling who it was. The odd thing was that she seemed to be carrying something up the stairs in the middle of the night. Reaching for my cell phone, I confirmed that: 4:10 a.m.

Too tired to think much of it, I went back to sleep. When I scrambled off the couch at 6:30, I wondered if it was just something I'd dreamed. But as I headed to the stairs with the blanket draped over my shoulders, a blank section of wall in the foyer gaped at me like a missing tooth. A Theta Pi group portrait was missing from the wall. Had Hoodie Girl taken it?

Weird things were occasionally happening when you threw forty girls into one house.

I headed upstairs to take a shower.

A few hours later as I waited to meet with the police in Mrs. J's quarters, I tried to ease my nervousness by soaking up her small apartment: the open mystery novels on the end table, the puffed-up pillows on the floral-patterned couch, the graduation photos of Jan Johnson's two sons, who now had kids of their own. What would it take to give up your life and live like a nun, administering to forty girls, carting them to urgent care, negotiating with the cooks, and chasing the repairs on an old house?

I'd made a lot of sacrifices during my gap year. By day I was a member of a cleaning crew, scrubbing toilets, coaxing grease from stovetops, and mopping floors. Rubber gloves and a mask were my friends. At night I worked as a hostess and food runner at a small Italian restaurant. The night job was a thousand times better, but I have to admit I probably did a better job cleaning kitchens and bathrooms, gritting my teeth and getting in the zone. The restaurant called for a more outgoing, cheerful girl, someone who lit up the room, not someone like me who moved tentatively through the empty spaces and occasionally told people exactly what she thought. At the end of the summer, when I gave my two weeks' notice, the owner, Sal, asked me, "What's your name again?" That was the kind of impression I made on people.

Maybe my less-than-dazzling personality would finally work to my advantage with the police, who would wonder, "What could mediocre Emma have to do with Lydia killing herself?"

Nothing, I thought emphatically as I chewed on the cuticle of one thumb. I never meant to hurt Lydia. At one time she'd thanked me for everything I'd done for her; she'd been grateful. But that hadn't lasted long.

My heart lurched in my chest as the door opened and Mrs. J escorted a middle-aged woman into the room and introduced her as Detective Paula Taylor.

I had expected a woman, but not the twin of Oprah Winfrey.

"And you are Emma Danelski?" Detective Taylor patted my arm with a warm, intelligent, best-friend vibe. "Thanks for making time for me, Emma. I know you have a busy schedule, so let's get right down to it." She sat across from me at the little round table and typed my name into her iPad. "Danelski. So, Emma, Lydia wrote about you in her journals, and some of the girls mentioned that you had kind of a special relationship in these past few weeks. I'm wondering if you can shed some light on that. Any insights on why Lydia might have taken her own life?"

My face burned with guilt. Was I turning red? "We weren't

really close," I said, looking down at the peeling skin on my cuticle, "but I could see that something was bothering her. She had stopped going out, and I don't think she was showering. She wore this bathrobe all the time."

"The pink bathrobe," Taylor said, scrolling the iPad's screen. "I've heard a lot about that. It's tragic how many people knew Lydia was in distress, though no one was able to help her."

"Yeah. Well. What can you do to help someone trapped inside herself?"

"Sometimes there is nothing we can do. But sometimes we can get people to intervene. A parent or administrator. You have a counseling center here on campus, and Dean Cho tells me that, during orientation, every student is told that free counseling is available."

"It's free, but there are strings attached," I said quietly. "Last year, one of our sisters went there for help and got kicked out of school."

"They didn't actually kick her out," Mrs. J piped in for the first time. "They granted her a medical withdrawal."

Granted? As if she'd been given three wishes. "They told her she couldn't come back," I said. "Lydia knew what happened to Lexi, and she wasn't going to make the same mistake."

"Lydia told you that?" Taylor asked.

"She said that counseling was out. Besides, she wasn't raised that way. Problems were private for her. I mean, so private that she didn't admit to having any problems. Although we knew something was wrong. Believe me, we all tried to get her out of that bathrobe and out of the house."

"Was she dating anyone?" Taylor had a bright face when asking questions: brows raised, head slightly cocked in expectation.

"Lydia dated a lot of different guys. She was into old-school dating, and that kind of works in sorority life."

"Anyone special?"

"Besides her high school sweetheart? Not really."

"What about..." She flipped through her notebook and paused. "Graham Hayden. Do you remember her talking about him?"

"From last year." I was glad my hands were under the table, because she missed my fingers tightening into fists. How much should I say? "They went to the Winter Ball together."

"Was that a rough breakup for Lydia? I hear he broke her heart."

I wanted to ping the sister who'd given that up. "That was a long time ago, and I think they were still friends. Recently, she was talking a lot about her old boyfriend from home. Nick. She still loved him. She wanted to go back to Greece, back to the island, and see if they could make it work. She thought she could be happy again if she ditched college and lived in the sunshine with Nick."

"*Barefoot in the sun,*" Lydia had told me, "*and we'll have lots and lots of babies.*"

Lydia had become obsessed with babies. And after what I'd gone through, it killed me inside.

Detective Taylor's face was pinched in a frown. "I wonder where she got the idea to go to Greece. Do you know why she came up with that plan?"

"She came here from Greece. Her family owns an island there." The doubts I had tamped down for the past year or so now surfaced like quickly rising bubbles. "She returned there every summer when spring term ended."

Taylor was shaking her head.

"That's what she told us."

"It wasn't true," Mrs. J said. "I confronted Lydia about it last year when she was bragging about getting a limo to the airport. I knew all along that her parents weren't foreign billionaires, but I let the lie go until she was using it to make another girl feel inadequate. She promised me she would drop the ruse, but I guess she held on."

"So where was she from?"

"Salem, Oregon," said Taylor.

I tried to swallow, but my throat had gone dry. "And not from a wealthy family?"

"Her stepfather owns a dry cleaning shop and drives a limo on the side." Mrs. J bit her bottom lip, staring sadly through stray silver hairs. "He was the one who used to pick her up in the limousine, and that's how I had the chance to meet him."

"So everything she told us about Greece and her rich family was a lie."

The detective shrugged. "I suspect that she was embarrassed by her family. I'm still sifting through the web of lies she spun about her past."

"Wow." I stared down at my hands, pretending more shock than I felt. "If she was lying, you probably can't believe what she wrote in her journals. I heard she wrote something about me? Can I see it?"

She held up one hand dismissively. "The journals have been vouchered as evidence, and the writing is disjointed, like a stream-of-consciousness thing. She may even have been writing about her dreams. But she seemed grateful to you. She wrote that you saved her life." Her wide amber eyes turned on me, making me feel like a pinned butterfly. "Did you stop her from committing suicide in the past?"

"I didn't. I mean, not that I know of. We just talked a lot, sometimes late at night, and . . ."

Shut up . . . *shut up!* The truth kept trying to rise up, a steel pillar in my path, but I couldn't go there.

The voice of reason blasted me to stop talking. It didn't seem that Detective Taylor had anything that incriminated me. So why not just end the interview now?

I decided to play the sympathy card.

"It's hard to talk about her now," I said. This was true, but for reasons the detective wouldn't understand. "I feel bad that she didn't reach out to one of us. I don't think any of us knew she was coming unhinged."

"It's not your fault." Detective Taylor reached out and squeezed the hand I'd rested on the table. "Very often in cases of suicide, the ones left behind feel guilty."

If Detective Taylor had an inkling of the guilt that was eating away at me right now, she would lock me up and ask questions later. "I'm okay," I said.

"The counseling end is not my bailiwick, but I know there's guilt." Taylor squeezed my hand. "I hope you'll take advantage of some of the grief counseling services Dean Cho is setting up."

Had she not heard anything I'd said about the black hole at the campus counseling center? I wouldn't be showing up there, but I shrugged to let the topic drop. "I need to go. I've got an exam in my Anatomy class."

"We're about done. I'm just now wondering about some of Lydia's references in her journal, and here's where I have to be frank. More than once she called you an angel of death."

"What?" I was sure I'd heard her wrong.

"An angel of death." Detective Taylor nodded. "I thought it was a strange nickname for a sorority sister. It sure got my attention. Any idea why she might call you that?"

"She must have been talking about someone else," I said, trying to keep my voice from shaking with panic. *Such an idiot, Lydia. You think I killed the baby?*

"I'm a nursing major." My pulse was thundering in my ears as if I'd just run a mile. *Stay calm.* "I try to help people, not harm them. She must have been talking about someone else."

"Maybe. But there are a few times when she mentions a blue-eyed killer. And now that I've met you, well . . . You've got amazing eyes. Were you the blue-eyed killer?"

A dull pain stabbed at my racing heart. I sensed that my face was red, probably looking guilty as hell. "I don't know what that means, but I'm not a killer."

"Do you think Lydia was writing in some sort of code?"

I shrugged. "Honestly, I don't know."

"Well, we know Lydia was in a vulnerable place, and you

were a close friend. Is there a possibility she was coerced into jumping?"

"I've been wondering about that. Lydia didn't take direction well. She was stubborn, but she stood up for her convictions. That's probably why she spent three years on the Rose Council."

"That's the leadership board of Theta Pi," Mrs. J explained.

"But anyone can be influenced, right? I heard that someone else was on the bridge," I said, staring directly into the detective's brown eyes, silently daring her to say that she suspected me. "Do you know who that was?"

Something shifted between us; it was as if I'd scored a point. "We're investigating the pedestrian on the bridge." She cocked her head to one side. "So you know Rory MacFarlane?"

"Everybody knows Rory," I said. "But yeah. We've met."

"Rory was in the last Winter Olympics," Mrs. J interjected. Another useless comment. "He almost won a medal in snowboarding."

"So I heard." The detective kept her gaze on me. "He was very helpful. And I appreciate your honesty, Emma."

Was she being sarcastic? I couldn't tell.

"Did you ever talk with Lydia about the other suicides this fall?"

"I don't think so. It's not something my friends and I talk about. We try to keep things positive. Except that now, with Lydia . . . it's been rough."

"That's understandable." The detective sat back in the chair, seemingly disappointed. "I'm sorry to press you, but I had to ask. Lydia's mention of you was one of the few things that made us wonder if her death wasn't a suicide. I'm glad to put these questions to rest."

"I have a test to study for. Are you finished with me?"

"For now, at least." Her smile brought me no relief.

I was on the hook.

Alarm flared in my chest at the thought of the Pioneer Falls police labeling me as the "blue-eyed killer," sticking a photo of me up on one of those white boards and just waiting until I stepped out of line, jaywalking or drinking, so that they had a reason to toss me in jail.

Was I on their list?

The possibility sent apprehension thrumming through my veins as I rose from the table. I hoped that Detective Taylor didn't notice my hands trembling.

CHAPTER 14

After the interview I felt a little sick and off balance. Had the detective been giving me a subtle jab? Her professionalism hadn't completely covered the fact that she didn't entirely trust me. What had Lydia written about me in that journal? I didn't have time to worry about this over coffee or a late breakfast.

I escaped to the suite and tried to make some sense of the human skeletal system, the most recent unit of study in my A & P class. Everyone said that Anatomy and Physiology was the turning point for nursing majors, the class that weeded out the weak from moving ahead. Merriwether's program provided human cadavers for us to dissect and study in the lab—a mixed blessing. Working on human cadavers provided excellent training for us, but I could never forget that I was working on a human body. A hand that once rinsed dishes, a cheek that had been kissed. At the beginning of the term, various body parts had haunted my dreams. Now I greeted the corpses with a feeling of respect and gratitude, and I think that kept them out of my psyche.

I opened my notebook and the air left my lungs. There were two hundred and six bones in the human body, and I needed to be prepared to identify them all. Oh, why hadn't I started studying this yesterday, when I still had a chance?

I pulled up a practice exercise on Quizlet and let out a yelp. "I am so dead."

"You okay?" Isabel appeared from her room, where she'd been tapping away on her laptop. We were the only two in the suite, but I figured she wouldn't hear me with her earbuds in.

I threw up my hands. "I thought I had a grip on this material, but I can't focus, and I've got the exam tonight."

"Oh, no." Her dark eyes seemed impossibly large in her sweet face. "Well, you still have the afternoon. Want me to drill you?"

"It's not about memorization. I just can't do this now."

"I'm sorry." She sank down on the sofa beside me and stroked my arm. "Maybe your professor will give you a makeup test."

"He's a hard-ass." The doubled-over, bearded Dr. Lamont had reminded me of an old crow perched on the edge of the desk. "No extensions. No makeups. No excuses."

"If you tell him about Lydia, I bet he'll soften up," Isabel said.

"Trolls like Dr. Lamont do not soften. They wear their bitterness like a badge."

"Did you talk to the police?"

I nodded. "Detective Taylor looks like Oprah."

"Did it go okay?"

"Fine." I hated myself for lying to someone as kind and pure as Isabel. I knew she would be sympathetic if I told her everything, but I couldn't.

"Do they think it was suicide?" she asked.

"Sounds that way. But listen to this. Lydia lied about Greece. She lived with her mother and stepfather in Salem."

"What? Not even a cool part of Oregon like Bend or Portland?"

"And her stepdad owns a dry cleaners. She didn't lie about riding in a limo, because he drives one."

"No way!" Isabel pretended to fall off the sofa. "I'm so disappointed. Not because she wasn't rich, but because she felt like she had to make up a lie to impress us."

"Lydia could be incredibly boring—even with the stories of her billionaire grandfather in Greece. I thought she was like a . . .

slice of white bread. No surprises, no texture or spice. But now that she's dead, I realize I had her all wrong."

"Was she a jalapeño pepper?" she asked, brows lifted.

"More like an onion, with one layer after another," I said.

"And she makes you cry," Isabel added.

Isabel had a way of capturing the truth. "I can't deal with this right now. How am I supposed to take an exam when my head is about to..." My cell phone began to chime. "Explode." I saw that it was Mrs. J. I sneered at the phone, then put her on speaker.

"Emma, are you still in the house? I need your help."

"I'm in my room."

"Lydia's mother is here to collect her things, and I told her she could meet some of the sisters who were close to her daughter."

Isabel gave me a monster shriek face.

I pressed my free hand to my jaw. "I'm studying right now. But she should meet Tori and Courtney. Violet, too."

"Violet is in class, and the other two are not answering my calls or texts." Mrs. J's voice was tight as a rubber band about to snap. "I would expect better of Theta Pi girls. I expect support and generosity. This is putting me in a difficult situation."

"I'm sorry," I said, rubbing the back of my neck where the muscles were bunching up. "It's just that I have an exam tonight and—"

"This is a horrific, once-in-a-lifetime occurrence for Mrs. Drakos." She spoke in a lowered voice laced with furor. "I need you down here to represent your sorority."

"I'll go with you," Isabel said quietly.

"All right," I told Mrs. J as I slammed my textbook shut and let it drop to the floor. I was pissed, but what could I do? "We'll be right down."

"No. Meet us up in Lydia's suite. You can help Mrs. Drakos pack."

Mrs. Drakos was a thinner version of Lydia, with the same black hair but styled in an A-line bob and a similar thick cable-knit sweater that hid any hint of her shape. Her face was gray, and mascara was smudged under her eyes. When I saw the tears glimmering in her dark eyes, the muscles in my chest tightened with guilt. I'd been obsessing over my exam and arguing with Isabel on the staircase about which of us would have to "touch" Lydia's clothes—a sudden task that gave us both the creeps—while this woman was trying to clear up the belongings of her dead child. The sorrow that vibrated the air around her broke my heart. I wanted to cry, not so much for Lydia but for her mother.

As Mrs. J introduced us, Mrs. Drakos's sad eyes searched our faces. "I'm sure Lydia mentioned you. I heard of Courtney, her roommate. Where is she, in class?"

I nodded, suspecting that Courtney was killing time at the student union or some café to dodge this task.

"Lydia loved her friends here at school," Mrs. Drakos said. "She always talked of her sisters."

"Aw." Isabel's eyes were also shiny with tears. "And we loved Lydia."

"We're so sorry for your loss." I knew that was the thing to say. I'd heard it plenty of times after Mom and Delilah died.

"Thank you. And it's good of you to come down and help."

"That's what sisters are for," Isabel said earnestly.

Mrs. Drakos patted her shoulder. "Such good girls. We were glad when Lydia pledged a sorority. She had no sisters, and she was always mad at her stepfather and me for not giving her a brother or sister. An only child."

That shed some light, though it didn't completely explain her self-absorbed personality.

"But here at Theta House, Lydia had more than forty sisters," Isabel said. "That's hard to beat."

"And she had Nick." Maybe it was foolish to get so personal, but I wanted Mrs. Drakos to see that we really knew her daughter. "Wasn't that her friend at home? A former boyfriend?"

She shook her head dubiously. "The only Nick in Lydia's life was Nick Jonas, but that was just a crush, of course."

Isabel held her arms wide. "He's great. I saw him in concert once."

"I'm sure Lydia told us about a boyfriend named Nick," I said. "Maybe it was someone she liked at school."

"Maybe a little crush, but she didn't date in high school. It was hard for her, being overweight."

What? Middle-class and overweight and her boyfriend was accessible only through Twitter?

"Boys made fun of her," Mrs. Drakos added. "Kids can be cruel, but it's hard to see it happen to your child."

"I'm sure it is." I couldn't keep the disappointment from my voice as it became clear that the Lydia we'd known was a lie. There was no Nick—no boyfriend at all in her short life. A life in which she'd been bullied for being overweight. That was too bad, but my sympathies were diminished by annoyance. I hated being lied to. When I'd been in the emergency room after the accident, no one would answer my questions about my mother and sister, and a few people told me that everything would be fine. The first nurse who stood there and told me my mom and sister had died—that woman was a hero.

"Look at that! Her sweaters." With moist eyes, Mrs. Drakos patted a stack of folded sweaters in the closet as if they were pets. "So much stuff! I don't know what to do with it. All this, it won't even fit in my car. Maybe you girls will find some things you want to keep?"

My eyes met Isabel's as an awkward panic set in. We had both decided that there was a definite eeriness about going through a dead girl's possessions. No way were we keeping anything.

"Our rooms are pretty full, too," I said apologetically.

"But we should take the Theta Pi stuff." Isabel pointed to two file boxes that pledges had decorated with the Greek symbols for Theta Pi. "Lydia was recording secretary and historian. She has some photos and notebooks with the minutes from our meetings."

"Take them, of course." Mrs. Drakos waved at the closet.

I reached up for the boxes, but they were heavier than I'd expected. Isabel took one side, and we eased them to the ground and took a peek. One was filled with a mound of photos; the other had files that seemed better organized. "I guess we'll store them in the ritual closet for now," I said. It would be too weird to have them in our suite. Isabel and I placed them by the door.

Mrs. J jumped in. "Anything you don't want to take home we can arrange to donate to Goodwill." She surveyed the room—a tidy open closet, its shelves full of fat sweaters and folded jeans, boots, and shoes. As dorm living went, the room wasn't bad, except for the top of the dresser, where bottles, packs, and tubes of makeup were scattered, some open and leaking so that the dresser surface looked like the palette of a crazed artist. "If we work together, it won't take us long." Mrs. J pointed to the top shelf of the closet. "There's her suitcase. Emma, would you get that down, please? Mrs. Drakos, did you bring anything to pack her possessions in?"

"No." Mrs. Drakos wrung her hands. "I wasn't thinking about this. I came mostly to make arrangements for the body. . . ."

Hearing her say that word sent a shudder through me as I pictured the shell of Lydia, drained of all life, but haunting at times with traces of identity like tattoos, scars, or nail polish. This was the consequence of working with cadavers in my anatomy class—the visuals of dead bodies in my mind.

"The arrangements are complicated," Mrs. Drakos went on. "Her body must be driven down to Salem, and there is a special company to do it. Not just anyone is allowed. But they're telling me I must wait for the autopsy."

"It must be so difficult," Mrs. J said, capping an open tube on the dresser. "Let me grab some plastic bags from downstairs. Girls, help Mrs. Drakos make three piles. Things to donate, things to take, and things to throw away. I'll be right back."

"So, Mrs. Drakos, where should we start?" Isabel unzipped the suitcase and set it like an open clam on the floor.

"I wonder if . . ." Mrs. Drakos hesitated, sifting through the closet. "I could sell things. Maybe on consignment or a yard sale. She had so much, so many nice things. So why?"

It was the same question we'd been asking. Lydia had possessed a room full of clothes, jewelry, and makeup, like any other girl I knew, but the question was, Why wasn't it enough to keep her in the game? Of course, material goods don't make a person happy. But why wasn't Lydia's full, fortunate life enough to keep her alive?

"Tell me what you want to keep and I'll pack them in the suitcase." Isabel kneeled beside the suitcase. "Her sweaters?"

As if she'd just discovered a secret, Mrs. Drakos took a folded burgundy cardigan from the closet and held it in front of her. "Oh, my girl!" She pressed the sweater to her face and sobbed into it.

Isabel tipped her head up and shot me a desperate look.

"Mrs. Drakos . . ." I put one arm around Lydia's mother and she folded me into a hug. "I'm so sorry," I said quietly. I rubbed her shoulder as she wept in my arms.

We were standing that way when Mrs. J returned to the room.

"Okay, I've got trash bags." Her voice trailed off when she saw that Mrs. Drakos was having a meltdown. "Oh, dear. It's so hard, I know," she said, rubbing the woman's back. "If it's too hard to make a choice, we'll pack up everything for you, and we'll hold on to anything that won't fit in your car."

"No." Mrs. Drakos held the sweater out reverently, then placed it on Lydia's bed. As if tending to an infant, she delicately arranged the garment, straightening the buttons and smoothing down the sleeves.

"Such a pretty sweater," Mrs. J said. "The girls will pack it up for you."

"No. Give it away. Give it all away."

"But there must be something you want to keep. Something to remember Lydia by?"

Her cheeks were wet as she surveyed the room and shook her head. "She's gone. These things will only bring me sadness. Please, give them away. Give them away and close the door."

CHAPTER 15

"So wait," Mia said, holding her fork aloft with a cherry tomato skewered on the end. "Who took the photo?"

"I don't know for sure. I couldn't see who it was." The salad was overdressed, and I blinked as vinegar stung my throat. Eating was a chore with the constant ache in my stomach. "I crashed on the sofa in the parlor last night. At one point I woke up and saw one of the sisters carrying it upstairs."

"So who took the picture?" Angela asked, clapping her hands to get quiet at the dining table. "Come on, people. Fess up. That blank spot on the wall ain't working for me." There were more than twenty of us at the big, long table in the dining room, but Angela had a voice that carried and demanded attention. Conversations at the far end of the table died down as people caught up.

"I'm talking about the Theta Pi group photo from the wall," Angela explained to the girls at the other end.

"I swear, my heart's gonna be broken if we can't find that picture. It was our pledge class, three years ago," Violet said, turning to Tori, who high-fived her. "The nine seniors are in that photo."

"Eight of us, now that Lydia's gone," said Courtney.

"Really? So the Theta Pi photo from our freshman year was stolen?" Haley, a senior nursing major who lived with her boyfriend off campus, rarely made any sorority events. She definitely had one foot out the door. "That's weird."

"Not stolen," Jemma said. "Someone just took it upstairs."

"For what reason?" asked Violet.

"Maybe they're going to scan the photo and post it on Facebook," Chloe said.

Tori held up her hands. "Why?"

"As a tribute to Lydia. It was her pledge class." Chloe glanced up and down the table with a defensive look. "I didn't do it. I'm just saying. Maybe."

"Not a bad idea, Chloe," I said. "We should check the study rooms. Maybe someone left it on one of the printers."

"If one of the sisters took it down, I'm sure it will turn up," Tori said.

"Or else we'll find it in a room search," said Megan. "The frame makes it kind of hard for anyone to hide."

"Come on, y'all, a room search?" Violet pressed a hand to her chest. "Are we living in a correctional facility?"

Courtney smiled. "Theta Pi Pink is the new black."

A few girls laughed, but Tori rolled her eyes. "Just chill on the picture, girls."

Sipping my milk, I shared her lack of interest in the missing photo. What struck me was the sight of the girl in a dark hoodie—echoing the pedestrian Rory had seen leaving the bridge. Could it be the same person? Had one of our sisters been with Lydia the night she died? If that was true, why wasn't the witness coming forward?

The only possible answer left me feeling sick inside.

Guilt.

Well, I could add that to the stack of stressors.

"Hey, Em, where you going?" Angela asked as I left the table.

"Work. I've got the afternoon shift." And I needed to fit in some massive memorization. I prayed for a quiet afternoon.

That night things went from bad to worse when Dean Cho turned up at Theta House as I was on my way out the door.

Recognizing her from student orientation, I tried not to make eye contact, but I felt her studying me as she waited in her short boots, leather jacket, and long black pencil skirt.

There was something sneaky about a university dean who looked like a kid. With a trim body, smooth skin, and eyes accented by stylish glasses, she could have been just another Merriwether student. The tip-off for me was her awesome haircut, an asymmetrical A-line, which you didn't see much on campus because most girls grew their hair long. As I stood by the door, wrapping a scarf around my neck, I heard Mrs. J tell her, "Oh, there's Emma now."

Great.

"Emma Danelski?" She introduced herself and extended a hand as I shot her a cautious look. "We need to talk." One on one, she seemed friendly and accessible, but I knew she had the heart of an unrelenting monster.

"I'm on my way to a class." I tried not to snap, but after dealing with Lydia's mother and losing any chance of studying, my disposition had soured. "An exam. I have to go."

"Then come see me in the morning." Like a magician grabbing a coin from thin air, she produced a card. "What time is good?"

"I have to work."

"Then the afternoon?"

"I have classes."

"You know, I can get you excused from a class, or get you some extra time on assignments." She placed a hand on my shoulder, looking around to be sure no one else was listening. "I'm intervening for Lydia's other friends, too, but please keep it confidential. I don't want to make it a blanket offer to everyone. People take advantage."

"I just want to keep up with the assignments," I said. "Things tend to pile up when you get extra time."

"How about Friday night?"

"Friday night I have a sorority function." Lydia's memorial ritual. Couple that with the Lydia Drakos Memorial Pancake

Event planned for Saturday, and it was going to be one hell of a weekend.

"So busy," Dean Cho commented.

"Yeah. That's what Merriwether's all about." If I resembled a sound bite from a recruiting video, I was trying to drive home the point that I had a life and I wanted people to let me live it.

"It's very important that I meet with you."

"Look, I wasn't that close to Lydia." And I was beginning to resent her for pulling me into the mess of her abruptly ended life. "She was depressed. Is that what you want to hear?"

"I know you cared about your friend," Dean Cho said, "but you're not really qualified to make that diagnosis."

"Then I give up. I thought you wanted to know about Lydia, but maybe I'm not *really qualified* to tell you about her."

Dean Cho pursed her lips together, a tiny gesture of annoyance. "Fair enough. Your anger is justified. But I'm here about the future. I think we all owe Lydia a chance to have her voice heard after death."

I loosened the knot at my neck. "That sounds creepy."

She eyed me with a deadpan expression. "Listen, I'm reaching out to you to try and build something positive from this. I'm assembling a student task force to address suicide prevention, and I'm looking for students with leadership skills to be a part of it. It sounds like you're busy, but the panel will certainly be a résumé builder."

Building a résumé for what? Nursing jobs were plentiful if I could just get through this program, but that wasn't going to happen standing here chatting. Everything seemed too hopeless right now. "I have to go. I have to buy Scantron paper before the exam and . . . I'm going to be late."

Dean Cho nodded imperiously. "Fine. Call me, or shoot me an e-mail."

As I turned toward the door, I caught a glimpse of Mrs. J's sourpuss of disapproval. Apparently, I couldn't do enough to right the wrong of Lydia's death. No, they thought I was too absorbed with my own life, all those brightly colored circus balls I needed to keep juggling.

I checked the time on my cell phone. Dean Cho had made me late. I broke into a run, careful not to roll an ankle on the uneven paving stones. I made it to the bookstore in seven minutes, but there was a line at the only open register.

"Fuck...," I breathed, sweating under my scarf.

Desperate, I found a student toward the front of the line who was buying a pack of Scantron paper. I paid him five bucks for one sheet—a deal for him—and raced out of there with the precious paper tucked into a notebook in my backpack.

The first drops began to fall as I darted out of the student center. I'd made the mistake of wearing my suede jacket. I slowed down to pop my scarf over my head, then took off again, this time motivated to move. But the rain pelted me, making it hard to see my way. I veered off the path and stepped into a mass of sodden leaves and mulch. My foot slipped and I went down, suddenly hugging the wet bricks.

The sting of my torn skin, the cold of the soaking rain, the stab of humiliation and defeat—everything combined to hit me with a cosmic slam.

I wasn't going to make it to class, and what was the point, anyway? I was going to bomb the exam.

The tears came hot and heavy as I pulled myself into a rumpled mass on the paving stones. The numbness I'd felt over Lydia's death had given way to shifting bouts of anger and despair. I was so angry at Lydia for pulling us into her troubled life, furious with her for not being strong enough or considerate enough to stick around. In that moment, with dirt under my fingernails and the cut on my knee smarting, I hated her. Yes, I hated her.

Some passing girl asked if I was okay, and I waved her off. Nothing was broken, just my former life. The downpour gave me license to cry all the way home without anyone noticing. I slipped into the back door of Theta House, careful to avoid

Dean Cho or the cops or even Mrs. J, who had been a pain in the ass lately. Like a criminal, I sneaked upstairs to my room. None of my suite mates were around. Whatever. I finished crying in the shower, then sat in my pajamas, trying to compose an e-mail to my Anatomy and Physiology professor that didn't sound sniveling or melodramatic.

> Since my friend and sorority sister killed herself,
> I have found it hard to focus.

That made me sound like a tepid moron.

> The recent suicide on campus was my friend
> Lydia, and I am still reeling from the news of her
> death.

Better. I rewrote it a few times, copied Dean Cho, and finally sent it off in surrender. Let him fail me if he wanted to be an ass.

I was tanking. A missed exam and no focus. I had the police, Dean Cho, and Mrs. J breathing down my neck, and I'd barely slept in the last twenty-four hours.

Sleep was what I needed.

I took two over-the-counter sleep aids, dried my hair, and crawled into bed. Hugging my pillow, I prayed for sleep to dull the thudding anger and despair. How great it would be to feel nothing.

CHAPTER 16

Emma's Freshman Year

Despite the stories of mean girls, hazing, and supreme bitch-ery connected to sororities, I enjoyed rushing and pledging Theta Pi. After a month of knocking around on campus, try-ing to make friends among the ever-shifting faces of thousands of students, I'd found instant friends while rushing. Maybe it was our own insecurity, but as soon as we found one another in our pledge class, Isabel, Angela, and I stuck together like glue, helping one another with schoolwork and just kicking back to talk.

I immediately wanted to adopt Isabel, with her round eyes and baby bird–thin body. Hard to believe she'd once been overweight, but she told me she had gone through years of binge eating in high school when her parents' divorce had up-rooted me. I got that. She still suffered from abandonment is-sues and PTSD, and she said she had her weight under control, though I rarely saw her eat anything besides raw veggies and water.

Angela and I had been the ones to choose Theta Pi, based on the incredible reception from girls like Kate and Theta Pi's rep on campus.

"They're not as focused on getting wasted as the Deltas," I said, "but they know how to kick it."

"And the Thetas aren't dirty girls, but they're not the God

Squad, either," Angela said. *"I'm kind of feeling like Goldilocks with the three bears. For me, the Thetas are just right."*

It didn't hurt that Theta House was one of the nicest hubs on campus, with plenty of bathrooms and small living suites instead of the massive sleeping porches that lots of sororities in the Pacific Northwest had to occupy. Orphanage-style barracks with more than a dozen triple bunks in the room. Not for us!

Sorority life seemed magical that first semester. At last, my mantra was becoming a reality. *"Are we having fun yet?"* I would ask my friends, and Isabel and Angela would laugh and high-five me.

The senior sisters welcomed us and spread their wings wide, introducing us to guys they knew, tutoring us in difficult classes. Kate was like a big sister to all of us, and Suz Ingrassio could make us laugh on the gray days. They made us feel like royalty. After years of a lonely, difficult grind, I was happy to be in the throes of an eternal sleepover.

Of course, there were the celebrity connections to elevate our status. India Taylor's father was a Hollywood film producer. Tori Winchester was rich and beautiful and hysterically snarky. Lydia Drakos was prim, from old European money. And one sister was rumored to be a cousin of Lady Gaga, but she played it down, saying she didn't want to be judged on something so *"ancillary."* I didn't mind ancillary. They thought it was cool that my father was a musician. Most girls had never heard of G-Dan, but they were impressed by his profile on Wikipedia.

Halloween night, when I met Sam, was the ultimate party weekend. We had finished the work on our homecoming float, that time-consuming paper dragon with the theme *"Theta Pi leaves the others draggin'!"* We'd made it through midterms, and Angela, Isabel, and I were making plans to move into Theta House after winter break. I had found my family of sisters.

I should have known that it couldn't last.

My downfall was a guy. I was sure Sam Mattern was the

one. *He wasn't always kind to me, but when he was, the sun shined on my world and held me in a warm glow. I wanted sunshine 24/7, and I began to plot ways to make him love me.*

Around the same time, my friends began drifting and fading into their own issues.

Isabel was sick all the time. "I have a tummy ache," she would say when I came to her room in the freshman dorm. She would crawl into the corner of her bed as I curled up beside her and told her about how Sam hadn't called me for two days or how I'd seen him laughing with a pretty Zeta girl at Starbucks. As Isabel had less experience with guys than I did, she fought off her fatigue to listen. "What are you going to do, Emma?" she would ask.

"Just keep trying," I said.

By November, we had to coax Isabel over to Theta House for meetings. Although she remained cheerful, she seemed to fade off while other people were talking, and she was always shivering cold, even after the room warmed up. Forget about hitting a party; Isabel could barely make it down the street.

Angela was spending more time with Darnell, having cooled on Theta Pi. She attended mandatory meetings and events, but never just hung out.

When I asked Angela about it, she swore me to secrecy and made sure no one was listening at nearby tables.

"I overheard some sisters talking about me," she said. "They were wondering why I hadn't pledged a black sorority."

"Who said that?" I asked.

"I'm not giving names 'cause you can't tell anyone anyway. You promised. But I'm just saying—you can probably guess."

"Tori? Violet?" I kept guessing, but Angela just scowled at me. "It can't be one of the seniors."

"Would you shut up and listen? Then she said, 'A girl like that doesn't belong in our sorority.' After I went through pledge week and initiation? I'm a fucking Theta Pi sister, and now they're saying I don't belong?"

"Oh, Angie, I'm sorry!"

"It's not your fault."

"But I feel bad for you, and pissed that we have a racist in the family." I picked at the seam in my paper coffee cup. "So what are you going to do?"

"Nothing."

"But you have to say something. Come on, Ang. You've never been shy."

"What do you think anyone will do if I tell them what I heard? You think your beloved Kate and her Rose Council are going to stick up for me and punish two of the older sisters who are about to be running the damned sorority next year? That will never happen."

Hope sank in my chest as I realized she was right. "What about chapter relations?" I said quietly. "You can send a note to chapter relations, anonymously, and ask them to address the problem. No one will get in trouble, but at least they'll talk about it and build awareness."

"Chapter relations?" Angela frowned. "Emma girl, you are so naïve. Chapter relations was the one doing the talking."

Chapter relations was Lydia Drakos.

My little family of sisters was drifting apart, and I couldn't let it happen. "Come on, you guys," I told them one Sunday morning when Angela and I brought Isabel bagels. "We made a pledge to be sisters of Theta Pi, and we're going to stick with it. I know it won't always be easy. The glitter has already faded from the time we pledged."

"Everyone was nice to us back then." Isabel, uninterested in eating, was hugging a pillow. "The senior girls spent time with us. They really seemed to like us. Now, they barely say hello."

"Not all of them," I insisted. I wanted to defend my big sister, Kate, but even she had pulled away with the excuse of preparing for a nursing job that would begin in January, during her last semester of college. "The seniors can see the end of their run. In a few months they'll be moving on into the real world. Getting jobs. Kate says it's a stressful time."

"It's like they already left us," Isabel said quietly, "and we barely know the other girls."

"We'll get to know them better," I said. "They're our sisters."

"Some of them in name only," Angela said. "I'd like a shot at those sisters who trash-talked me."

"Angie . . ."

"Seriously, I'm rethinking this whole sorority thing with the pretty white girls and their crazy theme parties and fake tans. What if we were set up? What if they bait the girls who are rushing? We think they select pledges based on qualities like personality and honesty. But what if they pick girls with parents who can pay the dues? It might be that simple." She picked the soft dough from the inside of a poppy bagel and rolled it in a ball. "They hook them in to collect their dues."

"You know that's not true," I said. "We know a few girls who didn't get bids from any sorority. We're the lucky ones. But we have to keep it together. The three of us need to stick together. I'm just saying, I'll always have your back."

"Aw," Isabel gushed, giving me a hug. "Of course I've got your back. You're the best friend, ever."

"Same." Angela patted my back as she hugged me. "You guys are the real deal. But you can't make me like the other sisters."

"I know," I said. Baby steps.

When I moved into the suite with Angela and Isabel in January of freshman year, I could feel things getting back on track. The planets that had been swinging out of orbit were aligned now, and our stars were shining brighter than ever.

"I feel like someone just let me out of a cage," Angela said as she helped Isabel string a set of red chili pepper lights up over the window. Her single room in the dorm had been like a cell, and she was sick of being the guest in the grotty dude shack that Darnell was sharing with some other players.

"The air here feels more peaceful and balanced," Isabel

said. *"Much healthier than the dorm. And with access to the kitchen, I'll be able to eat right again."*

After a scary episode in which someone found Isabel passed out in the women's room at the campus gym, Isabel had confided that she had an eating disorder. Angela and I had suspected, but it seemed best to have Isabel tell us on her terms. She said she had it under control now, and though she still had the body of a frail bird, her new diet gave her enough energy to get through the day.

"When do you think Sam will be by to check out our new place?" Isabel asked. Going along with the pretense that I had a real boyfriend, she had offered to vacate the bedroom we shared whenever necessary so that Sam and I could have privacy.

"I'm not sure," I said. "He's been so busy." Hanging out with everyone else but me.

Once again I texted Sam, inviting him to Theta House, telling him I would meet him downstairs and sneak him up to the suite. So many times over the holidays I'd considered ending it with Sam. He was only available on his terms, rarely when I needed or wanted him. And I knew he was hooking up with other girls. He said no, but the signs were there. I'd seen him walking and laughing with other girls on campus. And all those nights when he didn't answer my texts. Those weekends when he wasn't available. The entire winter break when I had begged him to meet me in Portland or Seattle so that I could escape my father's small apartment and get a Sam fix. I had missed him. But Sam had left me hanging, later saying he had "family stuff."

Are we having fun yet? Not quite.

When I considered the true dynamic between us, it was an off-balance symbiotic relationship. Sam was the bird that landed on my back and ate away the pesky insects. It felt so good when he dropped by to pick at the bugs, and he benefitted from it, too, but I could never count on him to land on my back when the bugs were biting.

Maybe we'd moved to a sexual relationship too quickly. But no one I knew held back sex when they were into a guy. And sometimes I worried that the sex was the only thing that kept him interested. When Sam teased that I was a *"wild woman"* inside, I felt hope for the rest of our relationship.

Until he left, and disappeared for four days.

Being a bit more jaded than the rest of us, Angela didn't buy into the magic of love. After a few weeks of watching my relationship with Sam, she brought it up one day when Isabel was off at class.

"You know," she said, her eyes on her cell phone, "you don't have to put up with his shit. Tell him how he needs to behave. If he doesn't step up, then dump his ass."

"I know he's unreliable, but nobody's perfect."

"Unreliable? Is that a nice way of saying 'lying piece of shit'?"

My eyes stung with humiliation, but I didn't want to cry in front of her. "Wow. I thought you liked him."

"I did, but now I can't stand the way he's working you over."

I softened. "I don't like it, either, but what can I do?"

"Lay down the law. Show him that he's got to treat you right if he wants to be with you."

"That won't work with Sam."

"Then cut him off. You got to have respect for yourself, Emma."

The thought of breaking up made my stomach ache with dread. How could I give up on the best thing I'd ever had? Sam had so much potential. He was my future.

"He hates when I try to control him, but I'll talk to him again about communicating better," I said, trying to keep that pathetic whimper out of my voice. "I don't want to lose him."

"You'll be losing a lot more if you let him sniff around any time he wants."

I turned away from her, humiliated that I was getting this kind of talk from a friend. What the hell was wrong with me? A feminist. A nasty girl. When people tried to push me around, I knew how to push back.

"Listen," Angela said. "I'm not judging you. Really, I'm just trying to show you a way out."

"I know that. Look, I'll figure this out. I promise."

That week I caught the flu. Although I managed to make it to class in between the bouts of nausea, I was in no mood to see anyone, Sam included. When Saturday rolled around and he hit me up to join him at an off-campus kegger, I told him I'd meet him there. I still felt queasy, but I figured that a decent meal and a shower would give me the boost I needed.

But as I started across campus with two other Theta Pis attending the party, the dizziness churned inside me again before we even reached the bridge into town. "You guys better go ahead without me," I said. India and Haley made sure I was okay, then continued walking.

Inky darkness loomed between the streetlights, but I felt too sick to care. I sat for a while on a park bench, and then vomited into a big smelly bin that reeked of dog poo. What kind of flu hung on for more than a week? Was I dying of something? Right now it felt that way.

After puking one more time, I pulled myself together and crossed the bridge leading into downtown. After a quick stop at the twenty-four-hour CVS on Main Street, where one of the older sisters had been looming, flirting with some guy, I headed home.

Back at Theta House, I used the guest bathroom downstairs. Just in case any of my suite mates were around upstairs.

Ignoring the knocking on the door, I sat on the toilet and stared at the stick long after the pink plus sign appeared. Minus meant negative, plus meant positive.

Staring at it didn't make it change. Plus, plus, plus.

I was pregnant.

CHAPTER 17

The desperate moan scraping from my throat pulled me out of the nightmare. Paralyzed, I stared up at the ceiling as my heart raced. The dream had been so bizarre I'd known it wasn't real, but still, it had sent me crashing into a panic.

One minute, Lydia and I were laughing about something, our feet dangling in the water of the fountain in the quad.

The next, she had fallen into the fountain and her body was rolling and floating in the dark-blue water, her skin pale as the moon against the cobalt tiles of the fountain. I thought she was lolling around, relaxing, until I saw that her limbs had ballooned and her face was bloated.

"Get her," someone whispered from behind me. "Help her!"

"Lydia!" I was reaching for her when everything shifted again. My legs kicked and thrashed frantically as I tried desperately to land on solid ground. This time she was down in the river and the landscape sank, down, down, down, as I knelt from the bridge two hundred feet above her.

"You let her go," the voice whispered in my ear. "You can't let go."

Wide-awake now, I clutched the sheet to my body and tried to breathe through the knot in my throat, the weight bearing down on my chest. My heart was thumping impossibly fast, a runaway train clicking along the tracks, and my face was burning up, feverish.

You're having a heart attack. Your chest is going to explode.
No, not a heart attack. This was pure panic.

I wanted to throw back the covers and peel off my pajamas. Open a window and swallow up clouds of fresh air. But the terror knotted up inside me was paralyzing. I couldn't lift my head from the pillow, let alone get out of bed.

The best I could do was to push back the covers with one quivering hand.

There. Some relief, some coolness, though the fear was still wound up around me. Part of me wished Angela were here, but maybe it was good that she was at Darnell's place. She didn't need to be freaked out by my whimpering and thrashing.

I pressed a hand to my chest, trying to coax my racing heart to relax, slow down, find tranquility. There was a brick in place of my heart, a smooth, rectangular brick aglow with love and peace.

My chest grew even tighter, heavier.

"No." I abandoned the brick image and tried to imagine the tension draining out of me, oozing from my fingertips and toes with each expelled breath. I closed my eyes to focus on the image, but all I could see was Lydia's pale white body glowing in the water like a white-bellied fish.

Breathe. Take long breaths, calming breaths.

I tried, but the air was thick with her presence, her flesh luminescent in the moonlight, her knowing smile hovering like the Cheshire Cat's. She was sitting on my chest, constricting my lungs, refusing to allow air in.

I was going to suffocate! I had to get out of the room . . . out of the house.

Kicking off the covers, I rolled onto my side and tumbled to the floor. This would be how they would find me, hugging my knees in my pathetic pajamas. Closing my eyes, I struggled to take in air and pull myself up along the side of the bed.

This was crazy. No one ever died of a panic attack, right? My heart was thudding like a crazed rabbit, but I pushed past the paralysis and got to my feet.

I flung off my satin pajamas and paused in front of my closet, afraid to open it, feeling her presence everywhere. Lydia's boxes sat inside—heavy, eerie tenants. I imagined the darkness inside the closet, where her pale skin glowed in the coffin of shadow. Ridiculous, yes, but I turned away without opening the door, grabbed yoga pants and a sweatshirt from the dresser, and wriggled into them. I carried my Uggs into the shared living room of the suite, where the air seemed even more syrupy warm and rotten. Had the furnace kicked into overdrive? In an old house like this it was impossible to regulate the temperature from room to room.

I barreled down the stairs, mindless of everyone sleeping, and turned toward the big kitchen. From her quarters at the front of the house, Mrs. J kept tabs on the main entrance, but I could slip out through the kitchen. To hell with curfew, I needed air to survive. Patting my cell phone and keys in the pocket of my jacket, I unlatched the bolt and stepped into a cool, leaf-rustling wind.

For a minute I slouched against the porch post, drinking small gasps of cool air and willing the strobes of panic to stop battering me.

The night offered escape. Therapy without walls or a ceiling. Sliding down to the porch steps, I fell into an exhausted slump as adrenaline ebbed. I was whipped.

Panic attacks always drained me, but I was grateful to recapture a calm, steady flame of peace. *Breathe in, breathe out, repeat.*

CHAPTER 18

Between the stabbing pain in his neck and the dull ache in his lower back and stump, Finn wondered if he'd been hit by a bicycle. When he tried to straighten and his foot hit the arm of the sofa, he realized he was at Jazz's place. Again.

For the second night in a row he'd gone for beers at Scully's, but this time it had been a strategic retreat from the kitchen, where she'd been preparing another tedious dinner. Fish sticks and Tater Tots. As if he were a five-year-old. As the sticks sat glistening in oil on top of the stove, he confronted Eileen, told her he was leaving.

With an hourglass shape and golden hair cut to fall softly around her heart-shaped face, Eileen was attractive. She would have no trouble finding someone to fill Finn's shoes.

But that night, once again, she had refused to accept his decision. "You can't leave us," Eileen said in a voice so low and sweet it was spooky. "I love you."

It had taken him more than two years with Eileen to realize that she probably had never been in love with anyone.

"You love the notion of things," he told her. "The notion of family and home, of husband and wife. But your picture of happiness doesn't include me. Any unlucky rising star in the history or economics or biology department at Merriwether could fill my role. I'm just a stand-in to make your picture complete."

"That's not true!"

"Not that I'm not a good catch," he said. "But for you, any male with a decent salary and a modicum of malleability would do."

"I don't know what you're talking about, but you can't leave us." She pointed to the living room, where their son was tugging the cushions off the couch, one by one, and toppling to the floor with the weight of each foam boulder. "Wiley and I love you and depend on you."

"I'll keep paying the rent on this house until the lease is up, and we'll work out child support for Wiley."

"But he needs his daddy."

Despite his guilt, Finn had come to see that it wasn't true. Wiley was still a mooshball of a thing, barely a toddler, and the baby had never bonded with Finn. "He has a good mother and caring grandparents. Plus your sister is crazy about him. That's more than a lot of kids have in this world."

"You can't do this," she said. "You can't break up our little family. I won't let you."

"Eileen, you can't stop me."

In a split second her demeanor flashed from sad to furious, and she shrieked, "Don't tell me what I can't do!" She wheeled around, grabbed the baking sheet on the stove, and flung it toward him, sending fried fish and potatoes flying.

"What the hell?" He batted the food away with one hand as the metal pan clattered on the floor. She'd thrown tantrums before, but this was the first time he'd been in the line of fire. "Do you think that helps anything?"

"It helps me to know I'm in control," she growled. "This is my house, and you are lucky that I've put up with your shit this long. Now sit down at that table and eat your dinner."

So the last resort was to bully him into submission? It was sad to watch the decline of a relationship, even a dysfunctional one like theirs. "That's not going to happen." He picked up the baking tray and placed it on the table, gently. "I'm not doing this to upset you, and God knows, I don't want to hurt Wiley, but I'm ending this, now."

"Oh, no you're not."

Finn held up one hand to indicate the doorway, where Wiley sat clutching one foot to his chest. He was an adorable kid, with piggy toes and chubby cheeks and his father's gleaming dark hair. A great kid, but not enough to tolerate a life with Eileen.

"Don't be scared," Finn said, lifting the boy into his arms. "Mom had an accident, but it's going to be okay."

Wiley spiraled out of Finn's arms, leaning toward Eileen. "Mama." The kid was attached to his mother, and that was okay. Actually, it was a relief. Finn handed him over to Eileen and made quick work of picking up the fish sticks and tots as she watched.

"I'm sorry," she said, adjusting the toddler on her hip. "I'm so sorry, but I love you so much. What can I do? I'll do anything if you'll just stay. Please. I'll change. I'll . . . I'll go back to work. That's what you want, right?"

"There's nothing to be done. Don't take this as a criticism of you. It's just time for us to separate. Strike out on our own paths." He rinsed his hands and fled to the bedroom to pack.

"What's her name?" Eileen called after him. "Tell me the name of the bitch you're sleeping with."

God, she was clueless, but the crazy act was just another facet of her attempt to take control, which he'd allowed for too long. His own passive-aggressive consent had brought him to this point. He grabbed a travel bag with toiletries and headed toward the front door. He would have to come back tomorrow, use the car to transport his clothes to . . . where? He could probably stay the night with Jazz, but he needed to find a small place that he could afford. Maybe just a room in a house.

Even if he had to resort to a boardinghouse, an uncomfortable living space was worth the freedom.

"What's her fucking name?" she shrieked.

He had to get out, let her calm down, let her turn her attention to Wiley.

"Lady Gaga," he called. He closed the door behind him and stepped into a new life.

Now he reached to pull the cord on the lamp, then swung his shoes to the floor and rubbed his neck. The socket of his prosthetic leg felt itchy, and he longed to get it off and get into the shower. Through a haze of dehydration and pain, Finn recalled the night in the bar that had brought him to sack out on Jazz's couch. After a burger, Jazz had toasted the start of Finn's liberation. Although Eileen had said she wouldn't let him go, her words couldn't keep him.

"You're a free man, my friend," Jazz had said, lifting a beer. "But just remember, rebellion is a process, and freedom is a gift you have to fight for every day of your life."

They had drunk to freedom, more than once.

Yeah. Finn roughed up his hair and checked the time on his cell phone. Just after four a.m. If he went home now, he'd be able to shower, make coffee, and pack a few things before Eileen and Wiley even woke up. Perfect.

Not that he was sneaking around. He would talk with Eileen after she cooled down. And if she held on to the psycho girlfriend role, he would extract his belongings from the house and make arrangements for Wiley without Eileen's participation. Jazz had been right about getting his ducks in a row; he needed to talk to a lawyer about setting up child support. It was up to him to make sure Wiley was taken care of. And then, the housing details.

Sitting here in the peace of Jazz's living room, he could see his way clear. Actually, if he persisted, he would make this all work out.

No doubt Eileen would muddy the waters. Of course she would. But this time, he would persist. Years ago she had sprung her trap, and he'd taken the bait. His mistake. But now it was time to get out before he died in captivity.

One of the worst things about a panic attack was the fear that it would happen again. In junior high I pinned a dream catcher on my wall, wanting to believe that it would catch twisted, evil scenarios before they floated into my dreams. It didn't work for me.

Steadying myself on the worn wood steps of the kitchen porch, I tried to weed through the questions Lydia had left behind. The fake identity she had concocted and sold us on didn't matter as much at the end—the thing that had compelled her to jump from the bridge. I might never know her reason, but right now I couldn't stop trying. I knew where I had to go.

That effing bridge.

The idea cut so close to the bone that it made my throat tight with anxiety. I figured that was a sign of its importance. I was on the right track.

The rain had subsided but the ground was wet and a mist hung in the air, painting everything with a gray haze. On a normal night I would have been scared to walk alone at four in the morning, but nothing about this night was normal, and the bridge wasn't far from Theta House, which seemed much more of a danger to me right now.

The translucent rings around the moon were beautiful, though Defiance always warned that they were the signs of a coming storm. Clumps of mist lingered in the street and lined the womb of the ravine, hinting of another world, a strange middle earth where people fly from bridges and never return.

By the time I reached the bridge, my heartbeat had slowed. My feet weren't so heavy anymore, and though my energy was still wiped out, it felt good to be moving forward.

The North Campus Bridge was a suspension bridge, probably the least picturesque of all the campus crossings. Sometimes when I saw it from a distance, I imagined how it would look if one of the cables broke, causing a chain reaction like in those old cartoons where one piano string pops and suddenly a hundred strings twang, whipping out of the lid. Lydia had probably chosen the bridge because it was closest to Theta House, definitely not for its beauty.

On the other hand, the falls on the north side did rank as some of the most beautiful in the area when the creek was swollen, as it was now. The whispering rush of water from the recent rain filled the air as I climbed the stairs to the bridge. If you ventured down to the ravine and the river was swollen from rainfall, the sound of the falls could be deafening as waves of mist covered your skin.

The novelty of walking in the gorges was shared by every Merriwether student. The administration had made a hike into the gorge part of the freshman orientation in an attempt to "demystify" the terrain. It also turned out to be an efficient way to get the litter, beer cans, and glass cleaned up at the beginning of the school year, tying into the environmental awareness unit.

At the top of the stairs I passed through the grid-like shadow of the west tower and peered ahead. My friends said a guard had been posted, but no one was here tonight. The rubber soles of my boots barely whispered as I walked from one dim pool of light to the other, measuring my steps to the spot where yellow police tape animated the center of the bridge. The police believed this was the spot Lydia had jumped from because they'd found her cell phone here.

Standing by the tape, I didn't feel Lydia's presence. It wasn't like the fear I'd felt standing at the closet door, or the sense of her in the familiar smells of the hallways and stairwells.

This wasn't her place, at least, not anymore.

Five years back, two other students had jumped from this bridge. An engineering student about to be kicked out of the program, and about a week later, his girlfriend followed. Defiance had a theory that their ghosts had coaxed Lydia over the edge, but that was too Hollywood for me.

The barrier at the side of the bridge was a short cement wall, around three feet tall, with a steel rail projecting a foot above that. I put my chin on the rail and peered out, trying to make out the rocks and water of the gorge below. With the clouds masking the moon, the water was a molten black, and the land was shadowed, but I could make out enough to feel weak and tingly over the distance between me and the earth below.

Leaning on the rail, I tried to feel her. "Lydia?"

There was no answer, of course.

"You were kind of a bitch."

The only sound was the rush of the water behind me. I sighed, dead on my feet, though not ready to leave just yet. I was about to camp out on the pavement when I noticed the gap between the top of the wall and the rail, around six inches. It was enough to slide my legs through and sit on the wall with the steel rail secure across my chest. My feet dangled precariously. This would be risky in flip-flop season, but my boots were on securely.

Hanging like a kid strapped into an amusement park ride, I tried to see my way through this mess . . . sifting through the guilt, anger, and frustration to come out on the other side. The practical side of me wanted to put Lydia behind me and move on, but something was holding me back.

Lydia.

I had learned that when people die, they leave behind more than just clothes and possessions. The emotional stuff lands on your doorstep like a truckload of gravel. All I could do was keep shoveling.

Finn was halfway home, entering the empty bridge, when he saw a flash of movement ahead. The wind moving the police tape? Something shifted in the shadows at the railing, a dark shape nearly hidden by a post. A person perched on the edge.

Shit. Please, not another jumper.

In the adrenaline rush that followed, Finn became acutely aware of the cool night air, the sallow pools of light from old fluorescent bulbs, the silence broken only by the rushing water of the falls.

That was the thing about crisis: It had the power to smack you awake in an instant.

It brought him back to the explosion that had rattled his brain and mangled his leg that sunny morning in Afghanistan.

And the night he'd been trying to crank on his PhD thesis when the call came about George, one of his commanders in Afghanistan, a West Point grad who'd been killed by a sniper's bullet.

Stay in the present, here and now.

He considered strategy. Tackle the jumper and pull him or her to the ground, or announce himself and start a dialogue?

His soft-soled boots whispered on the pavement as he approached, biting his lower lip. Slow and steady was the way to go. Didn't the cops spend hours trying to talk jumpers down when they had the chance? Negotiation. Validation.

Sometimes a desperate person simply wanted to be heard.

Negotiation was always best, but Finn didn't like leaving anything to chance. He stepped up the pace, worried that the person might slip away before he got close.

He couldn't let that happen.

A protective instinct ignited inside him as he broke into a run.

CHAPTER 19

"Don't do it!"

The gruff voice emerged from the darkness, scaring the crap out of me. I turned, saw him charging at me, and freaked. The subsequent jolt that ran through my body made my cell phone slip from my fingers.

"Don't jump!" He was closer now, a man in a leather jacket barreling toward me in an uneven gait.

My eyes flashed from him—dark hair, Johnny Depp–brown eyes, and a soul patch—to the bridge deck, where my cell bounced and landed hard. "Crap."

"Are you okay?"

"It's just . . . I dropped my cell phone. The way you rushed up on me—"

"Here." His hands clamped around my arm. "Let me help you down."

Normally, I would have told him hands off, but I could hear the concern in his voice and once I recognized him from freshman Comp I wasn't afraid. "Dr. Finnegan? What are you doing here?"

"That's my question for you. Come off the wall." He tugged on my arm. "Come away from the edge, before my heart leaps out of my chest."

He was legitimately scared for me. Holding on to the rail, I leaned back and slid one leg off the wall, then the other. He held on to my arm as I straightened and stepped toward the center of the roadbed.

"You're good, right? You're okay? Still in one piece?" His eyes were wild, his hand warm on my arm.

"Yeah. You can let go now."

He let out a breath of relief, then held his hands in the air. "Just trying to help. You scared the shit out of me."

"Yeah. Well, overreaction. I wasn't trying to jump."

"Let's look at the truth. You're here alone. Middle of the night." There was no accusation in his voice, only an argument for logic.

"It wasn't about suicide. I was just trying to understand, to put myself in her place. Lydia was my friend."

His eyes searched my face. "Then I'm sorry for your loss," he said. "Suicide makes it harder, doesn't it?"

"Yes." I turned away from his probing stare, stepped back toward the rail, and bent down to retrieve my cell.

"Wait! No! What are you doing?" He grabbed me by the waist and pulled me upright. "Get back here."

It was shocking to be touched by a teacher, but his manner was protective and swift. The way he pulled me up and set me on my feet made me feel like a little kid again. "Calm down, Dr. Finn. Just getting my cell phone. You made me drop it."

"Really? Maybe you shouldn't be texting while contemplating suicide."

I gaped at him as I picked up the phone. "Wow. That's cold. And sort of funny."

"Sorry. I'm just . . . just trying to lighten an intense moment with humor. I'm glad you're okay."

I could feel him studying me as I pressed the home button on my phone. The screen lit up. One crisis averted.

"Emma, right? You were in one of my classes."

"Last year." He was one of the better English professors, young and self-deprecating, an army veteran. Dr. Scott Finnegan, but everyone called him Dr. Finn.

He nodded. "I had Lydia in one of my classes this term."

"Really? That must feel weird."

"It's horrible. She came to me asking for more time and . . ."

"You said no?"

"I gave her some time, but now I wish I'd been more accommodating. I should have reached out to her. I should have recognized that she was suffering."

"You're overestimating your power," I said.

"You think?"

"Lydia didn't jump over an English grade. She barely cared about her classes." Having been forced to help her with a few last-minute assignments, I knew that academics were not high on Lydia's list. "She did just enough work to pass."

"Well." He scratched one sideburn. "I don't know if I should be insulted or relieved."

"It's not really about you, is it?"

He rolled back on his heels, off guard. "Okay."

"That's not what I meant. There are a lot of people crying and pouting over Lydia, but they didn't know her. They're just pretending to have a connection so they can get street cred for the tragedy. But you're the real deal. You're one of the few professors who take the time to get to know students."

He shrugged off the compliment. "Nice of you to let me off the hook, but it's hard to shake the feeling." He winced and looked away, toward the broken crime-scene tape, hanging limp in the damp air. "You were right. This isn't about me." He moved cautiously toward Lydia's spot on the bridge, leaning heavily on the railing as if he needed help standing. "Tell me about Lydia, then."

"We're in the same sorority. Theta Pi." Again, that wicked song lyric uncurled in my mind. *Theta born. Theta bred. And when I die, I'll be Theta dead. . . .*

"What were her best qualities?" he asked quietly.

My heart sank. "Ask me something else."

"Things she did that annoyed you?"

"Once she started with a story, she never shut up. Some

nights I fell asleep listening to her drone on about who sat where at a wedding or how to make moussaka." I moved back to the rail and stared at the mist below. "And now it turns out that a lot of those stories were lies. So I guess that's annoying, too. And she thought she was the authority on behavior, telling us that something wasn't proper or bugging us to make sure we had a proper date. That pissed me off, but part of that's sorority life. All the events that you need to hook up with a guy for."

"Sounds tedious."

"For me, it is. But Lydia loved being someone's date. Someone's princess."

"Like dating from a bygone era. Barbie and Ken. Cinderella."

"It's alive and well in Greek life."

"But you're not into it?"

"The dating protocol is a throwback. Kind of archaic." I didn't even want to touch on the way sororities and fraternities at Merriwether excluded the LGBT community. I felt bad about that, but sorority life gave me something I desperately needed. "I'm in it for the sisterhood," I told him.

"That working for you?"

I thought about the Theta Pis, the good and the bad. The current Rose Council was bossy and way too caught up in appearances, but my girls, my friends, they were my life. "It is." The mist was closing in around us, soft, protective. The privacy it offered made it seem that it was a perfectly normal thing to have a deep conversation on a footbridge in the middle of the night.

"I wasn't in a fraternity in college. I got my education later, after the army, but I can see how a supportive group of friends could save your life at such an alienating time."

"My sisters are my family now."

"And yet, you came out here alone. In crisis."

"Yeah. Maybe I didn't want to wake up my friends in the middle of the night because I was having a panic attack. I didn't want to be that girl." He squinted at me curiously. "You know the one. Self-absorbed. Keeping people up all night with her problems. Unaware that other people have lives." Why was there so much anger in my voice? I tried to dismiss it, but then realized who I was describing.

"I think I've met her." He glanced over his shoulder, toward Chambers Hall. "Energy-sucking, mind-fucking."

"That's the one," I said. "That was Lydia."

"And the plot thickens."

"I shouldn't talk about her this way. I can't believe we've been talking this long here, in the middle of the night. It's so random."

"I just happened to be walking by and I figured I'd save your life."

"I wasn't going to jump."

"I know. But I'm glad I was walking by."

"Same." Understatement of the year. Now that we'd stepped out of the conversation, I realized we were going to wrap it up, and I was sorry to see him go.

"So thanks for almost saving my life," I said. "I guess I'll see you around, Dr. Finn."

"What? You think I'm going to leave you in the haunted mist? I'm walking you home, missy."

"I'm right over there, at Theta House." I pointed toward the right side of the ravine, where the grim outline of the building was now masked by fog. "I can get there on my own."

"It's close. I'll walk with you."

"But you were going in the other direction."

"Can't do it." He shook his head. "Not that I don't believe you. It's just . . . with everything that's happened, I can't leave this bridge until you go with me."

I rolled my eyes. "This is harassment."

"And you could get me in a shitload of trouble. Or I could save your life. I'll roll the dice on option A, since option B is so critical."

That was the Dr. Finn I remembered from class, a sweet, animated nerd who valued his relationship with students. Just my luck. I'd been rescued by the rock star version of Super Mario when I didn't really need saving.

"Fine." As we started walking I noticed that he was limping. I was about to ask him if he was okay, and then I remembered that he had injured his leg in Afghanistan. Part of it was missing from an explosion. Which made him walking me home that much more of a sacrifice.

We passed a sign that read WE CAN HELP. CALL FIRST. It gave the number of a suicide hotline. Had Lydia noticed the signs, or had she been too lost in her daze to see?

THERE IS HOPE, read a sign on another post.

I was such a sucker for hope.

CHAPTER 20

During the short walk back to Theta House, I asked Dr. Finn what he was doing out so late on a Tuesday night.

"Walking?" he answered like a ten-year-old.

"Let's look at the truth."

"I don't think the truth makes for appropriate conversation between student and teacher."

"That's not fair after I spilled my guts to you. Okay, you look tired and a little rumpled."

"I'm always rumpled."

"You were headed to the town side of campus, where most of the professors live. Late night at the office?"

He gave me a look that said I should have known better.

"Okay. You were Skyping an associate in Moscow."

"Sweden, actually. They're talking about nominating me for the Nobel Prize in teaching."

"What?" For a quick second I believed him, and then he cracked a smile. "Come on. I'm not that good."

I let it drop, only because we were approaching the lawn of Theta House. "That's it. I'm going 'round the back, so... thanks."

"Listen." He put a hand on my shoulder, a solid grip. "If you ever want to talk, you know where to find me."

"Same with you," I said as he gave my shoulder a pat and

turned away. "And be careful crossing that bridge," I called after him. "Don't do anything I wouldn't do."

He glanced over his shoulder with a wry smirk. "I've come to hate bridges, but it's good to get to the other side."

"Wow. That could be a proverb. Kind of deep."

"I know, right?"

I sneaked in the kitchen door and stole upstairs, holding my breath all the way. For the next few hours I slept like a stone, torn from sleep when my alarm jangled. That early-morning wakeup call was a bitch, but it was worth the easy A in Art Lit.

As Angela and I crossed the North Campus Bridge on the way to class, I imagined Dr. Finn and me, two broken people standing there inside the torn crime-scene tape.

"I came out here last night to think," I told Angela. "I woke up with a panic attack, and I had to get out."

"Aw. You should have called me."

"In the middle of the night?"

"What about Isabel and Defiance? They wouldn't mind."

"I just had to get out . . . and fast. I ended up running into Dr. Finn from English." I told her that we had talked for a while, and it had helped smooth out my anxiety.

I was still awed that we'd talked so openly out on the bridge. Most people would have just ushered me home or called the cops, but Dr. Finn had gotten involved and engaged. He reminded me of my older brother—reticent but easy to talk to, respectful but warm and encouraging. That made sense, since Dr. Finn and Joe were probably around the same age, both pushing thirty. Talking to Dr. Finn reminded me that I owed my brother a call, though I knew I wouldn't do that. Although I always enjoyed spending time with Joe, a phone conversation would only punctuate the awkwardness of distance and time. No matter how much I wanted a family, there was no going back to the time when I had an older brother who picked me up at soccer practice or swiped oatmeal cookies as soon as I got them out of the oven. With Mom and Delilah gone and Dad in emotional retirement, the web of family had dropped away, leaving Joe and me calling to each other from distant islands. He was married now, living a very different life, and I had started down my own path at Merriwether.

"It's weird to run into a professor in the middle of the night," I told Angela, "but if I had to choose, Dr. Finn's a good one."

"He always made me laugh. But I feel bad that I wasn't there for you, bae. Next time call me."

"I didn't want to be a pain."

"You know I can go right back to sleep if I want to. What do you think caused it?"

"Just everything. Classes and work and the normal shit. All the questions about why Lydia killed herself, and the police detective pressing me about it. Detective Taylor seemed annoyed and suspicious. As if I pushed my own sister off the bridge."

A sigh hissed through her teeth. "And you were so nice to Lydia. You were one of the few people who would listen to her stories. And you took care of her when she was sick, Nurse Emma."

"I take care of everyone."

"But still, you deserve major credit."

"Tell that to Detective Taylor. She scares me. And Dean Cho wants me to be on some stupid suicide squad, and I missed my A & P exam last night, which is a matter of life and death in the nursing program. And my stomach has been off for the last two days."

"You a mess, girl."

We paused on the steps of Chambers Hall, looked at each other, and laughed softly.

"Good thing you're here to help me keep it real," I said.

Although it had been a rough night for sleep, Finn was actually whistling as he walked into the English department Wednesday morning. Mrs. Noble, the department secretary, twinkled her fingers at him but didn't miss a beat of her phone call, telling the caller that there were no guarantees without making an appointment. Finn checked his mailbox—an archaic practice, and yet there were two flyers there, one about a department meeting. Inside his office he added the meeting date to his calendar and fired up his PC.

Life was good. He sat down at his desk, took a sip of his coffee, and savored the smooth, bitter taste. Yes, good.

Last night's bridge incident had been the wakeup call Finn needed. The glimpse of Emma's life had made him realize how imminently solvable his own problems were. Time to put aside the hesitation and self-pity and keep moving ahead.

Because he had a purpose.

That morning he had received an e-mail from Dean Cho that outlined a suicide prevention task force she was forming—finally a positive, proactive step from the university's office of health services—and Cho had offered him a position on the panel.

Yes, yes, and yes.

Since their abrupt meeting a couple days ago, they had volleyed a few e-mails, with him suggesting programs that might help students, and Cho enumerating costs and restrictions. Issues of privacy, costs, and student rights had to be respected. While their correspondence hadn't solved the problem, he had realized that Cho's heart was in the right place, and they had come up with a strategy to address it—a task force that included students, faculty, and administrators.

Seeing Emma on that bridge had sealed the deal for him, reinforced that he could reach students and help them. And now, with this opportunity, he was beginning to believe that he had come to Merriwether to fulfill a role that would be more meaningful and lasting than his mistakes with Eileen.

With more than an hour until his first class, he picked up two coffees and egg sandwiches at the campus Starbucks on his way to the admin building, a cranky structure that smelled like it had retained the original dust of its construction in 1896. Taking the steps two at a time, he made it to the second floor without spilling coffee onto the lids. Dean Cho's door was open, and he could see her at her desk, working on the computer. "Good morning," he announced himself from the threshold.

Sydney Cho glanced away from her computer monitor, her eyes flickering with recognition. "Well, look at that. It's my worst nightmare. Come in. Have a seat."

"I brought you a peace offering. An egg-and-cheese sandwich and coffee."

"Thank you." She took one of the coffees and cradled it in her hands. "I see you're partaking of the peace gift, too."

"Of course. The ritual of breaking bread together."

"You are so old school, Finn. And this has nothing to do with you squeezing in a breakfast?"

"You wound me," he said over a mouthful of sandwich.

"I've been hearing that a lot lately." She switched to a more serious tone as she sat back in her chair. "The students have rejected and criticized every program I've developed here, and so far—and I realize it's early, but still—the new policies do not seem to be reducing student suicides."

"That's why the task force is a great idea. It's a way to engage students while directly addressing their concerns. We have some amazing kids here, Dean Cho. Together we can do amazing things if they help tailor the program to meet student needs."

"You sound like you're running for political office."

"Can't help it. I get excited when I have a brilliant idea."

"And modest, too," she said as she unwrapped her sandwich.

He was glad that the banter had returned. Cho tended to take herself far too seriously. He rolled the paper from his sandwich into a ball and pitched it toward the trash in the corner. "Score."

"Do your students ever complain about your cavalier attitude?"

"Not to my face. And I'm not being facetious. This is genuine enthusiasm."

"I'm glad one of us is feeling upbeat about this. I can tell you it's not going to be easy to get students on board. So far, out of the three students I've approached, two have said no."

"Who did you ask? I'll find them and turn on the charm."

She frowned. "Do you really think that's a good idea?"

"Have faith, Dean Cho. We're moving on an important mission, and if you believe in that, it can't fail."

"I'll give you their contact info, but please don't come on too strong."

He rose and grabbed his coffee.

Later, when he got the students' info in an e-mail, he smiled at the first name on the list: Emma Danelski.

Serendipity.

After class as I walked into Theta House, my cell phone pinged with an e-mail. Dr. Lamont, my A & P teacher, expressed condolences and wrote that I would be allowed to make up the exam on skeletal structure. "Sweet." A weight lifted. My nursing career wasn't dead yet.

While I was on the e-mail server I looked up Dr. Finnegan's e-mail address and sent him a one-word message: *Thanks.*

Enough said.

The kitchen smelled warm and savory, reminding me that I hadn't had breakfast. The caterers were prepping for lunch— chicken tacos—and the smell of grilled chicken and chili beans made me wish I could stay. My stomach was probably rebelling because I hadn't eaten enough these past few days. Snitching was strictly forbidden, so I grabbed a yogurt from the fridge and filled a to-go cup with coffee.

"Oh, there you are." Mrs. J moved away from the big stove, where she'd been talking with Juana, one of the cooks. "The police were here again, asking about you."

That stabbing pain was back in my abdomen. "Detective Taylor? What does she want now? She could have called me."

"She didn't want to talk to you. She had questions." The flicker of suspicion in Mrs. J's eyes was like a jab to my heart. Why was our housemother turning on me?

"What did she want to know?"

"Character reference. She asked about your family and your background. She wanted to know if you'd ever been in trouble that I knew of. What your behavior was like here in the house."

"Oh my God, they're investigating me? Why?"

Her downturned brows punctuated a scowl. "You tell me."

"Tell you what? I always tried to help Lydia."

"I told them that. I know you had long talks with her."

"What about the rest? My family and . . ." I hoped that Mrs. J hadn't mentioned my dead mother or the crash. She was sort of fatalistic about the toll of loss in a person's life. As if a crisis damaged a person forever. "What did you tell them?"

"You've never caused me any trouble, Emma, and you've never been arrested before."

At least she'd been honest about that. "Wait. They're talking about arresting me?"

"That didn't come up, but they were fishing. I defended you as much as I could. Told them about your car accident—not your fault. And that I've met your dad. What's he do again?"

"He's a musician."

"That's right. Slipped my mind." She seemed to mull it over as damaging evidence that I couldn't be trusted because my father didn't run a corporation or own a franchise of gas stations.

"What else did they want to know?"

"They wanted to know your schedule and where you worked. Oh, and they asked if you owned a dark hoodie."

Another stab in my chest. "What did you tell them?"

"I gave them your schedule and told them yes on the hoodie. You girls posed in your black Theta Pi hoodies for rush this year. Every girl in the sorority has one."

"Well, I hope you told them that part."

"Of course I did."

"It's ridiculous. Everyone on campus owns a dark hoodie."

She squinted at me. "For someone who claims to have done nothing wrong, you're pretty defensive."

"Wouldn't you be?" I slammed an open palm against my chest. "For some mysterious reason I'm being investigated, and I would expect my housemother to stick up for me."

"I did what I could, but I can't stand in the way of a police investigation."

Too furious to respond, I took my yogurt and coffee and headed out to my next class.

CHAPTER 21

The rear rows of the amphitheater were full when I walked in. Class was starting soon, and most people liked the back of the room, either to exit quickly or to dink around on their laptops or text or sleep.

But I usually found Dr. Habib's lectures interesting, so I moved ahead down the steps and took an empty seat on the aisle of the third row. I was opening my spiral notebook when I noticed Dr. Habib at the side of the theater talking with someone. A woman with auburn hair in a perfect A-line cut. She wore a navy blazer and khaki pants and practical shoes, and something about the way she moved seemed familiar. Oprah Winfrey.

No. Detective Taylor.

They seemed to be wrapping up a conversation, and I was pretty sure I knew the topic.

With a nod, the detective said her good-byes and started up the stairs to the exit. Leaving my backpack open at my feet, I darted up the stairs behind her.

"Detective Taylor?" I called, following her up to the door at the top of the aisle. I had to call her three times before she turned to look back at me.

"Emma. Hey, there."

"I just heard that you were grilling Mrs. Johnson about me, and now Dr. Habib. Why are you trying to dig up stuff on me?"

"It's all part of our investigation. We need to make sure that—"

"Isn't Lydia the one you should be investigating? You should be talking to *her* professors."

"And we are. But it's not that simple."

I wanted to rail at her that it was very simple and I wanted to be left alone. But I was scared, and I didn't think it would do me any good to piss off a cop. "I just want to be left alone," I said, keeping my voice level.

"Listen, if Lydia was your friend, then I'm sure you want us to make sure she jumped of her own volition. That's why we're digging. I'm sorry if it's an inconvenience."

"Is this about the person in the hoodie who was on the bridge? Because it wasn't me."

"Do you have an alibi?"

"I was in bed. In my room."

"But no one was there to verify that," she said. "You see, we talked to your roommate, Angela, who said she stayed with her boyfriend Sunday night."

"But that doesn't make me guilty. It's not my fault that—"

She drew in a breath and held up one hand. "Just go to your class, okay?"

I didn't really have any choice.

Back in my seat, I tried to tamp down the anxiety and focus on the steady timbre of Dr. Habib's calming voice. This wasn't a panic attack; there was a very good reason that my hands were shaking as I took notes.

The police were investigating me, and I had something to hide.

Although I didn't see Detective Taylor for the rest of Wednesday, I couldn't shake the feeling that I was being watched. When someone glanced up at me from a table in the library, I saw suspicion in their eyes and worried that they knew something. As I walked along the paving stone paths and bridges on campus, I felt someone following me, matching my pace, slowing when I slowed. But when I looked back, I saw no cops or detectives, only students, male and female, minding their own business.

I told myself it was my imagination, that the police department wouldn't bother having me followed for such a small thing. At least, that was the way I rationalized it.

That night at dinner as I sat at the table picking at a slice of veggie pizza, Violet came up behind me and leaned in. "Hey, sweet pea. I hear you ended up with those archives from Lydia's room."

"They're in my closet. Do you want them?"

"Hell no. I'm overloaded with all the other offices I'm supposed to fulfill. I was just talking with Tori and she agreed. We're going to nominate you to take over historian and recording secretary. That would put you on the Rose Council."

"That's an honor, but I don't have time right now. Isn't there a junior or senior who wants to do it?"

"We need some new blood on the council. Most of us are graduating end of this year. And Lydia's jobs weren't so hard to do. It'll take you no time at all. But as your first unofficial task, I need you to pull some photos of Lydia for a collage. We'll use them for the ritual Friday night, and the memorial pancake supper on Saturday."

That damned pancake supper. It was idiocy to think that anyone could be honored with burned pancakes and drunken, horny students lined up for hookups.

"Don't you have photos of her online?"

"Only the one that's been going around." A thoughtful portrait of Lydia with her chin resting on her knuckles appeared online and in newspapers, and a framed copy greeted us from the makeshift memorial out front whenever we arrived home. It hadn't been a bad picture when it was first taken, but now I saw something creepy in her eyes, a dark shadow there that said, *I've got a secret.* "You've got our sorority history in that box. We wanted Lydia to make it digital, but who has the time? So you need to pull some pictures for us."

I couldn't say no to Violet, who did a lot of work for the sorority. "How many photos do you need?"

"A dozen or so? And choose another one to blow up. Everyone's getting sick of the picture we've been using."

"I'll see what I can find in the boxes."

"Don't look so glum. With the way Lydia loved herself, there should be dozens of photos."

"It's not that. It's just..." I looked around the table and lowered my voice. "I'm totally stressed about everything, and the police are investigating me. They think I had something to do with Lydia's death."

"Oh, that's no big deal. They got that young cop following you, too?"

"Detective Taylor? The Oprah clone?"

"No, there's another one. Pretty. She could pass as a student. She and Taylor have been following a bunch of us. Any girl who was Lydia's friend."

"Really? You, too?"

"Yup. Tori and Courtney, too. Tori stood up to them, told them to leave her alone or she'd have her daddy sue for harassment."

"Did that work?"

"Seems like it."

"But you didn't tell them to back off?"

"My parents raised me right. Besides, Daddy would be furious if he found out what was going on here, all these suicides. It's not the sort of environment my parents would want for me. So I don't care if they speak to my teachers and watch me walk from English to the student union. If that means I'll be left alone by my parents, the police can watch me all day long."

"Why didn't you guys tell me? I've been so scared, thinking I was the only one."

"I figured they were just going after the seniors, and honestly, I didn't want word getting around. I only knew about Court and Tori because they had us corralled together in the beginning. But don't let them get to you."

"I can't stand it," I said. "They're like vultures. The only time I feel safe now is here in the house."

"Don't you be scared, honey. Those officers got nothing on us. In a few days, they'll leave us alone and move on to some other case." She squeezed my shoulder as she straightened up. "Don't forget those photos, now."

"I won't." Turning back to my cold pizza, I wanted to believe Violet. I wanted to think that they would back off after a few days. But I couldn't stop the worry that niggled at my conscience. What if they found something?

That night I dragged the boxes to the center of our living area and opened them up on the floor. One box was loaded with standing files, none of which contained photos. I put that one away, but found the other box jammed to the top with photos that seemed to be piled up in no particular order.

"What a mess," I said as I grabbed a few photos from the top of the box. "Lydia was usually so anal about being organized."

Angela looked down from the sofa, where she'd been working on her laptop. "That's not Lydia's style at all. Looks like everything fell out and got slopped back in. What are you doing with the box?"

When I explained about the archives and the need for a collage, she got down on the floor and started digging through with me. A few minutes later Defiance joined us, calling for organization and setting up stacks of photos by the month and year stamped on the back. Isabel came out to the living room, but kept her distance, snuggling with a blanket and her cell phone on the window seat. She told us she didn't feel well, but I sensed that she was still uncomfortable being around the photo collection that had been managed by Lydia.

"You know, this is really Stone Age," Angela said. "Keeping our sorority history in printed photos. Does anyone have a digital copy of these? Maybe on Lydia's laptop?"

"The police have her laptop, but Violet says there are no digital files. I mean, people will have stuff they took on their phones. But as far as the official Theta Pi archive goes? You're looking at it."

"It's a little chilling to see her alive and smiling," Defiance said, pausing at a photo of a carefree Lydia with her arms up, her dark hair a stark contrast to her snow-white sweater. "If you forget about her bossiness, she was a beautiful girl."

I agreed. "It's good to remember Lydia before the bathrobe stage. Her smile, it used to light her up," I said, trying to ignore the desire to cry. Here was Lydia, alive and happy. Of course, these captured moments didn't hint at the darkness in her heart, but the photos pointed to the woman that might have been.

It took the three of us more than an hour to sort through the top of the box, which took us back through the last five years of Theta Pi history. We managed to cull twenty photos with Lydia in them. Nothing from her freshman year, which was odd, though it could have been buried in the bulk beneath.

"Let's stop here," I said. "We've all got other things to do."

"I can drop off the pictures we picked," Angela offered. "I'm on my way to meet Darnell. Who gets them?"

"Leave them with Violet," I said. "Thanks for your help, guys."

Isabel donated plastic Baggies to keep everything organized. I noticed that she held her breath as we covered the box and then tucked it back into the closet.

I got that. I think we all breathed a little easier with the photos stashed, the memories allowed to rest. Rest in peace.

CHAPTER 22

Thursday and Friday were more of the same, swimming against the tide, struggling my way to the surface to grab a breath. Classes, work, two hundred pages of reading, an essay, an article review. The makeup quiz for anatomy was painful, but at least I was able to answer most of the questions. Just in time to begin studying for next week's test.

Thursday night there was an awkward moment in the A & P lab when I found myself staring at a woman's hand, her fingernails still bearing a chipped coat of coral nail polish. It struck me that those hands had been touching the world a year ago. Buttering a slice of toast. Patting a child's shoulder. Cuddling a cat.

With all the mysticism of death, losing my mom and Delilah and now Lydia had taught me the reality of the survivor—the simple disappearance of someone from your daily world. *Now you see me, now you don't.*

I groaned when I got an e-mail from Dr. Finn about joining the suicide task force. As if I had time for some idiotic committee.

And there was the added suspense of knowing I was being watched and followed. When I scanned a crowd, I wasn't sure who was a cop and who was a student, so I assumed everyone had their eyes on me. The slightest rustle of a dead leaf sent my heart racing. Paranoia can really zap your energy.

I had to remind myself that I'd survived much worse things. The accident . . . the aftermath.

No one here knew the details of the accident, circumstances that had made me hate my sister for years after it happened. Delilah had insisted on driving, and then while on the road she had badgered Mom about a three-day concert my parents had refused to let her attend. All the classic ploys—all my friends are going, I'll pay for it myself, don't you trust me?—weren't working. In a tantrum, Delilah sent the car speeding ahead. Mom shouted at her to stop, but that made her go even faster. When the car went into a spin, I think Delilah regretted it. She yanked the wheel, and in the rearview mirror I saw a look of panic in her eyes. That raw fear, gritty and dank as mud.

"It wasn't suicide," I told my father afterward. "She was speeding, but she didn't mean to crash."

"We'll never know." He seemed so gray and wrinkled then, as if he had aged overnight. Only the ponytail at the back of his neck hinted at the cool, young dude he used to be.

We didn't discuss it much, but I made myself an expert on suicide to prove him wrong. I wanted to point to signs and symptoms to discount my sister's motives. I wanted to say, "See? Look at that. Definitely not Delilah." But the facts were inconclusive.

Ironic that I was here all these years later trying to convince the police of the exact opposite. *It was suicide. It was, you idiots. Lydia Drakos killed herself. End of story.*

Sometimes people just didn't listen.

White dresses, white candles, white flames. Each of us held a white, long-stemmed rose twined in crimson ribbon. The velvet ribbon had been Violet's idea—red to symbolize sorrow and heartbreak. The woven thread of color was startling against the field of white. We all wore our diamond-shaped Theta Pi pin, an engraved gold pin framed by tiny inlaid diamonds that occasionally winked in the light. The bright glow of white fabric and light against the muted shadows of the room always brought quiet and reverence to the usually noisy girls.

The semicircle of sisters surrounded a little table, a makeshift altar bearing photos of Lydia, a scarlet-red rose floating in a glass bowl to symbolize sorrow, and the Theta Pi banner with our sorority insignia. I inhaled the scents of wax and ceremony. Theta Pi rituals could be a little bit sanctimonious, but like church, they were just intimidating enough to make people behave and be their best selves.

Her eyes shiny with tears, Violet stood tall, holding the candle of truth with one hand and hugging the ritual book to her lace-covered bodice with the other. Her red curls shone, coppery in the candlelight. "The memorial for a dearly departed sister is called the 'Rose Beyond the Wall' ceremony. It's so rare that it's not in the book, but National sent us a copy. I know that, as ritual keeper, I usually conduct our sacred ceremonies, but tonight I . . . I just can't. And I say that out of pure love and devotion to Lydia."

Really? From what I'd seen, Violet and Lydia had just tolerated each other. But after someone died, plenty of people wanted to jump on the friend bandwagon.

"So I've passed the candle of truth to our president, just for tonight." With a nod, she stepped back into line.

Tori's heels clicked as she went to the altar, placed the candle of truth on a bare spot of tablecloth, and held up a nearly transparent sheet of paper. "Sisters, we are gathered here today to pay tribute to our beloved sister Lydia Drakos. Repeat after me: Dear Lydia, we love you and miss you."

"Dear Lydia . . ." We repeated the words in zombie voices. Was any girl in the room feeling this in her heart? I wanted to feel something deep, but it sort of seemed like business as usual.

Tori continued. "On this sad day, we bow our heads and remember you, Lydia Drakos, the Rose that has passed beyond the wall. Although you have left this side of the wall, the everlasting covenant of Theta Pi remains. Every sister's allegiance to Theta Pi is eternal, every bond will last a lifetime. . . ."

As she read on, my thoughts strayed and I suddenly wondered who here had taken the photo from downstairs. Was it the same person in a hoodie who had been on the bridge with Lydia that night? Keeping my head bowed, I scanned the faces around me, looking for . . . I don't know what. A sinister look? Mia and Megan stood holding hands. They weren't supposed to do that during a ritual, but Violet would probably correct them later. Violet was wiping tears from her eyes, and Courtney's lips were puckered in that sad puss that she used all the time lately. I'm sure she had no idea how infantile it made her look. Angela, Haley, Defiance, Jemma, Isabel, Chloe, Belle, Suki, and more than a dozen others. Most girls stood with their heads bowed. Their expressions were somber amid the circle of light.

I wanted to think the best of all these girls, my sisters. Aside from the nursing program, Greek life had been one of the big draws of Merriwether U because I knew that I needed a family that would hold me in their hearts and have my back and share my joys. I thought I had found that in this sisterhood. I hoped I was right.

"We stand here in memory of you today, Lydia." Tori addressed the photos on the table as if Lydia were hiding underneath, peeking out from under the tablecloth. "Each of your sisters is holding the flower of Theta Pi, a white rose, which means innocence and purity in the language of flowers."

Tori delivered the words smoothly, flawlessly, though I always expected her to stumble on the word *purity,* as most would consider her far from it. Tori had sex like a guy. She chose her partners based on looks, made them conquests, and bragged about it later. There'd been one or two "boyfriends" in the past year, but they hadn't stuck around long. Tori managed to find fault with them, and most guys didn't want to share their girlfriend with the defensive lineup of the university's football team.

"In loving respect to Lydia Drakos, we will drape her photo with the roses we hold. This is symbolic of our love and support for Lydia, the Rose Beyond the Wall." Tori stepped closer to the altar and placed a rose near Lydia's photo. "Sisters, as you come forward with your rose, take time to think of a message you would like to deliver to Lydia on the other side of the wall."

A message to the dead? I kept myself from frowning, swallowing back the cynicism. The language of our rituals was sometimes drawn from Christian texts, but this "beyond the wall" thing seemed a little macabre.

The air was tense with grief and silent tears. Although the sisterhood had come together in sorrow, we were still quite alone in our individual thoughts. Alone in birth, alone in death.

When I approached the table and saw the photos of Lydia—photos that made her appear to be contemplative, noble, loyal, and happy—that was the moment when I felt the pang of connection to the imposter in the pictures. Lydia had possessed none of these qualities, but she'd been a good pretender. I knew the girl who'd been a poser. I'd been prodded and manipulated by her, more than once.

You were mean to me, I thought, *and I'm sorry you died. But I'm not sorry I lied to you. I'm not.*

As I extended my rose, a thorn stabbed the pad of my thumb, puncturing the skin. I swallowed back a gasp at the sight of blood. I dropped the rose onto the table and backed away.

CHAPTER 23

"Just so we're clear," I told Tori, "I'm totally against this. I've told the sisters that, more than once, but I've been overruled. So here I am." I plunked the metal cash box on the table in the foyer of Theta House and took a seat in the folding chair. "I'll handle the door, but I'm not going to pretend this honors Lydia in any way."

"Wow, Emma." Tori placed the Ziploc bag of name tags and pens on the table. "I sense that you're upset."

Even as I was looking up at Tori, a bad angle for most people, she was beautiful, the lines of her jaw regal, her skin smooth with just the right amount of peachy highlights. I stood up again to even the playing field. "You can't pay tribute to one of our sisters with pancakes and hookups. It's just wrong."

"I'm sorry you feel that way," Tori said sweetly. "You should sign up for a session yourself. Sounds like you could use a good—"

"Hey, guys!" Isabel interrupted, skipping into the foyer like a five-year-old. It didn't help that she was swimming in the "Lydia Memorial" T-shirt Violet had ordered for us. "Did you know that we have gluten-free pancakes, too? I'm so psyched."

Tori gave a mincing smile. "Somebody's happy."

"For the pancakes," I said. "But she doesn't like the memorial thing. Do you, Isabel?"

"Me? Oh, well . . ." She hesitated to stand up to Tori. "Not really. I mean, I'll support the sisterhood's decision, but I think it's kind of eerie, using Lydia."

"To each his own," Tori said. "I hope you've got a lot of fives in that cash box, because there's going to be a shitload of girls and dudes here with twenty-dollar bills and big hopes. So Haley and Alexa are in handling the griddles in the kitchen, and we'll have a few girls in the dining room to make sure people clean up their mess. Last time those guys from Theta Tau thought they were cute with that syrup war. That can't happen again."

"I'm not in charge of the dining room," I said, touching the familiar diamond shape of my Theta Pi pin on my T-shirt. Before I pledged, the only T-shirts in my wardrobe had been plain cotton in black or white, but sororities were big on matching T-shirts or sweatshirts tailored to certain events.

"Don't be so spiteful, Emma," Tori said. "You know those frown lines around your mouth will be etched there forever."

I didn't have frown lines—I knew that much—but Tori had scored her point.

"I've got to make sure the babe cave is set up for the speed daters," Tori said. "Oh, and encourage the sisters to participate in the dating, at least to get things started. Last year we had a lot more guys than girls." She strode off, her heels clicking with self-importance as she crossed the tile floors. I never understood how she could stand to wear heels that high.

"Are you going to chill with me here?" I asked Isabel. "I could use help explaining things to the newbies."

"Actually, I was planning to be in on the dating. I've never tried it before and it might be cool."

"Izzy, this is a random four minutes to plead your case. It's fodder for a meaningless hookup. You get a lot more information on Tinder or OkCupid."

"But Tinder is so cold. I think everyone gets rated completely on their looks. If you're not, like, a supermodel, guys swipe left. It's a dead end for me."

"But you're beautiful," I insisted. I believed that, but I knew Isabel was hard on herself.

"I just feel lonely. Like there's no one there for me."

I slung an arm over her shoulder. "You can always talk to me."

"I know that, but it's not the same as being in love."

"I know." When I gave her a squeeze, the fine bones of her shoulder made her seem like a delicate bird in my arms. My heart ached for Isabel. I understood loneliness, but I had learned to suppress all the myths about romantic love, valentines, and soul mates. But her quest was so pure and genuine that I didn't want to discourage her. I just prayed that her heart didn't get broken.

"Anyway, Tinder hasn't worked out for me, so why not try this? I'll have time to do the first session before my shift downstairs." She leaned over the sign-up sheet and wrote her name and cell phone number in the girls' column. "Here's the fifteen dollars."

"Exact change. So you planned this."

"Maybe. Do I need to do anything else?"

"Make yourself a name tag. You'll be in the first group. Other people should start arriving in a few minutes."

"Okay. I promised Patti I'd help with the cleanup, so the first group is perfect." Her dark eyes seemed bright and round as quarters as she took a chair next to me. "I just saw Defiance in the kitchen, and she told me something special is going to happen tonight. Something about the November Super Moon in Virgo that stands for beginnings."

"I thought you weren't into New Age stuff."

"I am when it's positive."

"Aw."

"I know. I'm adorable," she said.

"Who could resist you?"

We made a few last-minute adjustments, moving the table farther from the door and posting signs for PANCAKES in the dining room and SPEED DATING downstairs. That was when I noticed that the photo that had been removed from the wall was now returned.

"So the picture's back. Anyone know who returned it?" I asked, moving closer to the group portrait.

"Nobody's mentioned it," Isabel said.

It wasn't hard to find our senior girls in the photo. Tori, Violet, India, Haley . . . and there was Lydia, smiling and composed, her chin lifted to an unknown future. I squinted. The portrait seemed kind of washed out and faded, but maybe it had always been that way.

My attention was drawn away when the front door opened and three guys came stumbling in like baby bucks finding their footing. Tall and lanky, as if their bodies had been stretched out. Obviously underclassmen, probably athletes.

"Hey, guys?" Isabel chirped. "Are you here for speed dating or pancakes or both?"

One guy with dark hair and a triangular patch on his chin opened his eyes wide. "We want it all!"

I went over to the table to get them set up. "That's fifteen dollars for the first session of speed dating, and five for unlimited pancakes."

As they were paying, a handful of girls came in bringing a cloud of one of those sweet perfumes that smells like cake batter. Giggly and awkward and overly made-up. Moving like a swarm of bees, they bumped into the guys and backed up and lined up. Definite signs of pre-party.

"So how does this work?" one girl asked. "The speed dating."

"They'll go over it all downstairs," I said, "but basically, we'll do twenty people at a time. Ten girls and ten guys."

I noticed that the guys were also listening intently. Apparently, their first time, too. "The ten women will be sitting down," I said, "and each guy will go sit with one, exchange first names, and talk till the bell rings. You get four minutes. When the bell rings, you write either yes or no next to the person's name on your paper, and you move on. Four minutes with the next girl, and the next. Then keep going until you get through all ten."

"So if we give a girl a yes, we leave with them?" asked one of the tall guys. He had a crew cut and pale gray eyes, a fine profile that was overwhelmed by his oversized Merriwether hoodie.

"Not quite," I said. Good thing this presumptuous guy was on the shy side. "You need to give every girl a chance, and don't ask personal information beyond first names. Well, not too much. We'll keep track of everyone's contact info," I said. "Besides, each girl is also giving you a yes or no after you talk. When your session is over, we'll compile the stats. If we see that two people both wrote yes, we'll text that couple with the name and contact info of the other person."

There was excitement in the air, as if people were going on to a TV game show. I didn't mind that, though it still annoyed me to think of Lydia being connected to these festivities.

"If you're speed dating, make sure you get a name tag," Isabel said as a line began to form behind the group of girls.

For the next half hour, I kept busy with the steady flow of students at the door, some of whom I knew from classes or Greek events. There was only one student on campus that I wanted to avoid, but I didn't think Sam would have the nerve to come to Theta House after what had happened. Sam had broken my heart and stomped on it, and it was my sisters who had helped me piece my soul back together.

Our first session had begun and our second session was nearly sold out when some Omega Phi brothers appeared in the queue. With mixed emotions I spied Rory MacFarlane among his friends. I was glad to see him, but disappointed that he was into the speed-dating thing.

"Hey. How's it going, Emma?" His eyes caught mine with a heavy look.

I felt glad that he remembered me, but that was Rory. Everyone liked him because he had mad skills on a snowboard but was still genuine and down-to-earth.

His friends were doing the speed dating, but Rory wanted pancakes only.

"So you're the hungry one," I teased.

"I came for moral support." He tapped one of his friends on

the arm. A husky guy with a dark beard and thoughtful eyes. "This is Charlie. He wants to talk with you when you have a chance."

I didn't know what to think about that, but I was fairly sure I'd never met Charlie before. "Hi, Charlie. I'm kind of busy now, but I'll come find you when one of the sisters takes over for me."

"Cool." Charlie nodded and moved down the line with his friends, while Rory swung around the table and took the empty seat beside me.

"Okay if I sit here? I'm not up for pancakes just yet."

He smelled of citrus and maybe woodsmoke, that slight hint of fragrance that made you want to move closer and breathe deeply. He wasn't wearing the knit cap, so I could take in the full effect of his poster-boy good looks. His hair was shiny, probably freshly shampooed. Reason for that great smell. "Sure. You can play bouncer if someone gets crazy."

"Not me." He held his hand up. "I'm all: Make love not war."

I kept my focus on the next person in line, trying not to be rattled that Rory was sitting beside me talking about making love. Of course it was an expression, I knew that, but still, it was cool. His presence kept me on alert as I made change and explained the dating process to the new arrivals.

"What's up with your friend?" I asked Rory as I waited for two girls to fill out their name tags. "What's his name again?"

"Charlie Bernstein. It's about Lydia. He feels really bad. Wants to talk to someone who knew her."

I was about to say that I wasn't that close with her but stopped myself. It was time to own the fact that I'd had a relationship with Lydia, even if it was a bit twisted.

We were starting to get a lot of people who wanted pancakes only—people who'd gotten baked on weed and wanted to burrow into a snack. From the dining room came the buzz of conversation and laughter, while the living room housed people waiting for the next session. They generally separated into packs by gender, talking quietly as they checked each other out across the room. It was a high school dance with a twist.

When I got the line down for the time being, I went into the dining room to snag somebody. I found Angela, wiping her hands on a damp rag. "People can be so disgusting," she said.

"Cover for me at the door for a few minutes?"

"Yes. Please," she said, tossing the rag onto the sideboard.

Rory and I plucked Charlie from the other Omega Phis and stepped out to the front yard, where the lights and flames of the memorial to Lydia still glowed at the center of the lawn. My gaze combed the street for a lone detective, waiting and watching, but aside from a male jogger who was fixing his shoe, no one was traveling alone. If there was a cop out there, he or she was probably sitting in one of the cars parked on the other side of the street. I turned away from the street, which gave me a chance to watch the steady stream of people heading into Theta House.

"So what's up, guys?"

Rory clapped a hand on his friend's back. "Charlie wanted to talk to you about Lydia."

When I turned to Charlie, the color seemed to drain from his face. "Wow. This is so awkward, but I'm really sorry." He struggled over the words.

I looked away. "Thanks. We're still feeling it."

"I feel really bad because things weren't completely right between Lydia and me. We went to the spring formal last year and..." He patted the breast pockets of his plaid flannel shirt, then dug one hand into a pocket of his jeans. "I have this for you. I was supposed to give it to Lydia, but that never happened. I'm really sick about it. I mean, she told me she could wait till I got it together, but..."

Trying to make sense of it, I watched as he pulled out a wad of cash.

"I was hoping you would take this," he said. "Get it to her parents or...maybe sorority dues or something?"

"Lydia loaned you money?"

"Not exactly a loan," he said, turning to Rory. "I just owed her this."

"For what?"

He squeezed the curled bills in his hands. "It's embarrassing. I would have paid her right away, but I didn't have the money. I work the desk in Pittock Hall. Night security on weekends. But part of that goes to my room and board."

"I gotcha. It's hard when you're paying your own way, right? I work at the library."

He nodded, extending the folded bills. "I'll feel a lot better if you take it. It's all there, four hundred dollars."

Enough for a hundred pumpkin lattes, a semester of books, an online shopping spree.

Still . . . it wasn't for me.

"Honestly, I wouldn't know what to do with it," I said. "Did you talk to Lydia's best friends? Tori . . . or Courtney. Do you know them?"

"I know of them. A guy like me can't get close to girls like that. They're, like, *tens.*"

I felt for Charlie, knowing that it was true. It made me wonder how I'd gotten connected with bitchy fat-shamers, though I hadn't known that when I'd pledged Theta Pi. "Wow, Charlie. I guess I can take it and find a way to get it to Lydia's mom. Or maybe if she owes money to Theta House."

"Whatever. I just need to know my part is done."

He handed the bills over, his cheeks puffing as he blew out a breath of relief. "Man, that's a weight off my mind."

"This feels kind of weird," I admitted, "but I promise, I won't keep it for myself."

"Whatever. I just needed to get right with her. You know? Thanks for helping me straighten it out."

"Sure thing." I slipped the cash into my pocket, feeling as if it might burn a hole through the lining.

CHAPTER 24

Back inside, I expected Rory to go off with his frat brothers, but he lingered behind the table as Angela told the students in line to hold on while she surrendered her post.

"All these people in the hall are in for session three. We just need three more girls to fill it. And I don't know where we're going to put all the pancake people. Girls are starting to sit on guys' laps."

"Which may be a whole new form of speed dating," Rory said.

I couldn't help but smile at that.

"You're laughing, but some of those guys are beasts, and we're in deep shit if the dining room chairs start breaking. Who's the comedian?" Angela asked, and I introduced her to Rory.

"You're making me go back to that crappy job?"

"Thanks for covering," I said, pointing her back toward the dining room.

She plodded down the hall with a sigh. "I'll be glad when this is over."

"You and me both," I called, and then turned to the next person in line, a girl with a team jersey, tight cornrows, and a big smile. "Dating, pancakes, or both?"

"How does the dating thing work?" she asked, squinting curiously.

As I launched into another explanation, Rory took the seat beside me and started setting up a sign-in sheet for the fourth session.

At one point I turned to Rory and asked if he was going for pancakes.

"I'll hang with you. If that's okay. Not like I'm stalking you or anything, but I wanted to talk to you."

Oh-kay. Not to sugarcoat it all in my mind, but this was turning out to be a better night than I'd expected.

Working side-by-side, Rory and I made it through selling tickets to five more shifts of dating, and way too many pancakes. Around one a.m., people started coming in for pancakes to go, and though we had no containers they didn't mind walking out with stacks of flapjacks on paper plates. Theta House would probably reek of burned grease and maple syrup in the morning, but we had delegated the freshman sisters for cleanup duty.

It was after two when our line seemed to dry up for good. Someone had turned music on in the dining room, and some people were dancing in the living room. We had strict orders from Mrs. J not to let the night evolve into a party, but the warm, sleepy glaze over the room didn't come close to a gathering anyone would object to.

I was stacking up the leftover name tags as Rory scoped out the pledge class photos in the foyer.

"This is you, right?" He pointed to the middle row, and looked at me. "You look pretty much the same."

"It's just from last year. I was an old pledge. Gap year and all that."

He moved his finger down to the caption. "Emma Danelski. That's your last name?"

"Yes, and please, no jokes."

"What, you don't like your last name?"

"The boys in grade school used to torture me with a string of Polish jokes."

"That's not cool. Unenlightened little brats. I'd never do that, Danelski."

"Thanks, MacFarlane." I lowered the lid on the cash box and gave it a lift. "This thing is heavy. I think I'd better go upstairs to count it." I pointed to it, mouthing the words: "A lot of cash."

"I'll go with you." When I gave him a skeptical look, he folded his arms. "What? Is there a rule?"

"Of course. But come on." In the world of rule breakers and followers, I leaned toward the followers, which made it edgy and thrilling to be leading a guy upstairs and carrying thousands of dollars under my arm.

The suite was empty and dark, all my roommates working downstairs. Someone had left a window cracked open, and the air was cool with the smell of smoke from a wood fire, probably from someone's backyard fire pit. I closed it and set the cash box on the table. I kicked off my boots as Rory sat cross-legged on the rug.

"Honestly, I've never seen this much cash before. Sort of makes me nervous."

"Cash is such a liability," he said. "Pretty soon we'll be a cyber-cash society."

We set to work putting the bills in stacks, which we counted twice. I found some rubber bands from the drawer, and we bundled everything up and tucked it back into the box.

"More than two thousand dollars," I said. "Not bad for a night's work."

"And your overhead?"

"For pancake ingredients and name tags? Less than two hundred dollars. Are you a business major?"

"That's the plan. It's so dry, but I'm good with numbers. How about you?"

"Nursing. I need a job when I get out, and I'm pretty good with people. I'm sort of the house nurse here."

"Do you like science?"

"I know how to use WebMD."

"What was Lydia's major?"

"I don't know. Sociology or liberal arts. She was going for her MRS degree. Why do you ask?"

He pointed to my T-shirt. "It's her party, right? But I didn't hear anyone but Charlie mention her."

"Exactly what I've been saying." I told him how my objections to having a party event in Lydia's name had been buried by the sisterhood. "I wouldn't have participated at all, but it was a mandatory event."

"That's ironic. I wanted to come so I could find you and talk about Lydia." He leaned back against the foot of the couch and rubbed his eyes. "This thing is messing me up. Seeing her jump from the bridge, that's all I can think about. It's very disturbing."

"It's a trauma," I said. "I'm sure I would be a wreck if I saw something like that."

"I can't get it out of my head."

"It helps to talk about it."

"I feel that," he said, "but for most people on campus, it's just a sad news event. The bros think I'm stuck on it; they don't get it. The only time I feel semi-normal is when I'm with you."

"Because I knew her and we can talk about her?"

"Not so much. I think it's just you, Danelski." He took my left hand and held it to his chest. The dim lamplight behind him accentuated the angles of his jaw, and again I could smell his shampoo, a soft citrus, mixed with the scent of his skin. "You'll make a good nurse. There's something about you that's reassuring. Kind of comforting."

"I've heard that before," I said. "I'm like everybody's best friend."

"Yeah. Maybe more than a friend." He leaned closer, and oh, I wanted to breathe him in. "If you want."

He didn't have to wait for my answer.

On Sunday, as Rory and I sat in a booth at Oogey's feasting on plates of eggs, bacon, and waffles, a wrinkle developed in my romantic euphoria. "Wait a minute. You've been talking with Dr. Finn? Scott Finnegan, from English?"

"About this suicide task force," Rory said. "He got my name

from the police report and sent me an e-mail, and we got to-gether yesterday. I thought the task force was a good idea. Maybe a way to help me get my head away from remembering that night."

"So you're going to be on it?"

"I'm in. I met with Dr. Finn yesterday for a while. He men-tioned that he asked you but you turned him down."

"I can't do it." I took a sip of water, trying to get this straight in my mind. "I don't have time for something like that."

"Think about it. It'll be like therapy. It's a résumé builder. And I'll be there."

"You make it tempting, but still. I've got a killer Anatomy class this term, and I work whenever I have free time." I stabbed a piece of cheddar-spinach omelet—a special treat for me. We were only here because Rory was treating and I wanted it to be a regular Sunday thing, getting together with him. But I didn't want "us" to be a result of some wacky professor's per-sistence. "Hold on. Did Dr. Finn put you up to this? Is that why you came to the pancake supper last night?"

"I'm not an asshat." He put his coffee mug on the table and rotated it in his hands. "I knew about the party and wanted to see you. Besides, I'd promised Charlie I'd help him with his weird closure thing."

I hadn't forgotten about Charlie Bernstein and that wad of money that I had stashed in a bottom drawer as if it were someone else's balled-up love letters. "What's the story on that money?" I asked.

"He says that he owed her. I figured it was a loan."

"But he denied that. And Lydia wouldn't have had the cash to give out. She claimed to be rich, the granddaughter of a bil-lionaire, but it wasn't true. I mean, four hundred dollars? No one has that lying around, unless you're a . . . drug kingpin."

"Do you think Lydia . . . ?"

"No, definitely not. That girl had a lot of mysteries, but she wasn't dealing drugs out of Theta House. We would have noticed. Our housemother is fairly observant." I knew there had to be a simple explanation. "Can you just ask Charlie about it, sometime when he's relaxed? Make it a dude thing."

"He's just one of the brothers. It's not like we ever talk."

I gave him a hard look.

"Fine. I'll see what I can find out." Using a fork, he chased the last triangles of waffle on his plate. "What about the task force. Are you in?"

I cupped the ceramic mug with the googly-eyed Oogey's logo. "I'm thinking about it. Dr. Finn would be good to work with, and it would be nice to have an impact on something that's so broken. The student health policies are useless, and maybe if students designed a program—"

"It would be more effective in targeting the problems?"

Our minds were already working in tandem; a little scary. "They should invite some of the students who led those protests against the health center."

"Great idea."

"And there's this guy named Stephen Kim—I see him all the time when his group gets together in the library. They call themselves Merriwether Faith in Action, an interfaith prayer group. Stephen said they couldn't get Asian-Americans to join when they called it a support group because it seemed shameful. A cultural thing. Stephen should be on the task force."

"So you're in." He smiled, and it made something inside me sparkle.

"I didn't say that. I've got so much to juggle."

"You can't say no. You're a helper. Nurse Emma."

I felt myself sliding into that gooey, warm glow of attraction, and although it was the wrong time and place in my life, I couldn't latch on to anything to stop my fall down the rabbit hole. And in my heart, I wanted to slide down, down, down and be with Rory.

But last time, it had been a mistake. Painful and costly. By the time I'd finally stood up for myself, Sam had eroded my soul down to the nub of boulders and tree roots.

"Let me think about it a while." I put the napkin on the table and slid out of the booth. "I'll be right back."

As I moved toward the restroom, I passed the waitress, an obvious student, serving a latte at the next table. The female diner had the look of a professor kicking back on Sunday with hair pulled back from brown freckled skin, black raincoat, jeans, and a big leather bag. There was a notebook open on the table with coffee and a croissant. She was talking with the waitress when I passed by. I didn't think anything until my gaze swept her notes and I recognized my name.

What the . . . ?

I paused behind her and took a longer look.

E. Danelski & Rory. $400. Drug kingpin. Theta House a drug house? Charlie. Dr. Finn. Merriwether Faith in Action. Stephen Kim.

"Oh my God. You're spying on us! You're a cop?"

The woman glanced back at me, her tight expression all the proof I needed. I'd blown her cover. She'd been caught. Though she wasn't doing anything illegal, eavesdropping is not cool.

"Don't I even get Sundays off?" I demanded. A stupid thing to say, I know, but I was pissed. "I am so sick of this!"

"You and me both." She closed the notebook and flipped open a leather sleeve to show me her ID: Officer Tamara Caldwell, Pioneer Falls Police Department.

I pushed the badge and ID card back at her. "Don't you have some real criminals to catch?"

"That's exactly what I'm trying to do. I guess you haven't seen the news today, but Lydia Drakos's autopsy results were released this morning. There was a press conference at the precinct. The medical examiner found bruises on Lydia's neck and there was damage to her larynx."

Rory and I exchanged a confused look. "What does that mean?" he asked.

"Those are signs of manual strangulation," Caldwell said. "Your friend was murdered."

CHAPTER 25

Standing in a sea of yellow maple leaves that covered the ground outside Oogey's, Rory and I stared at the screen of his phone, watching Chief Blue deliver a written statement about the death of Lydia Drakos.

"I'm really sorry to be bringing you folks this news today," Blue said. His bass voice was clear and professional, but his rueful expression showed his humanity. "The physical evidence indicates that the actions of the attacker, the strangulation, at the very least contributed to the victim's death. At this time we are officially investigating a homicide. We will be casting a wider net, and following up on interviews with everyone who knew the victim. As always, if you have any information that might lead to the apprehension of this individual, please call our crime tips hotline any time, day or night."

"Holy crap." Rory looked from the phone to me, unable to process. "So she wasn't alone on the bridge that night. That person I saw in the hoodie must have been—"

"Trying to hurt her. Or kill her." My gaze skimmed the paths and buildings around us with a new point of view. An edgy fear that a killer was out there, ready to strike again.

"Shit. I wish I'd gotten a better look at him. Not to be morbid, but Lydia didn't make a sound going off the bridge. So maybe she was unconscious and he pushed her."

"Or she," I said. "The killer could be a girl. The police know that. They've got a cop following me to Sunday brunch."

"They're way off on that theory. Unless there's something you haven't told me?" He was joking, but the question made me feel a little wobbly.

"I didn't kill Lydia," I said.

"And the cops must know you're an unlikely suspect. Everyone knows men are behind most violent crimes."

He was right, but the image of some guy choking Lydia, manhandling a girl who was a little out of her mind and very vulnerable in her pink robe and nightgown... I shuddered, shoving my hands into the pockets of my jacket. "Probably a guy," I agreed. "And it had to be someone she knew. Lydia walked out of Theta House in her nightgown by choice. I know people are going to be frightened by this news, and it's awful, but it's not like some killer came into our house and kidnapped her during the night. She left the house with this person. She probably walked willingly to the bridge with him, too."

"Could it be an old boyfriend?"

"She dated a lot, but no real boyfriends."

"So a lot of possibilities there. Or somebody she knew from class or a club?"

"Her only extracurricular activity was Theta Pi and Greek life."

"Then the cops will be looking closely at the frats." He pulled me into his arms, looking down on me with concern. I felt safe there, less scared. "I'm worried about you."

"Yeah." My cheek to his sweatshirt, I breathed in the smell of Rory, woodsmoke and fabric softener. "If it's not the cops after me, now there's a killer out there."

"Don't worry. I'm going to be your escort on campus."

I lifted my head, looking up at him. "That would be great, but our schedules don't always jibe. You've got classes, and your workouts, and—"

"We'll figure it out. You gotta stay safe."

"I will. I won't be wandering off with strangers at night.

Not without my sisters." I wondered if they'd heard the news. Word would travel fast, not just through Theta Pi, but all the Greeks, all women on campus. Besides that, a mass e-mail would be launched from Dean Cho's office, advising of the incident and warning all students to travel in groups.

"This is going to scare the crap out of the Theta Pis," I said.

"Not just them. Everyone's going to be on alert."

"I'd better get back."

As we walked back to Theta House, Rory made yet another pitch for me to join the task force, and this time I saw how it might work. I'd be spending time with Rory, and I could pull in some vital people like Stephen Kim. It would look good as an extracurricular for my nursing job applications. Besides all that, I thought it might ease my conscience to be doing something constructive to reach suicidal students.

"I don't know when I'm going to find the time to do it," I said, "but I'll e-mail Dr. Finn and get the details."

"Cool." When Rory slung an arm around me and pulled me close, it seemed so natural, as though we'd been together for years. He looked down at me to make sure it was okay, and I stared back with that warm, tender feeling that made my knees go weak.

Sam used to hate public displays of affection. He wouldn't even hold my hand when we were walking on campus.

His pissy behavior made me appreciate Rory's kiss that much more.

When we got to Theta House, all hell was breaking loose. I could hear the panicked voices from the front porch.

"You'd better go," I told Rory. He'd been planning to come in—his confidence tended to calm people, and all the girls liked him—but I hadn't expected such a big reaction. "Sounds like they're freaking. You don't want to have to play big brother to forty girls."

"No thanks." He kissed my cheek. "I'll call you later."

Inside, it was like a bad funeral parlor scene. Some girls

were huddled together on the sofas in the living room watching a handful of freaked-out sisters egg one another on into meltdown phase.

"It isn't safe!"

"I want to go home!"

"Do you think he's watching us now?"

"What if he wants to kill us? We're like sitting ducks."

My quick assessment revealed that these were all freshmen and sophomores. Yes, I was a sophomore, too, but because of my gap year and birth date, I had two years on most of these girls.

"There is no random killer out there watching us," I said. "Think about it, girls. Lydia was killed out on the bridge. Rory saw her there, talking. The killer didn't break in here and pluck her from this house in the middle of the night. She went out there on her own. She knew her killer."

"That doesn't make me feel any better!" Mia wailed.

"Where's Mrs. J?" I asked. It was her day off, but this was an emergency.

"Defiance went to find her," Isabel answered from the sofa, where she was sitting with an arm around Patti, stroking her sandy-brown hair while Patti dried her tears.

"And Tori? And Violet?" I asked. Where were the seniors?

"Up in Violet's room, I think," Chloe said. "They said something about a Rose Council meeting."

I rolled my eyes. They were probably drinking shots and laughing about the poor frightened freshmen. That crew seemed to think they were immune to the problems of the rest of the world, but they might be at risk, too.

My mother's pragmatic, nurturing streak kicked in as I turned to the frightened girls. "All right, listen, guys, everyone needs to calm down."

"But we're so scared," Patti sobbed.

"And he could be out there!" Mia pointed to the windows. "We don't know why he killed Lydia. Maybe he hates sororities. Maybe he hates Theta Pis!"

I stood my ground. "Maybe he does, Mia. But if we freak out and give in to fear, we're not going to be prepared to protect ourselves, are we?"

"But I can't stop shaking," she said.

"I know that feeling, but we can't give in." I put my hands on her shoulders and guided her over to a chair. "We can't let him win. We are going to stick together on this. We're going to support each other and stay safe. Right, girls?" My gaze passed over all of them, willing them to calm down. Maybe I'm not a natural leader, but I wasn't going to look the other way while these little lemmings dashed off a cliff.

The front door thumped and Mrs. J came in with a bag full of books. "Oh, my goodness, I just heard. I can't believe the police didn't give me a heads-up."

"Lydia was murdered, Mrs. J," Mia moaned. "And he's out there. Any one of us could be next."

"Mia, please, calm yourself. We don't need your drama at this moment in time." Mrs. J unwrapped her scarf as she scanned the room. "Really, girls, this is not such an unusual situation. We've had discussions about date rape, about things getting out of hand with a guy. I'm not saying that happened, but you girls know what you need to do to stay safe. This was not some random strike at Lydia. The assailant probably knew her. And not to blame our dear Lydia, but she did go wandering at night. Alone. I hope none of you take a risk like that."

Guilty, but I wasn't giving myself up.

Another hour of soothing the panic was about all I could take. I went upstairs to the suite and found Defiance painting her toenails as she took an online quiz in Earth Science. Defiance has a cerebral side that's a little scary; she can ace tests and quizzes. Her downside is public speaking. I think her accent bothers her, and she gets nervous when she has to do a presentation.

"You missed the crybabies." I sat on the love seat, then stretched out, propping my feet on the armrest.

"I had enough of them earlier. I sent a text to Mrs. J. That's all I can do." She clicked the cursor, scrolled down, and then went back to the nail polish. "I told them not to worry. They're not in danger."

"Well, they should be cautious."

"This person is not dangerous to them. But you? I'm worried about you, Emma."

A small boulder might have hit me in the chest. I sat up. "Am I in danger?"

"Not from Lydia's killer. It's something else. Something about the ravine. I keep seeing you down there, crying." She squeezed her eyes shut and shook her head, as if that would cast the image away. "I can't stop seeing you there. I'm sorry."

That damned gorge. Sometimes I couldn't stop seeing myself there, but I'd never told Defiance about it.

"Am I going to be okay?" I asked. "Do I get out of the gorge?"

She frowned, her dark eyes shiny with tears. "I can't see that far. There's trouble, Emma. I can feel it, but I can't see who it is. I don't want to scare you. It's just what I see."

"Okay." Was she reading my mind, or just picking up on my thoughts? You got on the same track when you lived with a person. I lay back down and stared at the ceiling, tracing the cracks along the edge as I tried to clear my mind, tried to wipe away the details of that day in the gorge. Trauma burns a deep scar. Yes, it might last forever, but I believed that one day I would wake up healed enough to forget that it was there.

I had known that Dr. Finn was a man of action, but I didn't know just how fast he could move until he asked Rory and me to meet him that night.

"Hey, guys." He moved from his desk to an upholstered chair as we sat down on the sofa. "I just heard about Lydia's autopsy results. That's awful news. You don't want to think about something like that happening at Merriwether, but no one is immune."

"In some ways it makes sense," I said. "Lydia seemed a little too proud to kill herself. A little bit of a narcissist."

"That's insightful. Narcissists don't commit suicide often.

When they try, it's usually a half-assed ploy to manipulate someone or get attention."

"Interesting." My mind flashed to the bridge scenario. Had Lydia threatened to jump to scare or manipulate someone else? Maybe they had argued and the guy in the hoodie had snapped. Infuriated. Reaching for her throat . . .

Rory was gracefully changing the subject. "How long do you think it will take to pull enough students together for this committee?"

"Here's the thing," Dr. Finn said. "If we wait for the university to set our task force up nice and pretty, we'll be waiting until next semester, maybe next year. I told them we need a meeting space and some stipends for the students on the force. Face it, you'll be taking away from time when you're working. They sent me these." He held up a stack of forms. "Bureaucratic bullshit."

"So you need help filling that stuff out?" Rory asked.

"Hell no." Dr. Finn tossed the papers over his shoulder. "We'll work around them. We'll throw some folding chairs in my office. And I'll lean on Dean Cho to get some stipends for you out of the health center budget. If that doesn't work, I'm sure she's got some emergency fund to draw on. She's all about supporting you guys on this."

"Are we talking about the same Dean Cho?" I asked. "The one who designed the policy that dismisses students when they ask for help?"

"That was a mistake, though it is one way of dealing with campus suicides. You'll see from the literature. We're going to give you guys a hurry-up condensed course in suicide counseling. Actually, I've got some handouts for you here."

He handed Rory and me each a thick packet of articles.

"Thanks," Rory said. "Some light reading."

At this point in the semester, that much reading was daunting, but as I leafed through, the titles caught my interest: "Healing from a Friend's Suicide"; "Debunking Suicide Myths"; "Guns, Depression, and Suicide." There were also numerous accounts of college students who had killed themselves.

"Back to Dean Cho," I said, winding back. "You're good at working around obstacles. Is there any way we can do this without her participation?"

Dr. Finn grinned. "Ha! You're not a fan."

"She revamped the health center so that they treat depressed students like criminals."

"I'm not here to unseat Dean Cho, but the health center—that's a problem for us to tackle," Dr. Finn said. "Don't shake your head at me, Emma. You've got to trust me on this. We will make it happen. We will change things for the better. Dr. Cho has been tasked with an important mission, and she knows her program has been missing the mark; she's on board now, and ready to move ahead."

Although the hysteria at the house settled down after the first day or two, the sisters tried to travel in packs, especially at night. When that wasn't possible, we took Mrs. J's advice and used the campus escort service. Sometimes we had to wait for them, but everyone was frightened enough to accept the inconvenience.

On my recommendation, Dr. Finn and I met with Stephen Kim and begged him to join us. Stephen brought along Suzie Yamaguchi, another student who had helped organize the Faith in Action group.

"Last year, before finals, things got very intense and people were all strung out," Stephen said. "They don't talk about it, but I can feel it. People are ready to pop. They really need to talk. So we started a support group."

"Only no one came," said Suzie. "Just Stephen and me." She had creamy skin, lips that seemed to be in a permanent smile, and a blunt haircut with the ends dyed orange, as if they had been dipped in fire. "We didn't understand it, because many of our friends, when we see them in the pool hall, they want to talk and let off steam. They would seek Stephen out for one-on-one conversations about more personal things."

"But no one wanted to be associated with a support group.

They thought it sounded bad, like they were in therapy. Maybe crazy."

"Many Asian cultures have a stigma about mental illness," Suzie said. "You can't even talk about it. Stephen and I did some research, and we learned that Asian-Americans have a higher suicide rate than non-Asians. Seeing our friends and other students battling depression, that concerned us."

"So we started a prayer group that really acts like a support group," Stephen explained. "We pray together and that's good, but most of the time we talk."

Their biggest concern was the health care center, which people in their group had learned to avoid. "No one wants to take the chance of going there for help and getting kicked out of school."

"Exactly," I said, turning to Dr. Finn, who had no argument with that.

Twenty-four hours later, we had our first meeting. Dean Cho was absent by design. Dr. Finn explained that he wanted the group to get its footing before the intimidating university rep got involved.

Fine with me.

Dr. Finn took notes, his fingers moving rapidly over his laptop as Stephen introduced us to Calliope Daniels, one of the students who had organized protests against the university health center at the beginning of the year. With straw-blond hair cut short and fairies tattooed on her lower arms, Calliope had a rapid-fire way of speaking that would have been impressive in a courtroom, but she also could hold tight and listen. She was the head of the Buddhist society on campus, and she invited us to join in their chants for peace. "This mental health issue is my thing. I am all about it," she said. "But in full disclosure, I'm not going to sell out to the university to stay on this task force."

"That's exactly what we're looking for," said Dr. Finn.

The evil Dean Cho had recruited a grad student who was working on a doctorate in psychology. I wanted to dislike

Kath Schwartz because she came through Dean Cho, but her acerbic sense of humor won me over. "Me in a nutshell? I'm a gorgeous Jewish lesbian babe looking for a low-paying but rewarding career as a therapist. But don't hate me because I'm beautiful," she said. "I'll just be here in the background, profiling all of you for my doctoral thesis."

An awkward silence filled the room. "Seriously?" Rory asked.

"Only in my head," she said. "The curse of the psych doctoral candidate."

Dr. Finn brought in a teaching assistant named Chase Cruz, a dude with thick biceps and the tendrils of a tattoo climbing one side of his neck. Low-key and calm, Chase told us he felt in tune with the LGBT community on campus, and, as a teacher, was always trying to be sensitive to issues of depression and anxiety among students. He had transitioned from being a female during his freshman year in community college, and although he'd received a lot of support, there were a few haters, too. "People tend to be afraid of that which they don't understand," he said in a quiet voice.

"Tell me about it," Evers Garner said. He had high cheekbones, skin the color of warm cinnamon, and a booming voice that captured attention in a reassuring way. He talked about the isolation he'd felt after losing a friend to a drug overdose. "Whether it was suicide or not, the take-away for me was that a lot of people backed away after Monty died. They didn't know what to say, so they avoided his family and friends. Half of them didn't come to the funeral, and the other half came just to get the day off from school." Something about Evers seemed familiar to me. Later I learned that he was in the theater program and had starred in many of the campus productions.

In the first meeting we got to work outlining the ways we wanted to address the problem of suicides on campus. The student health center was at the top of our list.

"The treatment of suicidal students is despicable," said Calliope.

"And what about students like Evers? People who've lost a friend to suicide?" Rory pointed out. "When you're trying to pick up the pieces and sort things out, there's nowhere to go but your friends."

"And they aren't trained in grief therapy," Evers pointed out.

"Statistics indicate that a large percentage of students turn to their friends," Kath said, serious for the first time. "We think that fewer than twenty percent of students considering suicide reach out to a campus health center."

"Even if the health center offers anonymous counseling?" I asked.

"Seems to be that way." Kath pushed back a sheath of dark hair with one beautifully manicured hand. "This is what's published, but there's a good chance that suicidal thoughts and attempts are grossly under-reported on campuses. When an at-risk person gets talked out of it by a friend, it doesn't go into the stats. And since most students say they would confide in friends, we don't really know the scope of the problem."

After that, there was the issue of reaching out to all students with a positive mental health program. And then the issue of the bridges on campus. We wanted to make the bridges safer, "more challenging for suicidal students," Chase suggested. "Some of the footbridges are so open, it makes my knees shake. It just feels like an invitation to fall, and, believe me, I have no desire to go over the edge."

By the end of the meeting we had split into three committees, designed so that we could move faster in smaller groups with gatherings that catered to our schedules.

"But please, when you send out e-mails with content, copy the entire group," Dr. Finn said as the meeting broke up. "We want to keep everyone in the loop."

CHAPTER 26

From the cement plaza outside the health center, Sydney Cho could pick him out from among the students and teachers walking along the path between the two Edwardian brick buildings. Leather jacket dangling open in the cold. A slight limp that one might see as a swagger as he walked at a fast clip. Known by students for his enthusiasm in class, Dr. Finnegan had become a ball of energy since he'd jumped into the task force.

As he approached, she thought of the e-mail he'd sent her after the group's first meeting.

> The health center must die. From the ashes a
> new program will rise.

So flipping dramatic. At least he wasn't boring.

Sydney turned to the center, gold brick and mortar with brown buttresses that leaned out over the windows like prison bars. The building was typical of the Brutalist architecture that appeared on campuses in the 1970s. The building had a cold-hearted appearance, but was it truly a house of horrors as students were depicting it to be? Students didn't like the aggressive line of questioning from counselors or the quick removal of at-risk students from the campus. Kids didn't understand that those measures were taken for their own protection.

And the way Cho had been vilified for the program . . . The student activist Calliope Daniels had called her Cruella de Vil, suggesting that she killed puppies in her spare time. A bit of research would have enlightened them to the fact that Cho had not created this program out of thin air. She had modeled it after programs at Ivy League institutions and competitive universities across the country. Programs that reduced the suicide rate on campus.

At least, as shown in statistics.

"You know what I wish?" Finn started mid-conversation, no greeting, no pleasantries. "I wish we could be flies on the wall in there, listening to the intake interviews, the screening process, the counseling. I know, I know, privacy codes don't allow it."

"And right now there are probably no students in the clinic for counseling. I looked at the intake for the past two weeks, and not a single one. Students are coming in for strep tests and earaches and STDs. But our counseling center has tumbleweeds blowing through."

He gave a laugh. "I'm glad you see the humor in it."

She didn't. Cho hated being wrong. It had been a weakness all her life. When her parents chastised her for making careless mistakes, when her older sister teased her for making a mistake in her math homework. "*Wrong. Wrong. What's the matter, Sydney? Did you forget to wake up your brain today?*"

"You're beginning to recognize that it's not working for us," Finn said.

"That's what the students are saying." It was so hard to budge when your self-esteem was tied to being correct.

"Okay, then." Finn swung the door out and held it open for her. "Let's take a look and see just how bad it really is."

The waiting room with standard-fare vinyl seats was half filled with students looking bored and deflated. Most of them stared at their phones. Two had a laptop open and one was reading a book. Cho spoke with the receptionist, saying she had an appointment to meet with Dr. Dreyfus.

"He's seeing patients now. What's this in reference to?"

asked the young woman, probably a student. She was perky but persistent.

"Tell him Dean Cho is here."

Ms. Perky straightened in her chair at that. "Yes, ma'am." She turned to the other woman working behind the counter. "Do you want to tell him?"

"We'll wait until he's finished with his patient." Cho didn't want to throw her weight around, but she wasn't going to waste time here. Shouldn't an appointment time be respected? Dr. Dreyfus was the director of the clinic. Were they that short-staffed?

She turned back to Ms. Perky. "How long do most students have to wait to be seen?"

"Ten or fifteen minutes, if they have an appointment."

"If not?"

"It depends on how busy we are. For walk-ins, it's usually an hour, maybe—"

"Dean Cho. It's good to see you. Let's go back here and talk."

In the small, generic office with a scuffed floor and one fluorescent bulb buzzing, Cho introduced Scott Finnegan to Harvey Dreyfus, a thirtyish man with brown curls tumbling over his collar and rubber-soled shoes that could have used a shine. Well, she wasn't in Boston anymore, and maybe the West Coast kids liked Dr. Dreyfus's casual style. Furthermore, she wasn't in a position to review his work. When she had been hired, the board had stipulated that she was to focus on mental health, specifically suicide prevention, and she had. But now, watching this operation, she was beginning to wonder about the integrity of the entire health facility. It was supposed to be running smoothly with the other dean of health out on maternity leave, but it didn't take a degree in hospital administration to see the shortcomings.

Maybe they're just having a bad day.

"I'm sorry if we caught you at a bad time," she said. "As we discussed, Finn and I are here to review the procedures for treating students who come in seeking counseling."

"That's right," he said. "I have the questionnaire right here."

"I have a question." Dr. Finnegan leaned in. "If students drop in with a problem, maybe depression, or maybe they're considering suicide, how long do they have to wait out there?"

"If they don't have an appointment, it depends on our volume. Generally, they'll have to wait thirty minutes or more."

"Do they get priority?" Cho asked. "Do you perform some sort of triage?"

Dreyfus folded his arms. "We're not an emergency room."

Finn frowned. "That's unacceptable."

"We do our best."

"No one's blaming you." Cho had a talent for keeping her cool when the temperature was rising. "The broader question here is how we might better serve our student clientele. And if that means adding staff, we need to consider that."

"I'd be down for that," Dreyfus said, scratching the back of his neck.

Cho held back, but really, did he go to med school in a barn? He didn't instill confidence, and he was lacking in personal grooming. And yet, he had won a spot in medical school, while her applications had been denied based on test scores, those blasted MCATs laden with chemistry and biochemistry. That was back before they had added the section on social and psychological behavior, which she would have aced.

"So let's look at that questionnaire," Finn said.

Dreyfus handed them each a form. "We haven't done any psych evals for the past month. We used to get a spike during midterms, but not this year."

Cho wasn't surprised, considering the student complaints against the clinic. She glanced down at the page, a two-column list of questions:

Do you cut?

Do you binge eat?

Have you experienced a loss of appetite?

Are you a compulsive shopper?

Have you ever shoplifted?

Do you have trouble sleeping?

How many hours a night do you sleep?

Do you feel tired all the time?

Cho felt tired just from scanning the list of questions. She had reviewed the form before, but now, seeing it with a new perspective, she couldn't imagine trying to tackle the questions while in a depressed state. "It's daunting."

"But necessary. The provider goes over the answers with the patient to determine level of risk. If the patient is a significant suicide risk, we admit them to the hospital in Mount Hood. Otherwise, they're counseled and given referral information for private therapists and suicide hotlines."

"It doesn't give the student much choice, does it?" Finn said. "If you come in here with a serious problem, maybe clinical depression, you'll be pushed out of the university, unless you can come up with the dough for therapy."

"Well, they do get one free therapy session out of it," said Dreyfus.

"Just enough to verify the crisis. What would it take to set up free, long-term counseling for these students?" Finn asked. "A chance to meet with a mental health professional once a week to discuss coping skills and learn techniques to manage stress? A safe place to bring up emotional issues and learn how to increase self-esteem."

"We don't have the staff for that."

"Then what would it take? Hiring more staff? A larger facility?"

"I don't think that can be done at a university."

"But it is. Some colleges offer free counseling to all registered students. They've made significant progress in making students feel integrated in the health center."

"Really? It must cost a fortune to cater to individual students that way." Dreyfus crossed his legs with a laugh. "Personal therapy for free. That's pampering."

"I see it more as a way of protecting the university's most valuable resources: its students," Cho said. It was becoming clear that Dr. Dreyfus's scope needed to broaden on this matter. Actually, there were quite a few adjustments that needed to be made at the student health center.

Starting now.

CHAPTER 27

In the damp, cool November days that followed, as I watched my back and helped my sisters hold it together, I tried to focus on the task force. It was an effective distraction between worrying about the police and the killer on the loose. Seeing Dr. Finn in action, I learned what could be accomplished by breaking the rules. When the university told him to hold on, he found a way to make things happen immediately by working behind the scenes, calling in favors, improvising. Dean Cho seemed to be helpful in getting him what he needed, though I was still not a fan of the woman who seemed to be focused solely on her own business success.

We worked together on the task force for nearly two weeks before people started heading out for Thanksgiving weekend. In that time we had come up with a list—a platform, Dr. Finn called it—of recommendations, but we were still researching some options and shaping ideas. The Tuesday night before the holiday, Dr. Finn invited everyone to his office for a break, and people actually showed. When Rory and I got there after class, people were still hanging out, talking about their holiday plans and classes. Non-task-force stuff.

"Hey, guys," Dr. Finn called. "Come on in. Grab a slice."

Rory and I wove between Evers and Chase to get to the boxes on Dr. Finn's desk. There was still some pizza left, along with a Caesar salad that looked crisp and green.

"Mmm, is that artichoke on the pizza?" I pulled a slice onto a paper plate and added salad.

"Was that your last class?" Stephen asked me.

I nodded as I swallowed. "Anatomy lab. I thought it would never end."

"You're in Anatomy?" Kath put one hand on her hip. "Don't tell me you're cutting up human bodies."

"We are," I said. "At least, we were thirty minutes ago."

"Are you premed?" Chase asked.

"Nursing major."

"And they make you dissect human cadavers?" He seemed surprised. "Whatever happened to cats?"

"Gross." Kath made a choking gesture. "I used to want to be a doctor, but the human dissection was too much for me. And as a fan of *The Walking Dead* I can tell you, those badass corpses are relentless."

"Are they scary?" Suzie asked me.

"It's not so bad now. We try to be respectful, and really we're looking at structure, muscles, and bones. But one of them, we named her Elsa, she appeared in my nightmares for a while."

"Oh my God!" Suzie covered her face as the others reacted with laughter.

That's the thing about the dead: They evoke extreme emotions. You either laugh or you cry. Moving on to something more uplifting, I said, "So you guys are done with classes, too? Everybody going home?"

"My mother is picking us up in the morning," Stephen said, indicating that Suzie was with him. "Just back to Beaverton for turkey." It was a good-sized suburb west of Portland.

Kath was going to Vancouver to have dinner with her father, and then Portland to hit some clubs with friends. "But I'm coming back Saturday, because I can't stand the Sunday traffic."

Calliope was taking the bus down to Roseburg—a four-hour drive—and Rory was carpooling to Bend for a weekend at home. Evers and Chase were taking the shuttle bus back to Portland.

"What's up with you?" Calliope asked.

"I'll just be hanging here." With all the demands on my time in the past few weeks, I had some papers to write, and I was looking forward to having the suite at Theta House to myself. Defiance was cool with it, and my father was glad to be off the hook.

"What the hell, Orphan Annie," Evers teased me. "Left at the orphanage all alone?"

"And you." Kath smacked Rory's arm. "Step up and bring your girlfriend home for Thanksgiving dinner."

"I offered. She declined."

"But they haven't caught the dude that pushed your friend off the bridge," Evers said. "Are you staying in a safe place?"

"I'll be fine." I doubted that Lydia's killer was coming after me. "And I've got a few sisters to hang with," I said, smiling up at Rory. There were too many stressors involved in going home with him this early in our relationship. The parental approval thing, the question of sleeping together under his parents' roof or pretending to be chaste in separate beds while we sneaked around. And I knew he had some friends in Bend he wanted to catch up with. Also, the prospect of snow in the forecast would send him up to the mountain, and I didn't have the money or interest in learning snowboarding right now.

"How about you, Finny-fin-fin?" Kath asked.

"I'll be here, laying low. I'll see my son on Thanksgiving."

"Is he old enough to care about a turkey dinner?"

Dr. Finn shook his head. "More of his dinner still ends up on his bib than in his mouth. But we'll go to the park or something."

"We'd better go," Stephen told Suzie. "We're leaving early in the morning. Happy Thanksgiving, everyone."

We all called our good-byes as they headed out. At the door Stephen faced us, a deadpan expression on his face. "And may the task force be with you."

It had become our inside joke.

"May the task force be with you!" we answered.

"Jesus, we are a bunch of nerds!" Kath said.

* * *

With no classes on Wednesday, today had been getaway day, and though it was late, the Greek Row was still buzzing as Rory walked me back to Theta House. As soon as I dumped my stuff off, we were going to play some pool at the student union, and then spend some time in his room. Rory held his skateboard in one hand, my hand in the other. The lane in front of the frat and sorority houses was crammed with double-parked cars as people loaded up their gear to head home for Thanksgiving. Parents lingered by their cars or milled around on the front lawns of the big houses, some of them chatting while they waited to drive their kids home.

That would have been my mom if she were still alive. She would have been helping girls move their stuff and making jokes about being an Uber driver. As we passed Rory's house, some Omega Phi brother holding a chunky upholstered chair nearly fell out of the front door.

"Whoa, man." Rory rushed over to the steps to help. "I got the front," he called, pressing his back into the brushed corduroy and grabbing the frame behind him.

Calling instructions and moving slowly, the two guys maneuvered the chair down the steps and onto the walkway. Somewhere in the operation I realized the other Omega Phi was Charlie Bernstein, whose face was now beet red and damp with sweat.

"That is one heavy mo-fo," Charlie said.

"How the hell did you get it in?" Rory asked.

"The brothers helped." Charlie explained that he had thought he'd use the chair, but it was too much of a space sucker. "Taking it home now. Thought I could do it on my own."

"I'll give you a hand loading it up."

"Thanks. I'll be right back."

As Charlie went to get his car, I tapped on Rory's arm. "Come on, dude. This is the time to ask him about the money."

"Out here?"

"Go with him to get the car. He owes you now. Just go."

"You're so demanding, woman," he said, but he left his skate-board with me and jogged down the block to catch up with Charlie.

The temperature was dropping, but it was dry, so I perched on the half-brick wall that rimmed the Omega Phi lawn. I sat there scrolling through Instagram as I watched the scene on the street. Everyone was in a good mood, that adrenaline at the beginning of a holiday.

When a hot metallic-blue BMW rolled up in front of the frat next door, guys started hollering and cheering. I looked up and saw the guys ogling the car and high-fiving the driver, Graham Hayden. If there was any doubt of ownership on the beamer, the license plate HAY YEAH, Senator Hayden's previous cam-paign slogan, confirmed it. The Gamma Kappa brothers were mocking Graham for having an expensive car, joking that he'd stolen it from his father. Graham took it in stride, smiling and locking the car so the guys couldn't climb in. He pretended modesty, but you could tell he liked the attention as he hung near the car, buffing a mirror with the hem of his T-shirt. Al-though he wasn't a big guy, Graham was pumped. His usual wardrobe of shorts and a skin-tight jersey made that clear. He had a warm smile, and a thick head of dark hair that he kept perfectly styled, heavy on the top, smooth on the sides. It was no wonder that girls swallowed back sighs when he walked by.

Of course, Lydia had chosen a guy who was a Gamma Kappa. It was known as the rich guys' fraternity, sometimes called "Gown and Cappa" since its members had wealthy par-ents who could buy them a degree. At least, that was what people thought.

I knew that Graham had been interviewed by the police when they expanded their investigation of Lydia's death. Had they pressed him about their relationship, the way they had stuck it to me, or did they let him off easy since he was a soc-cer star and the son of a U.S. senator?

Graham's name had been on the list that Tori, Violet, Courtney, and I had put together for the police. Tori had been snotty about doing it at first, but Detective Turner had told us that if we didn't do it based on her request, we would be subpoenaed. That had changed attitudes quickly.

I'd been the "recording secretary," typing names on my laptop. Much of the time, Courtney had been talking the guys up, saying how they were so hot or so nice to her. "Can't we leave his name off?" she asked more than once. "I don't want him to get into trouble."

"The only way this will get him into trouble is if he killed Lydia," I said, resisting the urge to add "dumb-ass" or "stupid idiot." I used to think it was an act with Courtney, but lately I had come to realize that the source didn't matter. The result was always moronic.

Just then Charlie's car pulled into the Omega Phi driveway, and the guys popped out and made quick work of loading in the chair. In a minute, Charlie was thanking Rory, and we were on our way once again.

"So?" I wanted to skip backward in front of Rory to get the full story, but I held back. "Did he tell you?"

"He was paying for an abortion."

"Wait. What?"

"He said he got Lydia pregnant. They did it one time, and they used protection, but you know. Shit happens. I guess he was that unlucky two percent."

"It does happen," I said, staring ahead into the darkness.

"It's possible. The freaky thing is that he says it was his first time, and I believe him. Not that I'm judging, but I can see why he would go for someone like Lydia. His weight, the shyness. He's socially awkward. He spends most of his time gaming, and when he comes out into the sun he can't look a girl in the eye. So he hooked up with Lydia, and she said it was her first time, too."

I winced. "That I don't believe. She always tried to act proper and reserved, and she didn't give details about guys she'd been with, but I doubt Charlie was her first. She dated a lot of different guys, and she had a boyfriend. . . ." I stopped before I reeled off Lydia's lie about the childhood sweetheart back in Greece. Amazing how hard it was for me to part with some of the mythology of Lydia's life. "She dated Graham Hayden during her junior year, and she really liked him. She had to have lost her virginity then."

"This is a weird conversation," he said. "Can we not talk about other people having sex?"

"I need to run this by Tori. She'll know if it's true." I took out my phone. "I wonder if she left yet."

With most of the sisters on their way out, Theta House had the feel of a train shuddering to a stop. I left Rory waiting in the front living room with a handful of parents and ran up-stairs to Tori's room. The sorority president got to have her own room—the only single suite in the house—but I hadn't been in this room since my big sister, Kate, had lived in it last year.

"Tori?" I knocked. "It's Emma." I had texted her on my way home, not sure if she'd be around, and she had texted back that she was "gettin' the hell out, bitch."

"Hold on," she called. A minute later the door opened to Tori slipping on a wool backpack with a Native American print in bold colors.

"Nice backpack," I said.

"Don't you love it? It's a Pendleton. I just got it."

This girl seemed to have something new every day.

"I'm already running late, so if you want to talk, you'll have to help me carry my stuff down."

"Sure." I stepped into a tornado zone, with scattered clothes, books, papers, and even some dirty dishes that should have been returned downstairs. Tori had definitely made her mark on the room. "Are you catching a bus?"

"I'm driving, but I told my home friends I'd be back by nine." I'd forgotten about her car. Most kids didn't bring a car to campus as it cost a lot to keep it here. Two thousand for the year. Not an issue with Tori. She stood in front of the mirror, pumping lotion from a bottle and rubbing it into her hands. "We always go clubbing in Portland. It's our thing."

I went over to the bed, where a giant hard-sided suitcase lay open. "You taking this?"

"Yup. You can zip it up."

As I went to close the suitcase, I noticed a bunch of photos zipped into the net lining. I recognized Theta Pi girls in the pictures, and Lydia was in some of the shots. Older photos, many of them from their pledge training. That year the pledges had to wear matching pink T-shirts. If Tori wasn't in such a hurry, I would have taken them out and gushed over them.

Instead, I folded one side of the suitcase over the other and zipped it shut. I suspected that Tori was bringing those photos home with her as a part of the grieving process. Maybe to keep Lydia's memory close. Maybe to reminisce on her own, in her familiar room back home. Or maybe she wanted the pictures out of her room. In any case, it seemed better to leave it alone.

"So I'm glad I caught you," I said. "I've got some money in my room that's burning a hole in my conscience."

She sprayed perfume in the air and walked through the mist. Despite her insistence that she was in a hurry, she didn't have the same desperation to get off campus I'd seen in the younger girls. That need to sleep safe under their parents' roof after the scare here. "What are you talking about?" she said. "What money?"

"Charlie Bernstein from Omega Phi gave me some money he owed Lydia. He said she had needed it for an abortion."

"Oh. My. God." She slammed the bottle onto the dresser. "Are you shitting me?"

"That's what he said."

"And he wants us to think he was the father? Big, fat woodchuck Charlie?"

"That's mean."

"The truth hurts. But really? Lydia would never go for him."

"But she did date Charlie," I said, thinking of the big guy's sincerity—the sweat on his upper lip, the lopsided frown. "It took him a long time to save that money, and he seemed determined to get it off his conscience. Like some karmic debt. I think he's legit."

"Whatever." She scrunched her hair up, then turned away from the mirror and grabbed her purse. "Let's go. You can grab the suitcase. I've got all this stuff."

She had a backpack and purse, but I wasn't going to bitch at her now. I rolled the giant suitcase out into the hall. At least it had wheels. "So what should we do about the money?"

"Keep it. Give it back. Whatever it takes to keep him quiet."

"I don't think he's talking about it."

"Good. We don't want him spreading rumors that will ruin Lydia's legacy. She cared so much what people thought of her."

That part was true. With a deep breath I hoisted the bag up and started carefully down the back staircase.

"I'm going to run and get the car," Tori said, pushing ahead of me. "You can leave the bag at the door. I'll see you Monday."

I paused, trying to maintain balance with the weight in my right hand. "Have a good weekend," I said, but by then she was gone.

CHAPTER 28

With Rory's help, I left Tori's suitcase by the front door. I dumped my stuff off in the suite, which was empty, though Defiance wasn't leaving until Wednesday. Once we were clear of Theta House, I told Rory about my exchange with Tori. "She didn't know about it, and she didn't really care."

"That sounds like Tori Winchester," he said. "So do you get to keep the money?"

"No. I'm going to give it to Mrs. J and tell her I found it in Lydia's stuff. She'll make sure it gets to Lydia's mother."

He nodded. "From what you told me, sounds like they could use the money."

"Yeah." It would be a relief to get that hot money out of my drawer.

Since Rory's roommates were gone, I stayed over at his house Tuesday night. When I returned to Theta House to shower, I ran into Mrs. J and, for the first time, found out the "rules" for Thanksgiving weekend. Mrs. J was going off to visit her son in Ashland, but a local woman would check in during the day, distribute the mail, keep the fridge stocked.

"We used to close the house, but last year we had a few girls from California who couldn't make it home. I thought you'd be here with Megan and Suki, but it turns out Suki's parents are concerned about her safety, so they're sending both girls to a spa in Hood River for a few days." Her pinched look of assessment made me feel like I was wrong for not rushing home to my family. "And then there was one. Are you sure you want to stay? You'll be completely alone at night, and with everything that's happened in the past few weeks . . . do you really want to be here?"

I had spent years alone in our family house, not just the only child but the only person, and I had made peace with the quiet. But here, in this big, rambling house meant for dozens? It would feel odd, all right. Add in the fact of a killer on the loose and my prickly relationship with the police, and it would become a very edgy weekend. "Maybe I'll go home with Defiance," I said. "But I need to come back early. I've got work to do."

"That's fine. A few of the girls will be back on Saturday," she said.

Upstairs, Defiance was stuffing dirty laundry into a trash bag.

"Hey, does that offer to go home with you still stand?" I asked.

She nodded, a hint of a smile there. "My mother is expecting you. I knew you would change your mind again."

"Did you know Theta House was going to empty out?"

"No. But I could see you pouring water in the restaurant, eating my grandma's goulash at our table. I knew it would happen."

"That's amazing." And a little scary.

"My brother will be here for us at noon."

"I hope you're ready because the roads are a nightmare." Defiance's brother Stevo was a twentysomething dude with longish dark hair, a trimmed beard, a sweatshirt, and jeans so loose they seemed likely to slide off.

"Of course there's traffic," Defiance said. "It's the day before Thanksgiving. Everyone wants to get somewhere." She handed him the bag of laundry. "And help Emma with her things."

"Whoa, what?" He glanced over at me. "Hi."

"Emma is coming home with us, so you'll have to be nice to me in the car."

"I'm always nice. Emma, do you want me to carry that?"

"No, I'm fine," I said, hoisting my duffel back on one shoulder.

"Take it for her!" Defiance insisted.

"She doesn't want me to," Stevo retorted.

I smiled at the banter between the two of them. I wished I knew my brother well enough to tease him, but we were almost eight years apart, and he was already out of the house before the crash punctuated our lives.

Traffic was terrible, and we crept along the freeway at a steady roll.

"So, Emma . . ." Stevo's eyes appeared in the rearview mirror. "Did Defiance warn you about our big, loud family? We marry young and have lots of children. Too many kids."

"Never too many," Defiance said, smacking his arm. "Our family came to Portland from Europe many years ago and stayed, despite the city trying to chase them out a few times. My grandparents bought a house, but many Roma couldn't afford that."

"Our grandma's house is still the center of every family thing," Stevo said.

"It is. Some of our family still travel, following the work. It's a tradition born of necessity back in Europe when Roma were persecuted and forced to leave the cities or towns." Defiance turned to face me. "No one knows the number for sure, but they think more than 200,000 Roma were killed in the Holocaust." She turned back to face the front. "But our family was here before that happened. We're the lucky ones."

"That's a rich heritage," I said. "I wish I knew more of my family history. I only know that my father's great-grandparents came here to America from Poland."

"Our family lived in Poland once," Stevo said. "Defiance, maybe you and Emma are cousins."

"It doesn't matter because we're already sisters," she teased. Soothed by their conversation and the radio and the dull cement and grass rolling by my window, I dozed off. It was a good sleep, deep and peaceful. When I woke up we were navigating the streets of a neighborhood in northeast Portland where ranch houses huddled close to two-story houses with porches. The ranch house was mostly hidden by thick, overgrown hedges in the front. Stevo let us unload in the driveway and then took off to get back to work at the auto repair shop owned by an uncle. The delicious smell of chicken and onions filled the kitchen. A petite woman dressed in a floral blouse that extended to her knees, black tights, and pixie-like black boots turned from the stove to stare at us through large, round glasses. Her age was apparent in her silver hair and huddled spine, but otherwise you might mistake her for a retro mom with kooky glasses. "There's my girl."

Defiance gave her a hug and introduced me to her grandmother Kizzy. "Smells good," Defiance said.

"It's for later, but I'll make tea. Unless you want to visit with your friends. Nadia knows you're here."

"We'll hang out here, with you."

"I knew you'd say that." Kizzy waved us off. "Go. Get settled."

The house felt lived in and comfortable. I followed Defiance to her room, a mix of teen and tween with shag carpeting, a white-framed princess bed, a navy futon sofa. A colorful Grateful Dead tapestry covered the wall over the bed.

"The futon sofa opens up for you." Defiance turned on a salt lamp beside the bed and opened the blinds to let in the pale afternoon light.

"We can visit your friends if you want," I said. "Or you can go. I brought my laptop with me, and I've got some papers to write."

"They're not really my friends anymore." She took off her boots and flopped on the bed quilt. "Nadia and all those, they're good Roma girls. They got married and most of them have a kid already. I have nothing in common with them anymore."

"That's a different life. I can't imagine having a kid at this age."

"It's what my parents wanted for me." She propped herself on one elbow and raked through her hair with the other hand. "But instead, I'm the rebel girl. I want to do things my way, not take orders from a husband. My friends don't understand that. They don't like it. That's why I had to leave Portland State. Living here, I was stuck. Every day my parents were wishing for me to quit school and follow my friends. Now, at Merriwether, I can get away."

Defiance and I had more in common than I had realized. I unzipped my bag and removed the shampoo and conditioner. "Where are your parents now?"

"At the restaurant. They'll be there until late. Tomorrow we'll go with and help them serve the meal. Then, Friday, everyone will come here. That will be crazy and loud. And Saturday, we go back."

"I hope that doesn't cut into your holiday."

"Pull-leeze." She sat up on the bed and stretched. Her expanded chest showed off her major boobage, something that had never panned out for me. "Three days of this is about all I can stand."

"You must be a little relieved to be home. Your house is so cozy."

"For three days. After that, relatives and fish start to stink." She pulled a scarf down from the wall and arranged it around her neck. "Let's have some tea with Kizzy."

I sat at the table in the little window nook of the kitchen while Defiance poked around in the refrigerator.

"We're using the fancy china," I said, admiring the white, shallow cups with gold-rimmed saucers. "Nice."

"Are you hungry, Emma?" Kizzy asked. "I can make you a sandwich. Or we have apples, and grapes."

"I'm good," I said as the kettle whistled.

"Put some cake out," Kizzy told Defiance, who had just

placed two jars of jam on the table beside the sugar bowl. I ran my fingertips over yellow and blue flowers in the tablecloth— little daisy faces in a sea of warm crimson. The stainless-steel appliances seemed new, the cabinetry old, with some doors that didn't completely close. The white-and-blue vinyl floor was so well worn by the door and in front of the fridge that I could see the brown brick pattern of a previous floor. Everything had an easy, lived-in look—clean but worn and useful in its time. I wondered if my father's new place was similar to this. Then it struck me that he might be close by. It was strange to think that he could be just down the street, but I was getting used to the emotional distance between us.

Stop thinking about them—the family you don't have. I did this to myself over the holidays, mostly because I missed my mom. But there was no bringing her back, and I wasn't going to pretend I had a relationship with my father or brother. Nah.

"We usually put lemon and sugar in the tea," Defiance said.

"So we can read each other's tea leaves," Kizzy added as she brought the teapot to the table and began to pour. "But you don't have to."

"I meant, do you want milk?" Defiance asked.

"No milk for me. Is that a Roma custom? The tea reading."

"Not. The two of us like to do it because we're psychic, but my mom thinks it's obnoxious."

"She doesn't like the gypsy stereotype." Kizzy sat down, straightening her filmy blouse. "But for Roma, fortune-telling is a kind of therapy. A good Samaritan gives a friend good advice, right?" She added two dollops of jam to her tea and stirred. "Sometimes I have clear eyes to see a problem that's got you all muddled. Tea reading is more about finding answers to a problem than learning about a future that's cast in stone."

"So how does it work?"

"It starts with a question." Defiance sat down with a tray of spice cake. "As you drink your tea, you focus on a question you'd like the leaves to answer." She nodded toward her grandmother, who was quietly sipping. "Meditate on it, and start to take long, slow breaths, like in yoga class. You think on this question the whole time you drink. When you get to the end of the cup, you must keep the leaves in, maybe sift them out with your teeth so they stay in the cup. And then, the rest you can watch."

I added sugar to my tea, watching for something special from Kizzy, who adjusted her big round glasses and took another sip. Other than the dreamy expression on her face, she was just an older woman drinking tea.

There wasn't much liquid in the small cups. Kizzy took the last sip, placed the saucer over her cup, and tipped the cup to let the last drops drain. "Okay," she said, righting the cup and passing it across the table.

"Okay." Defiance held the cup in the palms of her hands and let her eyes squint a bit as she stared inside. "I think I see a fish. Do you know what that means? Something about water?"

"The fish is the symbol of Christianity," Kizzy said. "My question was about our church group. What else?"

"I see a flower. A daisy, I think. See?" She showed it to Kizzy, who frowned.

"A flower means patience," Kizzy said. "I don't want to hear that. I was asking what to do with a bossy lady in our prayer group. She talks forever. The rest of us can't get two words in. No one can stand her. But patience? I'm running out of that for Mrs. Stella Digwell."

"There are two mountain peaks. Obstacles to climb? Or opportunities?"

"Mmm." Kizzy held up one finger. "I hope an opportunity to kick Stella out. Do you see a boot? Or a hook?" Defiance shook her head no. "What do I do about this woman? You can't kick someone out of prayer group."

"I don't know, but some of the tea is sticking together. A brown blob."

"That's trouble. Is it near the handle?"

Defiance shook her head. "On the other side."

"Good, then it's not my fault."

I held back a laugh. These two spun a strange mixture of the supernatural and humor.

"I guess I have to put up with Stella for now." Kizzy turned to me, her eyes magnified behind the round lenses. "Do you want me to read your leaves, Emma?"

"I wouldn't know what to ask." Actually, I didn't know how to narrow my hundreds of questions down, and the important questions couldn't be shared with Defiance and Kizzy.

"You don't have to tell us the question," Defiance said. Damned if she wasn't reading my mind again.

Before I could refuse, Kizzy opened the teapot and spooned some of the sodden leaves into my cup. "There you go. Are you ready with a question now? Let it float in your mind as you drink."

"You can ask about a guy," Defiance said. "Everyone wants to know about relationships."

"Love and happiness," Kizzy said. "It's universal."

But to ask about Rory seemed too superficial when so many other things cut deeper.

I cradled the cup in both hands and started to sip. Drinking in the question.

Will I get away with this?

They chatted as I sipped and focused. I thought of Lydia's death, my trip down to the ravine that awful morning, Detective Taylor pressing me, her dark eyes reading into my soul. And the baby. My baby. No amount of sugar in the tea could sweeten bitter regret.

When I was nearly finished, I swirled the cup in my hand and took one last sip, careful not to suck in the leaves. I fumbled a bit as I fit the saucer over the cup.

"I got it." Kizzy took it away and drained the liquid, an expert. She adjusted her glasses and scratched her nose as she stared into my cup.

"First thing I see is a long knife. You know, a very long one. A sword. In tarot cards, the suit of swords represents air. Action and change."

"Positive action?"

"It could be good or bad. That I can't see. It might also be a soldier or a cop."

The damned police. A pulse throbbed in my ear.

"Or it could signify something painful that cuts straight to the heart." Kizzy pressed a thumb to her chest and winced in mock pain. "Does any of this ring true?"

"All of it." The cops following me around. And trauma in my life? Past and present, take your pick.

"A sword could mean violence," Kizzy went on. "Or the opposite. Someone is championing you. A hero is fighting for you."

"I want to believe the hero part," I said, thinking of Rory. Or Dr. Finn? "But not the violence."

"Time will tell." Kizzy pursed her lips as her eyelids swooped low. "You have an owl. It's cute. Like a cartoon owl. That's wisdom. Is that you? I think so. You have a good head on your shoulders."

"Emma has good sense," said Defiance. "She'll make the wise choice."

I shifted in the chair, not wanting any choices on my shoulders. This tea reading wasn't supposed to make my life more difficult. I wanted an enchanted path to a happy ending. Not birds and swords and violence.

"Something else about the wise old owl." With her silver hair framing her face, her round glasses shining, and her huddled stature, Kizzy herself seemed owlish. "They sit and watch from the tree. They see all; they know all. They know so many secrets. And you have a lot of secrets, Emma. I can tell."

Defiance popped a piece of cake into her mouth, nodding. "You know that's true."

"Everyone has secrets," I said.

"Yes, yes. We're all entitled to hold some things inside. Some things would only do harm if they got out."

I nodded, relieved that Kizzy understood.

"But some secrets can be a heavy burden. Too heavy. They're like poison. They get stuck inside us, cramped and dark secrets that rot our insides." Kizzy shrugged. "Those secrets have to come out or else you just, you know . . . throw them up."

I nodded politely, trying not to get upset. How much of this was real? Kizzy's advice could have applied to anyone, right? I turned to Defiance, who was polishing off the small square of cake. "Are you going to have your tea leaves read, too?"

"Wait a minute." Kizzy scowled into my teacup, not yet finished. "This is bad," she said. "Very bad."

My heart was beating like the wings of a large bat in my chest. "What's wrong?"

"The tea is clumping again. It could mean trouble for you." She tilted the cup slightly. "Or maybe the tea is old. It shouldn't stick together like that." She showed it to Defiance. "Look at that. That's not right. And you saw it clumping in my cup, too. I think we should throw it out and brew a new pot."

Defiance frowned. "What's not right? So we see trouble in two teacups? You can brew tea all day long, Kiz, but the future is what it is."

"Such a rebel." Kizzy reached across the table and smacked her granddaughter's hand three times, somewhere between a slap and a pat. "Your parents named you well. So full of wind."

CHAPTER 29

Those days at Defiance's house gave me time to breathe. It felt good to be in a safe space, surrounded by people who wished me well. Thanksgiving Day we worked in the restaurant from eleven until nine, cleaning tables, serving food, and scrubbing bowls and pots in the kitchen. When it was through my hands were red and my feet were sore and swollen, but there was satisfaction in feeding people who wouldn't have had a dinner without us. My reward? That night, I slept for nine hours without waking up.

The next day was festive with all her aunts and uncles and cousins arriving with covered dishes and bottles of wine. Most of the women were dressed up in dresses and high-heeled shoes worthy of a wedding, and they all wore heavy makeup. False eyelashes! I was definitely underdressed. The men wore dress slacks and button-down shirts. When the cousins began to assemble, I got a sense of Defiance's issues with her family. The female cousins gathered in her bedroom, most of them with a baby on the hip, while the men stood together in the backyard smoking and laughing. It seemed that a lot more fun was being had out back, but we couldn't hang there; we didn't belong.

When it was time to return to campus Saturday morning, I felt ready.

"I feel like I was transported to another world for a few

days," I told Defiance as Stevo's car sped along the expressway. "Thank you for inviting me."

"Anytime," she said. "My father said you're a very hard worker."

"For a *gadji*," Stevo added.

"That means a non-Roma," Defiance explained to me as she smacked his arm. "Just drive, okay? No name-calling."

"It was a joke," he said. "You get that, right, Emma?"

"It's cool."

The part of the weekend that stuck with me most was the tea-leaf reading. Maybe it was Kizzy, her big heart and her obvious attachment to her granddaughter. Or it might have been Defiance opening up and acknowledging that some of the girls in Theta Pi were still cool toward her. For her tea reading she had asked if they would ever warm up, and the answer appeared to be that it didn't matter. The important thing was that she stay true to herself.

As we cleaned up the tea things, I asked if there was magic in the tea leaves.

"Let's put it this way," Kizzy said. "Those who don't believe in magic will never find it. But if you believe . . ." She shrugged.

The days I'd spent away from Merriwether had cleared my head and made me crave some alone time. The campus still had that tired, abandoned feeling, clinging to sleep and unprepared for the coming weeks of papers and finals. I got that. Snow had fallen on Mount Hood, and Rory texted that he wouldn't be back on campus until Monday. I spent six hours in the library, knocking off the papers that were due. That night there were nine of us back at Theta House, so we headed out to a Thai restaurant in town and shared platters of pad Thai and curry and chicken skewers. As we dug into our food and compared notes on who would be having a welcome back party Sunday night, the familiar comfort of sisterhood hovered over us. This . . . this is what I'd missed since Lydia had died. At last, things were swinging back into place.

"I have something disturbing to report," said Megan. "I

was at work today. You know, in the bookstore? And I was wearing my Theta Pi shirt. And this girl came over with her mom and told her, 'That's the sorority with the girl that was murdered.'"

Alexa made a gagging gesture. "Great. We're notorious now."

"People are strange," I said. "Did they at least say they were sorry for your loss?"

Megan stabbed at her noodles. "The mom just shushed her daughter and pulled her away. Like I had some contagious disease or something."

"I've heard some frat guys dissing us," Jemma said. "I won't say who they were, but they were calling us Theta Die."

"That is so obnoxious." Chloe slammed her cell phone on the table. "Who said it? We need to report them to the Panhellenic Council."

"Oh, my dear sisters, let's not go there." Suki looked around the table, fierceness in her dark eyes. "We're going to take the high road on this. These people who prey on others when they're in pain? We refuse to see them. They are nothing to us."

"Exactly," I agreed. "Don't engage with those guys. We're not going to be taunted."

"Or . . ." Defiance held up her hands, commanding our attention. "We could put a curse on them."

Silence.

"A curse would work," I said.

As if in one great sigh, we burst into laughter. And all at once the girls were asking Defiance if it was possible, could she do it? How did it work? Was she kidding? How long would it take? With a smile, I watched Defiance field their questions, telling them that she could cast a curse, but these frat boys were not worth the time or effort. She was winning some of the sisterhood over. Had the tea leaves been right?

The next day I was far enough ahead on my work to attend a work session for the task force. Kath, Chase, and I were the only ones back on campus, so Sunday morning we brought our laptops to Dr. Finn's office and set to work revising the various parts of our platform. As we worked, Kath threw out sardonic comments and Dr. Finn pointed out a few pitfalls in our ideas. No idea was too stupid to brainstorm in Dr. Finn's world, and at times I tuned out and focused on my own writing. Chase had a similar work style, quiet and dogged. At one point we joked that Kath probably had nothing written, and she turned her laptop around and showed us three pages of text.

"Don't you hate those multitaskers?" Chase said.

It was after noon when Dr. Finn ordered some meze platters from a Lebanese restaurant in town, and we took a break and pulled up chairs to the food on the big walnut desk.

"Do you ever use this desk as anything besides a dining table?" Chase asked.

"Sometimes it's a laptop holder." Dr. Finn picked up a spinach pie. "Mostly it keeps my coffee off the ground."

"I wonder why grape leaves don't taste like grapes?" Kath asked, holding up a grape leaf stuffed with rice. "They don't even taste like wine or grape bubble gum. They're probably not grapes at all. Probably manufactured in a plastics factory in China." Cutting and silly at the same time, Kath delivered monologues designed to lighten the intensity of our discussions. When things got serious, she could snap to sincerity in a heartbeat.

"You know," I said, "I think you're going to make a great therapist. But if that doesn't work out, there's a place for you in stand-up comedy."

"Thanks, Emma. Two professions that pay nothing and have no future."

After we ate, Chase packed up his laptop. "I have to go. I have two reports due online by midnight."

"I feel your pain," I said. "I submitted my stuff late last night."

"We're in the home stretch," Kath said. "One week of classes, then finals."

After Chase left, I got up to get the kinks out, and Kath stretched out on the sofa.

"I just need to close my eyes a few minutes to let it all hit rock bottom," she said.

"Don't let us keep you up," Dr. Finn said, perching on his desk. "I've been thinking about the health center, about our demands, and let me play devil's advocate here. I'm wondering if we're expecting too much."

"What?" Kath opened one eye. "You're selling out already?"

"Hear me out. I'm not giving up, but I also want to submit a plan that's doable, and it seems to me that we're asking a clinic to stretch themselves and perform the function of an ER, a women's clinic, and a counseling center."

"They may be small, but for a student like me, the health center is my only resource." I paced to the window and turned back to them. "I don't have a car. I don't have a doctor anywhere else. To get help I would have to pay out of pocket for a doctor and take a shuttle bus to Portland. I'm paying for health services here, and I need them to work."

"Good point." Finn rubbed his chin. "There seems to be a huge, yawning gap between the health care that exists and the health care that we need."

"And Emma is just one student," Kath pointed out. "Keep in mind, we've got twelve thousand students here on campus. That little overcrowded clinic is not big or functional enough to serve a small city the size of Merriwether. If they need to grow, let them build a new facility."

"We've been focused on the mental health part of the clinic," I said, "but they've failed at women's health care for a while."

"How so?" Kath asked. "I've never had to go there, but I've only been here a few months."

"A few years ago, they screwed up and ruined the life of a girl who had a baby on campus."

"Jennifer Saunders." Dr. Finn crossed his arms. "I was here then."

"Who's that?" Kath asked.

"A campus legend because of what the health center did to her. Oregon has that safe-haven law. If someone brings a baby to a medical facility, they're supposed to take the baby, no questions asked, no ties. She brought her baby in, and they screwed her. Told her parents and messed with her scholarship money. And her father was a minister, so she had the wrath of God crashing down on her, too."

"Isn't that a violation of the privacy act, too?" Kath asked.

I nodded. "But Jennifer didn't sue them. I don't think she knew any better, and her parents blamed her, not the school."

Kath covered her face with her hands. "Grrr! Things like that infuriate me. How did you find out about it, Emma?"

"From the girls in my sorority. It's a cautionary tale now. Whenever someone needs to see a gynecologist or has birth-control issues, they try to avoid it. A lot of my friends go to their doctors at home. Some of us take the bus to a free clinic in Hood River."

"That's a hike," Kath said.

"But it's the closest place." I remembered going there with my sisters. The dusty motes circling in the sun of the waiting room. The pocked ceiling tiles that I'd stared at so long I'd begun to see clown faces. The waiting . . . forever waiting for awful news, trying to hold it all in but failing.

"That's unacceptable." Dr. Finn sighed. "What's the point of having a student health center if the students can't use it?"

"The snotty white boys can go for their team physicals and high-five the doctors," Kath said.

"No, seriously. It's a problem."

"It is a problem." I looked out the window and stared down at the lawn, the morning frost long melted by the sun, though it would be back tonight. The cold would return with the dark. There was some foot traffic on the library plaza across the way, as people arrived back at campus and rushed to finish weekend assignments.

"I have a friend . . . she could have died. She almost did." In the weeks since it had happened, I had been hit with the pain of that day every time a candle was lit for a ritual. And when the memory came back, it rushed in like a ferocious wave. That familiar stab of desperation, the exhaustion and fear mixed with the strange glow of jack-o'-lanterns. Funny how memories wove themselves into your mind. The smell of candle wax, the sheen of a red latex costume cape.

"A friend?" Kath's voice was softer now, speculative. "Is that code for 'This happened to me but let's pretend it didn't'?"

"It was my friend," I said. "I can't tell you her story. I've been sworn to secrecy. But I can tell you my part, what happened to me because that goddamned clinic wouldn't take her baby."

"Did they turn you down?" Dr. Finn asked.

"We didn't go there. We couldn't take the chance that they wouldn't take the baby, or that they'd ask questions. Especially since the baby . . ." I hugged my elbows, remembering the initial shock, then the stark fear of being found out. "The baby was stillborn."

In the silence I could feel them processing, sympathetic but struggling to make sense of something that made no sense at all.

"I feel for you, Em," Kath said. "How'd you handle that?"

"Not well. I had never seen a newborn baby in real life, and I never expected to be holding a dead one."

I would never forget that night, the protracted pain and anguish. I thought it would never end. And just when I thought it was all over, the second nightmare began.

"You have to get rid of it," Tori ordered.

"I can't." The glaring candles of the sorority lounge made my eyes tear, but I didn't swipe at my cheeks. I didn't have an ounce of energy left.

"Take care of it now. We can't have something like that hanging around in Theta House."

"Like . . . how? What am I supposed to do?" There was no taking the baby to the clinic; we'd gone through that scenario too many times and ruled it out. A cold tremble gripped my body, and I was so thirsty. My skin was hot, my lips dry, and I

felt as if I'd just run ten miles through a blistering desert. "I can't do this. I can't."

"Of course you can. And you will." Tori snapped her fingers at Courtney. "Material Girl? Help Emma clean up her mess."

Back in the room, neither of us wanted to touch the baby girl covered by fluffy white towels. I had wrapped her up, wanting her body to be cozy and respected.

"Here. You can put it in this." Courtney unzipped a backpack and told me to drop it inside.

Not it. She. A baby girl.

I leaned over the laundry basket and parted the terry cloth, just to see her face. Except for her bluish lips, she seemed perfect in every way, with tiny nostrils and eyebrows so fine they were nearly invisible. How did it happen that a perfect baby just didn't breathe like all the others? My anatomy failed me and I imagined that she was hollow inside, like the rubber dolls I had toted around as a toddler.

"Come on," Courtney said. "The longer it's in here, the creepier this room gets."

"She's just a baby. She didn't do anything to you."

"Just put her in here."

The infant was so heavy in my arms and I swear she still felt warm, but then she was all wrapped up and heat was pumping in the house. My arms trembled as I tucked her into the backpack, giving her a soft landing.

Courtney's face puckered, and she leaned away as she closed the zipper. "There you go." She hoisted the pack and groaned. "God, it's heavy. Turn around." I braced myself as she slipped the backpack onto my shoulders, then stepped back, hands on hips. "There you go. No one will ever know. You can walk right out of the house and no one will be the wiser."

I tried to remain erect despite the weight of her pulling me into the earth. "But where do I go?"

"Do I have to think of everything? Just dump it somewhere. Find a trash bin."

Trash?

I could never . . . Bile rose in my throat at the thought of it. A dead baby's body mixed in with the paper coffee cups, half-eaten veggie burgers, and crumpled tissues. The wave of sickness made me teeter forward, and the weight on my back would have taken me down if Courtney hadn't caught me.

Courtney was surprisingly strong under that blond lace-cookie veneer. "Now go. Do it now, before everyone's awake and full of questions. We can't let people figure it out."

Figure it out. Didn't they know? I had been stuck in the room all night, assuming people knew, but . . . "It's a secret? No one else knows?"

"Only the Rose Council. Now get going."

In a daze of exhaustion and fear, I staggered out the door, relieved to leave the humid room. The hallway swayed back and forth, setting me off balance, and I had to run one hand along the wall to keep from toppling sideways. Down the stairs I plunged, dodging faces and conversation that floated around me, detached and without meaning. Once outside, the cool air offered some relief, but as I plodded down the street my sense of direction faded away.

Where was I going?

The dead baby on my back weighed me down, pulling me into the earth.

Back to the earth. The ravine.

I knew I was headed that way, just to get out of sight and away from people and to think. Think. Think what to do with her.

I turned off Greek Row on the block, wanting to avoid any sisters or frat brothers who might be out early. As I cut down a side street I spotted Sam Mattern heading my way.

Sam . . . Not now! I just couldn't . . .

The muscles in my shoulders and back tensed. Would he know what I was carrying in my backpack? Would he sense it?

I had avoided him for months, skipping certain parties and dropping classes when I knew he would be there. But still, even with the time apart, as we drew closer to each other, I felt

*the heat of awareness, the softening in my chest at the sight of
eyes the color of a tropical sea and shiny dark hair.*

*He was close now. His eyes flicked my way and he smiled.
"You look like hell, Danelski." And that was it. He kept walking, as if we were old buddies, casual friends.*

Bastard.

*I walked to the bridge, then cut around it, taking the well-
worn trail used by kids looking to find a hiding place among
the rocks for sex or smoking weed or drinking or all of the
above. A few yards down, in the shade of bushes and the tall
steel towers, I stopped and removed the weight from my back.
Something about it had just felt wrong. I brought the pack
around and slid it over my chest. Better. The weight of the
baby was more comforting there, pillowed against my breasts.
I imagined her fitting into the concave angles of my body, at-
taching herself like a real baby.*

My baby.

The version I told Dr. Finn and Kath was sanitized a bit. I
didn't mention any names, of course, and I streamlined the
narrative, telling them that I had sneaked the infant's body out
of Theta House inside a backpack and taken her down to the
ravine for a secret burial.

"With the baby hanging in the cradle of my chest it took a
long time to make it down the path. You know how the trail
weaves back and forth? It seemed like hours, probably because
I was so tired and achy. I'd been up all night and I'd been dealing with some virus.

"When I got to the bottom, the noise of the water rushing
over the rocks scared me. It just seemed wrong. I moved away
from the rapids and went to the sheltered spot under the
bridge where you can hide behind the brush. I sank onto a
boulder and closed my arms over the backpack. The bundle
was keeping me warm, and we just sat there. I talked to the
baby, telling her maybe she was lucky to be gone from a world
that can be a terrible place. No one could see me, so I took the

baby from the backpack and sat there for a long while cuddling her. It made me feel better to stroke her face and tell her everything would be okay.

"That was when the baby flinched. She moved. I freaked at first, staring at her. I was so tired and achy, I thought maybe I was hallucinating. But then, as I was watching her, she jerked again. I had read that sometimes bodies move after death, like when the air drains from the lungs. I know it sounds creepy, but it wasn't. At that moment it felt right to be holding her. I kept stroking her skin, soothing her arms and shoulders and tummy, and I talked to her in a soothing voice as her little body continued to twitch. I told her she was going to be okay, that she was going to a good place.

"Stupid lies, but I wanted to comfort her, and I think dying people at least understand the tone of our voice. And as I was talking to her, she opened her eyes."

I would never forget that moment, those dusky gray eyes rolling lazily.

"I thought it was some kind of involuntary reaction, like a muscle spasm or something. Her final good-bye. But no, her eyelids stayed open and the pupils moved, as if she were trying to focus.

"And then she started squirming in my arms, turning her head and burrowing into the crook of my arm.

"So real and human.

"A real baby girl, alive and making little squeaky sounds."

I turned away from the window and found Dr. Finn and Kath staring at me, riveted.

"She came back to life."

CHAPTER 30

Dr. Finn's hands were pressed together, fingertips tucked under his chin in awe. "Emma . . . I don't know what to say."

"I do. That's a fucking amazing story, and you're my hero." From her prone position on the couch Kath thrust a fist in the air.

"But I didn't do anything that special. Maybe it helped her when I held her in my arms. Some doctors think that helps. I searched on the Internet and found a handful of incidents in which newborns came alive after they were pronounced dead. One doctor from Cornell suggested that it was the act of the mother holding the child that brought it back. He believed that the mother's warmth, the sound of her heartbeat and her voice, might have guided the child back to life."

"Fascinating." Dr. Finn was blown away. "You're talking about a miracle."

"I think it was." My worst nightmare that had turned into the best day ever.

"So then what did you do next?" Kath scrambled up on the sofa, tucking her legs under her. "Did you drop her off at the police station? That's what the safe-haven law is about, right?"

I dropped my head down and rubbed the back of my neck, letting my hair cover my face. Mostly to avoid looking at them. "I can't tell you that part."

"What? You can't cut us off before the rest of the happy ending!" Kath was freaking. "It is happy, right? How's that baby girl now? I need to know."

"Wow," Dr. Finn said. "And I thought I was the compulsive one."

"We're talking about an innocent baby here."

I straightened up and faced Kath. Now that I'd gotten the story out, I felt a little light-headed. Burden lifted. Maybe Kizzy was right about some secrets needing to get out into the light. "I think she'll be fine. She has a chance to have a good life."

"But where? In a foster home? Is she with Child Protective Services?"

I shook my head. "I can't tell you anything else, okay?"

"But you said she's fine." Kath nodded. "I'm holding you to that. You did the right thing. Good job, Emma." She leaped from the couch and gave me a big hug that startled me, coming from Kath. "You want to get in on this, Finn?"

"I'm okay, but thanks for sharing that with us, Emma. And as I've always told you, anything you say in here stays within these four walls."

I gave Kath a squeeze, then leaned back. "It *did* have a happy ending, but the moral of the story, my point was that this baby might not have died in the first place if the mother was able to get health care at our clinic. Students need medical care they can trust. Now."

With darkness pressing in, Finn offered to walk Emma and Kath back to their respective homes.

"I already texted the campus escort service. They have someone at the library," Kath said. "Emma and I will walk together and meet them there."

"I have a private escort," Emma said drily. "Usually, there's a cop waiting for me."

Kath scowled. "For what?"

"The police suspect Emma was involved in Lydia Drakos's death."

"What? This is crazy town." Kath zipped up her red leather laptop case and slung it over one shoulder. "What the hell is that about?"

"I'll tell you on the way," Emma said as she headed out of his office.

"Oh, snap! Another story."

Finn walked them out through the dark building, noting a tin on the empty reception desk with a sticky note bearing his name. He put it out of his mind as he held open the front door. "Are you sure you don't want me to walk with you?" He hated knowing that some dick was out there, lurking. A predator.

"We're good!" Kath waved him off.

He stood on the threshold and watched their progress. Not even six and the sun was long gone, campus streetlamps casting halos in the misty air. He planned to shoot some pool with Jazz later, but for now he'd stay here and get some work done. Since he'd moved into the basement apartment with a grad student named Gordon, Finn was spending most of his time in his office. The view sure beat the basement, and here, with the task force and his teaching, there was progress and growth. It was more spacious than the new place, and a hell of a lot more peaceful than living with Eileen.

On his way by the reception desk he picked up the tin, saw they were cookies, and took one. Peanut butter, one of his favorites. He didn't have to open the note to know they were from Eileen, but he did.

I made these with Wiley, she had written.

Right. Maybe Wiley had hand-mashed the butter.

We miss you so much! When you coming home, babe?

The cookie was good, but the note made him gag. Like the lyrics of a Christmas song.

When had she come by? He didn't like her coming around here, especially when he had people in the office. With this being the tail end of the holiday, the building was quiet as a tomb today. Had she waited out here for a while, feeling sorry for herself?

He left the tin at reception, took out his phone, and saw

that he had six missed calls and two texts from her. When would she give up?

He called her.

"Hi, honey." That drizzled-honey baby voice. "Did you get the cookies?"

"Yup. What were you doing here?"

"Silly. I dropped off the cookies."

"Did you bring Wiley?"

"He was napping at my parents'. He was so tired from helping me mix the batter. He poured the sugar in all by himself."

"Phenomenal. Eileen, you've got to stop coming here."

"How else am I going to see you, if you—"

"You're not. I've moved out, okay? It's over." How many times did he have to say it?

She sighed, and for a moment there was blessed silence. "When I was making the cookies, I thought about the holidays. Remember last Christmas? We were so happy then."

"See? That's not true. I hate to burst your bubble, but I wasn't happy. I wanted out of the relationship, and you wanted an engagement ring. What part of that scenario translates to happiness for you?"

"You're so mean. And here I was just leaving you some cookies. Who were you talking to in there, anyway? I was going to knock, but the woman kept going on and on."

His jaw clenched. "You were eavesdropping. Spying?"

"I was checking to see if you were free. Who was the girl, anyway?"

"It's none of your business. You know, there are privacy laws. You shouldn't be snooping around my office, or anyone's for that matter."

"Don't freak, Finn. I just came to see you."

"Don't. Just . . . don't come around anymore."

"That means no cookies for you," she teased.

"I'll survive." He hung up and dropped the rest of the cookie into the trash can.

CHAPTER 31

When the campus escort dropped me in front of Theta House Sunday evening, a shiny car sat in the no parking zone in front of the house—a BMW with the license plate HAY YEAH. Two people were twisted around in the front seat. I stopped staring when I realized they were making out. Ugh. Definitely against Theta Pi rules.

I turned away and headed up the lawn. Someone had removed the burned-out candles and dead flowers from the Theta Pi sign, but the lights and teddy bears and photos remained. There were a few added pumpkins, plastic tiaras, and Mardi Gras beads that made the sign look like a tombstone. Behind me I heard the door of the car close. I waited a beat, then turned to discover Graham Hayden's mystery date.

"Hey, Tori. Got a new boyfriend?"

"Maybe." She pressed a finger to the corners of her lips. Lipstick check. "What are you doing?"

"Just got back from a meeting." We headed up the path to the front porch. "That suicide prevention group I told you guys about. Inspired by Lydia."

"Right. How's that working out for you?"

"Fine." I went in for the kill. "Wasn't that Graham Hayden? Lydia's boyfriend?"

"No. I mean, they dated, but that was a long time ago."

"But she really liked him. And we have that rule about staying away from a sister's guy," I said. We were on the steps now, and she was rooting through her designer bag, desperate to find her key and get away from me. "Or does that not count when the sister is dead?"

"You're such a bitch, Emma." She jammed her key in the lock and opened the door.

"But welcome back," I called after her. "Hope you had a good one."

Upstairs in the suite, Isabel and Patti were in the living area with photos spread out in stacks on the rug. They had spent the weekend together at Patti's house—probably a good thing, since Isabel's mother had a way of lashing out at her and throwing her back into bad eating patterns. Isabel had been spending a lot of time with Patti in the past few weeks. Another good thing, as far as I could tell. Patti knew how to calm Isabel's anxiety, and Isabel seemed to add a spark to Patti's deadpan affect.

"Hey, how was your holiday?" I asked as Isabel popped up and gave me a hug. We exchanged stories about our weekend and then started going over the stacks of photos on the floor.

"Aren't these the photos from Lydia's room?" I asked.

"The archives. Violet asked us to sort them out," Isabel said.

"She begged us," Patti added. "She didn't have time and National has been asking for photos of Lydia. They're doing a special tribute to her in the *Theta Pi Journal*."

"I thought you didn't want to go through her stuff," I said.

Isabel wound a lock of hair around her fingers. "Patti told me that was dumb, and I got over it. But we can't find a single picture from her pledge class. Not even one with the other girls. And we've gone through everything."

"Really? That's odd." I stared down at the photos of smiling girls. "Well, we know there's a photo of Lydia's pledge class down in the lobby."

"That's the thing," Patti said. "Violet took a closer look at it and it's horrible. All blurred and gray. Like someone took the original and left a photocopy."

"I don't know what to tell you," I said. "The hoodie girl must have made off with our original."

"National isn't going to like that," Isabel said.

Patti shrugged. "They'll get over it."

I liked that about Patti. She didn't get ruffled easily.

"Well, if you really need some photos from that pledge class, ask Tori," I said. "She's got quite a few." I had seen them in her suitcase.

"I didn't think of that." Isabel pursed her lips. "Other girls in the pledge class would have pictures. I wonder if Courtney has some, too."

"Ask her at dinner," I suggested.

"Okay if we leave these photos out?" Patti asked. "We'll pick up after we eat."

"You guys go. I'll put them away," I offered, wanting some alone time to mellow out.

When they left, I changed into my pajama bottoms and a sweatshirt and sat on the floor for one last look at the archives. I set aside the photos they'd pulled that included Lydia. Damn, that girl had a mysterious smile. I had always thought it was calm and placid, but now, looking at these pictures, I saw a crimp in her smile. A glimmer of pain. A crystal goblet with the tiniest chip in the rim.

The really old photos were still in their envelopes, and I did a quick check of those to make sure Lydia's pledge class hadn't slipped in by accident. Nope, nothing there.

I had started to put the bagged photos back into the box when I realized that the bottom of the plastic file tub wasn't plastic, but cardboard. Actually, it was a separate cardboard box, black like the plastic tub.

"I found you!" I said as I lifted it out, sure that the missing photos had to be hiding in there.

But when I took off the lid, there was cash inside, wads of twenty-dollar bills held together with clips or rubber bands.

My fingers touched the edge of the bills, some of them crisp, some of them worn soft as money tended to be. "What was this for?" Lydia had never served as the Theta Pi treasurer, and I couldn't imagine that a girl my age would keep her entire savings hidden with sorority stuff in the closet. Everyone had a bank account, an ATM card, and a Visa card. What the hell? This was like falling into an old mobster movie.

Or drugs . . .

I lifted the packs of cash carefully to see what lay beneath. At least there were no bags of capsules or pills or powder. If Lydia had been dealing drugs . . . I didn't know if our Theta Pi chapter could come back from a scandal like that.

I did find a small spiral notebook, not much bigger than a dollar bill, with a list of names inside. I flipped through the pages and saw that there were more than fifty names of guys, all males, some of whom I recognized as Merriwether students.

Were they lists of potential boyfriends? When I was in junior high I had lounged on the pillows of my friend's bed and made lists like that . . . the very basic "if he likes me I'll like him" prospects. But this one went on for pages, and most names had a pert checkmark beside them.

Rory's name wasn't there, thank God. As I was scanning the list and came to Charlie Bernstein, I paused and stared at Lydia's writing. So was it a boyfriend list? Charlie wasn't the only nerdy guy on there.

And no check beside Charlie's name. What did it mean?

I didn't have time to deal with this now. A quick count of the wrapped bills put the money at more than sixteen thousand dollars. What? Wait. My second count came in the same range.

"Crap, Lydia," I said under my breath. "What was all this about?"

This was too much to pass along to Lydia's mom through Mrs. J. No one had this kind of money sitting around, unless they were hiding it. I thought about contacting the police, a possibility, but it didn't seem to be part of Lydia's murder investigation, and Detective Taylor would probably make it all out to be a prostitution ring.

That thought stopped me cold.

Lydia as a prostitute?

She'd always talked about what was "proper." But the cash and the list of names fit what I would imagine in a business like that.

A glum feeling came over me as I put the box with Lydia's cash in my closet and started reloading the photos into the plastic bin. I wanted to be done with this crap, but there was no way I could get it off my mind until I figured it out. That meant a confrontation with the last person I wanted to see right now.

Tori's room was messier than before, with clothes spilling out of her open suitcase and something nasty growing in the glasses on the windowsill. It was surprising that she could emerge from this den looking so fresh and lovely.

"You again." She held a stick of eyeliner aloft. "I don't have time for this." She rolled her eyes and walked away from the door, leaving it to fall closed in my face, but I pushed at it and stepped in.

"I'm going to the movies with Courtney and India. And no, you're not invited," she said, drawing a dark line under her eyes.

"This is Theta Pi business, sister, dear," I said calmly. There was something about her nastiness that fueled my fortitude. "I'm here about the photos you took. The pictures from your pledge class? The photos of you and Lydia when you were freshmen."

"You're crazy."

"I saw them in your bag before you left." Stepping over a thong that had been dropped to the ground, I went over to the open suitcase. The photos were gone from the empty net lining. "What did you do with them?"

"Um, I don't know what you're talking about?"

"The photos from your pledge class, and others of you and

Lydia. You went through the archives, didn't you? You must have done it when the boxes were still in Courtney and Lydia's room, before the police even got to them."

She turned away from the mirror to stare at me, less hateful now as wariness edged in. "What if I did? The archives belong to all of us."

"Right. We share them, but you can't steal from them. What was it about those photos that you had to have?"

I had thought long and hard on this since I'd seen those photos in her suitcase. Had she wanted them for her own collection, to feel connected to Lydia? That seemed too compassionate for Tori, and if it was true she could have easily had copies made. No, not that. There was something in those photos that Tori didn't want us to see. Something about Lydia's killer? Clues leading to who had put their hands on her neck and choked the life out of her?

"They're gone, okay? I destroyed them."

"What? Why would you . . . ?" I sputtered, trying to hold back my frustration. "What the hell, Tori. That's the property of Theta Pi."

"I had to get rid of them. They were so awful, they made me sick. So yes, I took them home and I shredded them, okay? Now get off my back."

"Why did you destroy them?"

"I told you, I didn't like the way I looked in them."

"All of them?"

"Pretty much. It was a bad year for me, and Lydia, she was such a bitch about it. I asked her to let me have the pictures in the archives, just to airbrush myself, and she refused. Then she started taunting me, threatening me that she was going to publish them on the university's Greek Page and send them to National. She could be such a bitch. She wouldn't give me the photos, but she promised to keep them hidden if I paid her money."

"Blackmail?"

"It was just Lydia being a bitch. I didn't care about the

money. It was the way she made me squirm . . . and she was supposed to be my friend. My pledge sister."

That had been some pledge class. Callous Violet. Lydia the blackmailer. Tori, Queen of the Divas. And Dumb-ass Courtney. The other pledges must have been shell-shocked by that crew.

"So if you paid her, she agreed to keep the photos hidden away."

"Yup."

"How much did you pay?"

"A thousand dollars."

That could account for part of Lydia's stash, but a small proportion.

"My mom gave me the money," Tori said, "but it always bothered me to have those pictures sitting around. Like they would float to the surface one day. So when Lydia died, the first thing I did was get rid of them. After the cops searched her room, I pulled them out of the bins. The whole envelope of pictures from our pledge class, just to be sure."

"But, Tori, to destroy them? They couldn't have been that bad. You're fucking beautiful!"

"I know, but not always. I used to have . . . well, I wasn't always this perfect." She turned to me. "I'll kill you if you ever mention this to a soul, but I got my nose fixed the summer after freshman year."

Plastic surgery. I should have thought of that. "But to destroy the photos . . . you really can't think you can get rid of every record of what you looked like back then, do you?"

"Why not? I got Violet and Courtney to delete my pictures from their files. I fixed the photo from the lobby downstairs."

"Yeah, I figured that one out. Not a very good job."

"Why are you in my business, Emma? First Graham, and now this?"

"I just can't stop caring about my sisters," I said. Maybe I was a pain in the ass, but apparently not as bad as Lydia. "Why did Lydia torture you about those photos? Do you think it was about the money?" Something that Lydia had plenty of, but I wasn't going to divulge the treasure to Tori.

"She never really seemed to need money," she said, staring into the mirror. "It was about having me under her thumb. Lydia was a secret control freak. I hated that."

"Lydia did like having power over people," I agreed.

"Who doesn't?" Tori capped her eyeliner and straightened her shirt. "We're done here. Two conversations in one day. We're good until after Christmas, Emma."

"Like, wow! I mean, really," I said, pouring on my best millennial-speak. "I'm so honored you remembered my name." I was out the door before she could shoot back.

CHAPTER 32

The hallways were full of sisters returning at the last minute, and as I dodged rolling suitcases and laundry bags, my head pounded with confusion. All that money. The list. Blackmail. And destroyed photos.

Beneath the pretense of friendship, Tori had nurtured a bud of hatred for Lydia, and Lydia had given her a pretty good reason to be pissed. But had Tori been pissed enough? Enough to lure Lydia out to the bridge and kill her?

Back in the suite, Angela, Isabel, and I shared a group hug, while Patti and Defiance sat on the window seat and smoked. I went to my room to talk with Rory, who was staying at a motel on the mountain with some guys on the snowboarding team. He was so animated and pumped about the snow that I didn't want to bring him down. At one point I did ask him about the person on the bridge.

"That guy in the hoodie," I said. "Could it have been a girl?"

"Could've been. It wasn't a large dude, like a football tackle or anything. It could have been a medium-height guy, or a tall-ish girl. Why?"

"I've been rethinking things. What if the hoodie person was one of the Theta Pis?"

"Wow. Rotten to have a traitor in the group. And scary, too. Do the doors in your house lock?"

He was half kidding, but the grain of truth put me on edge. What if Lydia's killer was right there in our house?

"Hold on a second," Rory told me. He was talking to a guy in the background. With the noise from conversation and the TV behind Rory, this wasn't the time for a detailed conversation.

"You have to go," I said. "We can talk tomorrow."

When we hung up, Angela was in the room unpacking.

"I heard what you said about the hoodie person," she said as she hung a shirt on a hanger. "Are you talking about the bridge? You think one of the sisters killed Lydia?"

"I don't know what to think." I stretched out on my side, leaning on my balled-up pillow. "But I just found out that Tori was no friend of Lydia's." It felt good to tell her about the blackmailing incident, which Angela immediately dubbed "Nose-gate." We talked about the meanness involved on both sides.

"We've got our share of mean girls," Angela said. "Every sorority does. The vow we made to always have our sisters' backs, always support them, always love them? It sounded good at the time. But you can't turn your back on some of these girls. Some of these senior girls? They're nasty!"

"Yeah. They recruited a bad batch that year. The question is, Are any of them nasty enough to kill Lydia?"

Angela groaned. "It's hard to imagine a sister doing that. But if I had to pick one? Tori would be my choice. That girl is cold right through to the marrow of her bones."

"God, I wish I could get a straight answer out of Tori," I said.

"You don't believe Nose-gate?"

"That's one of the few things I do believe. That and the fact that Tori is now seeing Graham Hayden."

"What?" Angela gaped at me. "How'd you find that out?"

I filled her in. "Tori doesn't want me to tell anyone," I said.

"But it can't be a big secret if she was macking on him right in front of the house." Angela sat on the bed and rubbed lotion onto one knee.

"Right. She's probably going to go public with him soon. Lydia's been gone a few weeks."

"But I don't like the sound of it. Not one bit. Maybe it's just because Tori seems to be getting everything she wants now that Lydia's dead."

"The queen bee." Like in a hive. Where all the sister bees toil and sacrifice and die to protect the queen. That bitchy queen.

That night the house was mostly dark when I crept down the stairs to the kitchen. I couldn't sleep, and my stomach was growling. I'd skipped dinner, but then I hadn't been hungry five hours ago. I moved cautiously, grateful to see light streaming into the hallway from the kitchen. Violet stood at the sink, washing an apple.

We talked about nothing as she made two cups of tea and I considered telling her about Tori and the photos. Violet would be pissed at Tori, but even she wouldn't stand up to her. And if Violet hadn't figured out the connection between Tori's nose job and the disappearing photos by now, she was hopeless.

As I ate a yogurt and some almonds, I watched her methodically wash three apples. I'd seen this before. It was some weird ritual because she was hungry but afraid that eating this late at night would make her fat. Whatever. I tossed back two almonds.

When she got to talking about Lydia's final memorial ritual—"The best ritual ever," according to someone at National who'd liked Violet's blog—I edged into the topic.

"If you can put on your treasurer hat for a sec, I was wondering if Lydia was holding on to any cash for the sorority? From a previous fund-raiser?"

"Of course not. It all goes into our account at the student bank."

"Oh, yeah. Of course. And what about Theta Pi dues? Do you know if she owed anything to the sorority?" I asked. "Was she up-to-date?"

"She was all paid up." Violet took an apple from the fruit

bowl and twirled the stem off. "Lydia always paid for the whole year up front. It was one of the reasons I believed the story about her family being wealthy. Why are you asking?"

"Well . . ." *Think fast, Emma.* I wasn't going to tell her about the huge stash. So I diverted. "Someone, a frat guy, came to me with some money he owed Lydia. He said he was paying her back for an abortion she had?"

"Did he?" Violet didn't flinch. So she wasn't surprised. "That big-mouth Jacob Rizzo."

I paused. Had I heard correctly?

"Lydia was spitting mad at that boy."

"Wait," I said. "Jacob Rizzo got Lydia pregnant?"

"I'm sorry, Emma, if this hurts you, but Lydia did not confide everything to all her friends."

I wanted to tell her that I was beyond having my feelings hurt. There was much more at stake, more than Violet could have imagined. I wondered if Jacob was on the list upstairs.

"Lydia was a very private person in her weird way," Violet went on. "I wasn't really that close with her, but I found out about her little problem with Jacob in a roundabout way. I was sworn to absolute secrecy, but I guess I can tell you now. Lydia got pregnant with that boy, and she had to have an abortion. You know, that pill you take in the first eight weeks? It's super-expensive. Like six hundred dollars. So she asked him for the money. It's only right. But that boy refused to pay. How do I know it's mine? he says, all high-and-mighty. Disgraceful piece of poo."

"Not to ask the obvious, but why didn't she use birth control?"

"She always did, and Lydia was such a detail person." Violet buffed an apple on the sleeve of her sweatshirt, then returned it to the bowl. "Lydia would never slip up. But sometimes, things happen. The condom breaks, and you know how the rest of it goes. That was just her bad luck."

This faulty condom excuse was becoming a regular refrain.

A noise at the kitchen door startled us. It was long after Sunday night curfew.

Violet moved closer, grabbing my shoulders and hiding behind me. "Oh my God, it's the boogeyman."

I would have laughed at that if I weren't so on edge.

The bolt clicked and the door opened to reveal a girl hanging on to a guy with wild curly hair. "Hey." He noticed us immediately. "I got a special delivery."

Courtney slid from his shoulder and staggered over to the kitchen island. "Hi." Her hands gripped the counter, but she had trouble standing up straight. "Hi, you guys. I love you."

"You are drunk as a skunk," Violet declared.

"She'll be okay." The dude at the door was already turning away. "See ya, Court."

"He's so nice," Courtney gushed. "Bye-bye," she cooed as the door closed and she turned her glazed eyes on us. "I'm so glad you guys are still up. I love you!" She swayed dangerously but held on to the counter. "Do you want to dance? Dance party upstairs in my room!"

"Oh, no, you're not, lil miss." Violet skirted around the kitchen island to throw the bolt and lock the door. "Your room is my room, and I am going to bed."

"Just a little dance party. Dance...," Courtney sang. "Dance..." She lurched forward and doubled over.

I closed my eyes at the sound of vomit splashing onto the kitchen floor.

"Oops." Courtney straightened, wiping her mouth on the sleeve of her lambskin jacket.

"Lord A'mighty, you are going to wake up Mrs. J and the entire house." Violet had the stern tone of a parent. "And I am not covering for you this time."

"But you're my sister, sister," Courtney hissed, stumbling toward Violet. She tried to put her arms around Violet, but was pushed away.

"Get off me. You reek!"

"I'll take her upstairs," I offered.

"Not to my room! I will not have her throwing up in my suite," Violet insisted.

"Come on." Sidestepping the puddle, I put one arm around Courtney's waist and guided her toward the hallway.

"Who is going to clean this up?" Violet hissed in a loud whisper.

"I've got my hands full right now," I said in a low voice, lugging Courtney up the bottom steps. Behind me Violet gave a grunt of frustration. Ha ha.

Courtney's chin rolled toward me. "Are we going to a dance party?"

"Lift your feet. That's it. We are going to my room. And you are going to sit on the floor with your head in a trash can."

"You're the best friend ever," she gushed.

"I know." Up in the suite, I helped Courtney lower herself to the floor so that she could lean against the love seat. She was still flopping around, but climbing the stairs seemed to zap her enthusiasm.

Her head lolled back against the sofa cushion and she looked up at me with hooded eyes. "What are we doing tonight?"

"Shh. People are sleeping. We're chillin' right here."

"Hanging with my homegirl," she said with a huge grin. At least she was a happy drunk.

I moved the coffee table back to give her space and opened a bottle of Gatorade from our stash. "And we're going to talk. Quietly."

I handed her the bathroom trash can with strict instructions to use it if she needed it and sat opposite her on the floor, a safe distance away. "Tell me where you went tonight." As long as I had to babysit Courtney, I figured I might as well squeeze out some information while she was in this animated phase of intox. "Out there alone? Did you even know that guy who dropped you off?"

"That's Mitch . . . Mick. He's a Gamma Kappa." She leaned her hands and chin on the rim of the can. "And I wasn't alone. I was with Tori and the Gown and Cap-ahs." She laughed as if she'd just made up the funniest joke in history.

"What happened to Tori?"

"She's still there with her new boyfriend. But shhh! Don't tell anyone. It's a secret."

"Do you mean Graham Hayden?"

She gaped at me. "How did you know?"

"I guess it's not such a secret. But it seems like a major back-stab to me. I know Lydia is dead, but still, she was a sister."

Her lower lip jutted out in a pout. "Lydia is dead."

Oops. I couldn't let her fall into a pity session. "Maybe Lydia wouldn't have cared. I'm not sure she liked Graham that much."

"But she did. Lydia loved Graham. She had a plan. They were going to get married and have little babies. A big, beautiful family. She was going to marry a senator's son. Did you know his father is a senator?"

"Yup. So Lydia liked him?"

"She was in love with him! He was the one she called Nick. It was her code name for him because she didn't want everyone to know who she was talking about because . . . because he wasn't as into her yet. He didn't know it, but she was going to marry him and he was going to become a senator, too. With little baby senators all around. And I was going to visit her in the governor's mansion. We were going to drink fancy cocktails and have a dance party. We had plans . . . we picked out her bridesmaids' colors. She and Graham looked so good together, with their black hair and dark eyes and . . ."

As she babbled on I didn't point out that senators don't live in the governor's mansion. I didn't comment on the wedding plans or the deluded crush. But as I processed it all, my thoughts shifted to Tori and her move toward Graham.

"Did Tori know that Lydia was into Graham?" I asked.

"They used to argue about it. Tori told Lydia she should move on, that he was a ten and Lydia was an eight. But Lydia refused to give up on him. She told me that's the power of love; that you hold on no matter what people say."

Hold on to a crush? An infatuation. A sad chill settled on my shoulders at the thought of Lydia clinging to a fantasy of love. Her Nick. Her Graham. Her dream of a happily-ever-after.

"But she didn't get to marry him. Poor Lydia." Courtney's voice was nearly hoarse now as she bumped along into a crying jag. The inevitable tears of a drunk teen, the predictable ending of a girl's college drinking binge.

"It's sad," I agreed. "Even sadder that Tori was probably plotting to get Graham for herself."

"She always liked him, but she stayed away," Courtney said. "Out of respect for Lydia."

Did Tori really stay away? I wasn't so sure of that. I'd never known Tori to sacrifice anything she wanted.

"Aw, I miss Lydia so much," Courtney moaned.

"I know. I was going through the archives and I found something weird. A lot of cash. I think it was Lydia's money. Do you know anything about it?"

"It was hers," she said sheepishly.

"How did Lydia get thousands of dollars?" When she didn't answer, I gave her a nudge. "Courtney, you shared a room with her. Was Lydia working as a prostitute?"

"No! Of course not. She would never do that." Courtney lifted her head from the bucket and slumped down to the floor. "Lydia was too proper. She just . . . she figured out a way to make guys pay her money. She was so smart." She curled into a fetal position.

The list of names. The cash. The guys owing money. Oh, so smart. How much had Violet said it cost? Six hundred dollars. Times how many names in the book? That would account for the mega-cash Lydia had accumulated, minus her expenses.

"Let me guess. She would bag a guy, tell him she was pregnant, and then demand money for an abortion."

"How did . . . how did you know that?"

"But the poor doofus didn't get her pregnant, so she just pocketed the catch. Yeah, she was smart. Except that she had to have sex with those guys."

"You're disgusting," Courtney whimpered, mashing one

cheek against the floor. "Everything is spinning. I can't make it stop."

"Take deep breaths."

Bone-tired but stuck on this new discovery, I went to the closet and dug through my backpack until I found the business card for Detective Taylor. I didn't want to betray a sister, but these events were far beyond the secrets I'd promised to keep. Nothing in our ritual or initiation elicited loyalty for a sister practicing blackmail and extortion. I decided that the police needed to know that Lydia was no angel, and the list of guys who might have been angry enough to wrench her pretty neck was more than fifty names long. And then there was Tori, who may have been so battered by Lydia that she had killed her to stop the torture. Had she killed Lydia? I didn't think so. But as a suspect in the case, I could only gain by passing this information on to the police.

I called the detective's cell phone, but got a recording. Of course. She wasn't going to answer in the middle of the night. The morning would be soon enough.

CHAPTER 33

It was happening again.

Monday morning, as Angela and I left our art class, a fire truck blocked our view of the ravine. "Is there a fire?" I asked two firefighters standing behind the truck.

"You're okay. We're here for backup. Police action down in the ravine."

As we moved around the truck the blue and red lights of police vehicles flashed over the rocks and bald dirt of the ravine. This time, they were farther down the river, near the Stone Bridge.

"Not again. I can't." Angela grabbed my wrist, starting to freak out. "I can't take this."

I turned to the firefighter, a lanky, gray-bearded man, who was opening the door of the cab. "Did someone else jump?"

"I'm not supposed to say."

"That means it's a suicide," Angela said. "That's it. I'm putting in a transfer."

Graybeard looked around and stepped closer, leaning down toward us. "Someone reported a homeless man hiking down under the Stone Bridge. The cops went down to move him out, but found some, uh, human remains in the process. A dead baby."

A dead baby. A baby in the ravine. How could it be?

My heartbeat thudded in my chest as I tried to make sense of it. *Not mine. Not mine. Not mine.*

Angela and I gaped up at Graybeard, who held up his hands. "You didn't hear it from me."

"Got it." I ignored my thudding heart as I tugged Angela toward the bridge, but the pressure in my chest made it hard to breathe. "I can't believe it," I muttered. "It can't be."

"Really. A homeless man was carrying around a corpse? That is too gruesome."

This time there wasn't much of a crowd watching from the North Campus Bridge. All the action would have been around the Stone Bridge, but from a distance it didn't seem too crowded. I figured the homeless guy had been taken away, as well as the small body.

A baby's body. What the hell?

While I focused on easing the thudding pulse moving up to my throat, Angela stopped to talk with some guys she knew from the basketball team. Graybeard hadn't shared anything that most of the campus didn't already know. On a campus this size the removal of an indigent man was routine. But the baby—that was big news.

"This is not the first time the body of an infant was found in the ravine," Zeke Hartwell said, holding up his phone to read the Internet entry. "A male infant corpse was found in 1967 in the rocks under the Stone Bridge. The case was never solved. But that was the sixties. Free love and psychedelic drugs. Abortion wasn't legal yet." There was something calming about his comment, this twentyish geek with his big black glasses and sly smile. Maybe this was just another random abandonment. It had to be.

By the time Angela and I continued walking, my pounding heartbeat had faded and I was able to take a deep breath. Panic attack averted. I tried to think of good things to keep calm. Rory coming back from the mountain in the afternoon. My meeting with Detective Taylor to get this heavy weight off my chest.

I was starting to feel better when we swung into the front door of Theta House and nearly smacked into Charlie's Angels. Tori, Courtney, and Violet stood in line like an army of goddesses. Fierce, furious goddesses.

"The Rose Council commands your presence immediately for an emergency meeting." Tori's voice was low but chilling.

"That means now," Courtney said, trying to siphon off Tori's cool composure but failing in her hungover state. Her hair was flat, her mascara from the night before smudged.

"It'll have to be later," I said. "I have a class."

"This can't wait," Violet said. "We'll go down to the babe cave."

"I really don't have time."

"You can't refuse the Rose Council!" Courtney seemed offended. "It's in the bylaws."

Angela fixed her eyes on Courtney. "Scholarship is in the bylaws, too. Or maybe you missed that one."

That lit Courtney on fire, but Tori pointed a finger at Angela and warned, "You don't want a piece of this mess."

"Maybe I do," Angela challenged.

I was grateful that she had my back, but I wasn't up for a catfight. "Just chill. Let's go downstairs and get this over with."

"Fine." Violet led the way to the stairs. I mouthed a thank-you to Angela and followed.

Down in the babe cave a few freshman girls were set up, studying, but Violet shooed them away. I hated the way she stood over them as they nervously collected the index cards that had been set up in a grid pattern.

"Thanks, you guys," I told them. "We won't be too long if you want to come back."

They spared me a quick smile and scrambled out. When I turned, Tori had already set up a folding chair in the place of shame, in front of the large TV.

"Sit," she ordered. "And tell us what the hell you were thinking when you tossed that baby down in the ravine."

"I didn't toss her. I would never—"

"Well, they found her," Courtney interrupted. "The body was out there under the Stone Bridge. Not even covered."

"I can't tell if you were just careless or truly moronic," Tori said sweetly.

"We trusted you to do the right thing." Violet lit a candle and cradled it. The flickering light danced eerily under her heart-shaped face. "We thought you were an organized young woman who crossed her t's and dotted her i's. But this was unforgivable. It was out in the open for all the world to see. Not buried or anchored down in the rivvah or—"

"Anchored down in the river? Like that's *the right thing* to do?" I lifted my hands. "Seriously? You've got a sick mind. We're not mobsters."

"I just expected the job to be done properly," Tori said. "Disposal is disposal."

"I didn't . . ." I stopped myself, realizing I had been planning to bury the baby's body before the little thing came back to life. But these girls didn't know that part; I'd never told them about the miracle. It was in the second layer of secrets.

I wanted to remind them that they'd sent me out, sick and exhausted, with a horrible task and no clear plan, but I saved my breath and tried to calm them down. "The baby they found today? It must have come from someone else," I said.

"You're so full of shit, and now they're going to trace it back to us." Tori was freaking out, pacing and jiggling her fingers in the air like jazz hands. "I touched it. I wasn't wearing gloves. What if my fingerprints are on it somewhere? What if they think it's mine, or that I killed it?"

"My fingerprints are on it, too," Courtney said dully. "Oh my God, Tor. Maybe we'll go to women's prison together. We could be cellmates. But orange is not a good color for me."

Tori pressed her fingertips to her temples. "Do not call me Tor."

I tried to reel them in. "No one here is going to prison because *one,* I didn't leave the baby girl in the ravine. So it's got to be a different baby. And *two,* unless you have fingerprints on file, the police database will not make a match. And that's assuming that they can lift prints from the . . . the baby's body." I stood and faced them. A cool undercurrent of strength moved me along. "You guys need to chill. And I have to go."

"Wait." Tori squinted at me. "So what did you do with the body?"

"The less you guys know, the better," I said firmly. "But she's not in the ravine, okay? Whatever the police found—it's not the body of our baby."

The news had hit Finn like a punch in the gut. The remains of an infant just below the Stone Bridge. He thought of Emma, her beautiful, wondrous story. He wanted to believe it was true, but the facts pointed to something different. He sent her a text, asking her to stop in to his office after noon.

    It can't wait.

She stopped in on her way to the library. Her dark hair was wild and windblown, but she seemed calm. She tried to finger comb it as she walked in. "Something tells me this isn't about the task force."

"I know you've heard the news about the body in the ravine."

"That's all I've heard all day. It's awful."

"I have to ask you, Emma. Is that the body of your baby? Did it die eventually?" He had begun to wonder if the baby had not come back to life as Emma had told him. Maybe that was her fantasy, some sort of postpartum hallucination.

"No," she said cautiously, "and I told you, it wasn't my baby at all. I wasn't the mother."

"The mother was someone else in your sorority?"

"Someone else. A friend." She squinted at him. "You don't believe me?"

"But you were sick. Dehydrated. You said you ached all over."

"I was getting over the flu, and I had to pull an all-nighter."

"Okay. I'm sorry to bring it up again, but with the incident this morning, I had to ask."

"I get that." She frowned. "It's a weird coincidence, I know."

"Are you nervous about the police connecting you to the remains in the ravine?"

"Nope. Not at all. The miracle baby is alive and well."

"Thank God for that." That night on the bridge they had promised to be honest, to keep it real, and he didn't want to push too hard. Trust was a tenuous thing. Stretched too far, it snapped. "So what else is going on?"

"Besides the scandal of the day?" she teased. "You want more?"

"I guess one is enough."

She was waiting for me outside Dr. Finn's office. Another cop, this one with sparkle gel on her skin and hair styled to feather around her face. Nice try with the makeover, but she had blown her cover when I caught her staring as I left the office. She popped out of a chair by the receptionist's desk and just gaped.

Letting my breath out with a hiss, I turned away and trudged out. This one had to be new; she followed me out of the building without even trying to be discreet.

My teeth clenched as I skirted around a mossy section of the path and started uphill. I was getting so sick of being followed by the cops, annoyed at having to arrange a campus escort after dark. I wanted to turn around and yell at her. *If you didn't waste so much time following me, maybe you would have caught the killer by now.*

But I kept my cool. I was proud of myself for not getting rattled by the Rose Council ambush that morning. The confrontation had forced me to tap an unknown resource of strength, and now I was on a roll.

The sparkle gel cop peeled off as I went into the library. Maybe she knew I was scheduled to work there for a few hours. Whatever.

Needing to keep busy, I pushed the cart down the aisle and shelved books. There was something satisfying about this job, mostly because I imagined that a student might be looking for one of the books on the cart for a report. I liked being the one to make each book available.

The library was more crowded than usual, probably because we were creeping up on the end of the term and students were trying to complete all the papers and assignments that they'd left until the last minute. The buzz of conversation floated up from the crowded tables on the main floor. I glanced down and immediately spotted Sam down below. It was his voice that had caught my attention, and I paused near the balcony rail, listening as he explained something to the other guys at the table. He came to the punch line of the story, and some of them laughed.

Ha ha, so funny? Not so much.

I stole a look. I remembered the soft leather of the jacket slung over the back of the chair. The way his hair curled over the tops of his ears. The things that used to squeeze my heart weren't so dramatic anymore. Sam seemed like one of many guys on campus.

I let out a breath of relief. I'd been freed. Sort of. I wondered what time Rory would be back that night.

Mulling over ways to use the discovery in the gorge to further support the argument for improvements at the health center, Finn headed out of his office to teach a one o'clock class. It was definitely a point for discussion with Sydney Cho.

"Hey, Dr. Finn." Max, the student manning the reception desk, nodded. With a dark forest of facial hair, Max was looking particularly scruffy today, but then it was no-shave November. "You heading out?"

"I've got a class to teach. Catch you on the rebound."

"I won't be here," Max said. "I'm just filling in so Mrs. Noble can take lunch. Hey, right. I almost forgot. Your wife came by earlier."

"My wife?" Finn hesitated. "You mean Eileen. Actually, we're not married."

"Whatever. I told her you were in with a student, and she waited a while. But after your door opened, she got up and left in a fit. Really pissed. Should I have interrupted you?"

"No. Unless she mentioned an emergency with our kid, you did the right thing. Thanks." In his mind, Finn replayed the last half hour. So Eileen had seen Emma emerge from his office. Had it been the sight of a pretty young student that inflamed her? *Frailty, thy name is woman.* It would be just the sort of thing she would sink her teeth into and rip apart like a wolf devouring its prey.

On his way to class, Finn reluctantly called Eileen. He hated any contact with her now, but he figured it was worth the annoyance if he could nip her tantrum in the bud.

It was too late; Eileen had made some calls, to the dean of students and the police. "You think you're so smart, so secretive, but I saw that girl leaving your office, and I heard her talking yesterday. She's the one who took her baby down to the ravine. She's the baby killer!"

"You don't know what you're talking about. She's a student on the task force, that's all. And I shouldn't need to explain anything to you. You can't be prying into confidential university matters."

"Oh, I can and I will if it means protecting my family."

His jaw clenched in frustration. When would she see there was nothing to protect? "This is huge, Eileen. You might have even broken some laws, but right now you need to undo the damage. Call the police and tell them you were wrong. But, wait. You don't even know the student's name."

"Oh, I got her name. I followed her to the library and got everything I need to know. Emma Danelski, and she's a Theta Pi. I know what you've been up to with her . . . what she did. I know the truth! That student—Emma—she had your baby and killed it. She dumped it in the ravine as if it meant nothing to her."

"No!" He smacked a palm to his forehead. "Eileen, you're wrong about this. Listen, I have to teach a class, but you need to call the police back. Tell them you were wrong. Fix this now, or I'll drag you to the precinct and make you confess in person."

The line went silent, and then in a small voice she said, "No. I'm going to fight to save my family."

"Eileen, no—" He launched into a new argument, but she had already hung up.

CHAPTER 34

It was still light when I signed out of the library and headed into town to meet with Detective Taylor. I would do my best to keep this short. My friends would be waiting for me at the Turquoise Tiger, a hookah lounge in town where Defiance had promised to read tea leaves for us. Isabel had found out that we'd done it over the holiday, and she wanted in. As I crossed the parking lot of the police precinct, the front door opened. Two men in uniform came out and headed to a car. Behind them was a stunning young blond woman.

Tori.

I flinched, partly from guilt. I planned to tell the detective everything I had learned about Tori and Lydia. At least the parts I hadn't sworn to keep secret. "What are you doing here?" I asked her.

"What do you think?" She kept her voice low, but she seemed ready to pounce on me. "I had to come in and talk to them because of your effing baby. And that Detective Taylor is no bargain."

"What are you talking about?"

"They found something in the gorge with your name on it. They think it's connected to the body."

"What?" My earlier resolve began to sink away. "What was it?"

"I don't know. A towel or something."

The Theta Pi towel. The baby had been wrapped in two towels, and I had peeled one off and tossed it into a pile of debris.

"You'd better go in there and take responsibility, Emma. I already told Detective Taylor that the baby they found in the ravine is yours. Step up and take responsibility or you're going to get all of us in trouble."

"I'm not going along with a pack of lies," I said. "That baby wasn't mine, and I didn't leave her in the gorge."

"But you promised to keep the secret. Remember? A Theta Pi promise lasts forever."

"I won't break that promise, but I'm not getting in trouble for something I didn't do."

Tori's lips pressed together, forming an angry crimp in her lovely face. "Just own it. You screwed up. You pay the price."

"I made a mistake last year—I was crushed by it—and since then you guys have used it against me, torturing me with the memory. You locked me in that room, forcing me to—"

"We thought you knew how babies were born. You have nursing training."

"I'm still taking intro classes. Not like Haley, who's been through clinical training. You made me deliver the baby because you knew you could push me around. You just wanted to pour salt on the wound."

"Oh, boo hoo, poor you." Tori's lips formed a pout, and for the first time I could see signs that those lush lips were not natural. Just like her nose. I wondered where else she had received BOTOX injections. Where else had a surgeon carved to create this beautiful monster?

"We took you under our wings," Tori said. "We treated you like a sister."

"More like a slave. Once you had me under your wing, you used me mercilessly. You rewrote the truth when the baby was born, to pretend she was mine. Do you know how that tortured me?"

Her jaw tensed as she glanced back at the precinct. "I am not having this conversation here. Just go in there and follow the story we agreed on. If you didn't do anything wrong, then there's no problem, right?"

"Not because of any help from you."

She shrugged. "Good luck with that. I'm going to meet my new friend for a study date. Yes, it's official. Graham and I are together."

"Congratulations. Do you guys ever chat about Lydia? About what really happened that night on the bridge?"

"You're cray."

"Does Graham know you were on the bridge with Lydia that night?" I watched her carefully, and the signs were there. The sudden breath. The averted gaze. "It was you in that hoodie, wasn't it?" I stepped closer to her and lowered my voice. "Did you kill her?"

There was a flash in her cool blue eyes—fear or guilt, I couldn't tell—as she backed away. "Get away from me!" She turned and strode off, her heels clicking on the pavement.

On the library steps, Defiance paused to answer Isabel's text, saying that she would meet her at Theta House and walk to the hookah lounge together. Defiance would have met her there, but Isabel, thin and delicate as a seedling, shouldn't be traveling alone on campus with the shadows that seemed to be present all the time now. Like the other girls in the suite, Defiance worried about little Izzy and her eating disorder. Lately she seemed to have evened out a bit, partly thanks to her new friend Patti. Defiance suspected that her roommate had a special relationship with Patti. It was never talked about in the sorority, but all behaviors existed everywhere. Patti was good for Isabel, but still, a fragile flower needed protection in a storm.

Be back soon, Defiance wrote. As she was tucking her phone into the pocket of her jacket, she looked up and saw Tori Winchester coming into the library arm in arm with a tall, handsome guy who could have modeled to be a Ken doll. The senator's son was hot, but stuck on himself.

She made eye contact with Tori, who gave her a wilting

look. Defiance didn't back down. "Hey, Tori." Her voice was coated with sugar.

Tori only frowned at her, but Graham said hello. An apprentice politician.

Seeing them together was jarring. Even after Defiance looked away, the image flashed in her mind. They were like the wedding cake figurines she had been seeing in her dreams. A beautiful couple, like the plastic bride and groom on top of a wedding cake. A perfect bride with her tall, dark, and handsome guy. Only Tori was blond.

She stared after them as the door closed, then made the sign of the cross. *There goes evil.*

Tori moved her knee ever so slightly under the table, brushing his leg just enough to get his attention but not enough to be obnoxious.

"Hey, bae." He put a hand on her thigh and smiled.

Graham had a perfect smile: square white teeth, not too much gum, and when he was happy his entire face lit up. They were still in the hot pants phase, that time when the slightest movement could be such a turn-on. Tori had never had a relationship that survived once the initial thrill was gone, but she saw long-term potential in Graham. Oh, pretty please.

They were in a private study room of the library, separated from the great room by a tinted glass wall. Usually, Tori liked the semi-privacy. It was the perfect place to make out without going too far. And sometimes the prospect of spectators outside made the kissing that much more exciting.

He slid his fingers toward her inner thigh, but she didn't encourage him. Emma's comment was stuck in her mind. This was too close for comfort. Although Tori was attracted to the thrill of danger, she'd never been teetering this close to the edge before.

"You okay?" he asked.

"She thinks I killed Lydia." That bitch had gotten the last shot in, and the barb still caused an ache in Tori's chest. "I don't mean to obsess, but it really got me."

"I get it. You're still upset about Lydia. And Emma's being mean to you."

"She is." Tori had plenty of experience shutting down bitches, but with Emma, it was harder. She was persistent, and she paid attention to things. It was difficult to fool a person who paid attention, and right now, Tori needed to get something past that nosy girl. Tori had something to hide, and Emma knew that. She could smell it like a dog sniffing out a bloody steak.

"What if she finds out that I *was* on the bridge that night?"

"So you walked your friend out to the bridge. You weren't there when she jumped. And you were a good friend to Lydia." Graham slid an arm over her shoulders and pulled her close. "Come on. You're worrying about nothing."

"Oh my God. What if she tells the police?"

"So what if she does? You didn't kill Lydia. Besides, the police don't care what Emma Danelski thinks."

"I don't want her dragging me into this with the police." Tori's parents didn't care about much, but trouble with the cops was one of her father's pet peeves. As a corporate attorney, William J. Winchester wanted a clean criminal record for himself and his next of kin. He would flip if his daughter were involved in a murder investigation.

"Look. Am I nervous? No. Trust me on this. Emma's got nothing on you. She's just freaking out because the police have been all over her since day one, and now, with the dead baby? Wow. She's the one who's in the hot seat, not you."

Tori hoped he was right.

CHAPTER 35

The meeting with Detective Taylor wasn't going well. Since she didn't immediately ask me about the discovery in the ravine, I started with my report. I had thought she'd be excited to be handed a chunk of information about one of her cases, but there was a glaze in her amber eyes as I told her about the possible love triangle between Lydia, Tori, and Graham.

"Did you investigate him? Graham Hayden," I asked.

"I can't give you specifics, but I assure you we have looked at every individual pertinent to the investigation." She reminded me of a taunt my sister used to say: Big words mean little nothings.

"Are you afraid of him?" I asked. "Because of his father."

"Let's just say there are certain people we need to handle with discretion."

That burned me, but I didn't back off. "You need to look at Graham again. It turns out that Lydia was really in love with him. She planned to marry him. It was a big dream of hers."

"And how do you know this?"

"She used to talk about it with one of the sisters. Courtney told me. Courtney Christensen."

She wrote that down. "Hearsay, but I can talk with Courtney." Although the detective had been poised to write since I started talking, she hadn't taken many notes. Wasn't all of this important?

"And there was bad blood between Tori and Lydia. Lydia was blackmailing Tori, getting money from her to keep these old photos of her from surfacing."

Her brows rose. "Nude photos?"

"Photos of Tori from freshman year, before she had her nose fixed."

"Oh, mercy. Are you serious? The way Tori talked to me about Lydia, you'd think they were best friends."

"They were playing each other. And besides that, Lydia was secretly making money. Some kind of business she was running." I told her about the box of money—thousands of dollars. She seemed concerned that I took it from Lydia's room, but I explained that it was offered to me by Lydia's mother after the police had searched the room. "Along with the cash was a notebook with the names of male students. At least fifty of them. I think she'd scammed them, probably since freshman year." I explained about two of the guys in the book being asked for money by Lydia to take care of an unwanted pregnancy.

"Really? I've seen a lot of rotten collegiate behavior, but that one hits a new low."

"Aren't you going to write it down?"

"I don't need to. We have security cameras recording us. They're standard in these interview rooms." Detective Taylor scratched her nose, refocusing. "These are interesting developments, but actually, I was glad you were coming in because I need to ask you some questions about the new case: the body of the child found in the ravine."

I maintained eye contact and kept very still. No reaction for the cameras. "Why does that concern me?"

"When we found a Theta Pi bath towel with your name on it down in the ravine, at first I thought it was coincidence. It's hard to say how half of the debris down there ends up sticking to the riverside. Of course, it's in our lab for analysis, and the medical examiner has not yet submitted a report on the body of the infant. But this afternoon we got a phone call, an anonymous tip, saying that the dead child found in the gorge was your baby. This caller saw you carrying an infant down into the ravine near the Stone Bridge. She said you had this child with a Merriwether professor, Dr. Scott Finnegan, and you disposed of it in the ravine."

"That's not true," I said. "It's not. And Dr. Finn is my friend. We're not involved with each other."

"I see." Taylor folded her hands on the table, an odd kindness in her warm amber eyes. "That part's not so important. The father. We women carry the burden in these relationships, don't we?"

"It wasn't my baby."

"Your sorority sisters claim that it was. I just spoke with Tori Winchester, and she says that Courtney and another sister, Violet Sweetwater, will back up her statement. You had a child born Halloween night. No one knew what to do with it, so you killed the baby and disposed of the body down by the river."

"No. No! I would never kill a . . ." The words died in my dry throat.

"This doesn't look good for you, Emma." Detective Taylor clicked her pen, her lips forming a frown. "We're still waiting on forensic results, but do you see the preponderance of evidence here? Your towel. The baby's body. Your sorority sisters. The witness who saw you carry that baby down to the river."

"No. This is not fair. It's not true."

"Then tell me the truth, Emma. A few people are saying that you took the baby down to the ravine early in the morning. It was the night after Halloween, and your sorority had a party. Tell me what happened. What did you do with the body?"

I shook my head. "I'm telling you, the body you found was not my baby," I said slowly. "I don't know . . . I don't even know what I'm doing here." I stood up from the table. I had come to the precinct with good intentions, wanting to help solve Lydia's murder, and I'd walked right into this sticky web. "I'm done here."

"I don't think so." Detective Taylor was on her feet, squaring off opposite me. "You need to stick around. We're not finished here."

"We're done. You can't hold me against my will." I had seen enough crime shows to know that. "Not unless you arrest me."

"All right then." She clicked her pen closed and tossed it onto the table. "Emma Danelski, you are under arrest for the murder of Baby Jane Doe."

"Where is she? She's so late." Isabel tapped another text to Emma and pressed send. "Maybe she forgot that we planned to do this?"

"Emma is too organized to forget." Defiance put the hookah aside and pushed a stream of smoke out through rounded lips. "Something's wrong. Angela hasn't heard from her, and she's not answering our texts." She wasn't one to panic, but she couldn't ignore the jab of pain that came when she visualized Emma at this moment. "She's not meeting us here. But I don't know why."

"Are you being psychic, or is that just common sense?"

"A little bit of both."

Isabel pressed her fingertips to her lips, panic approaching. "Oh my God, should we call the police? What if the killer got to her?"

"No. There's no reason to panic." There rarely was, but try to tell that to a nervous butterfly like Isabel. "The danger is not immediate. It's a threat. Like distant thunder."

"How do you know?" Isabel checked her phone, then tossed it back onto the table. "I'm going to get sick about this."

"No. You're going to stay calm and have some tea and smoke if you want."

Isabel hugged herself. "I don't do tobacco."

"You smoke weed, and Arabic tea and hookah go together

like peanut butter and jelly. Try it." Defiance lifted the teapot
and began pouring. The subtle aroma mixed with the smoke
to awaken her senses, stoking the blue flames of vision. "I'm
going to do a reading for myself. But really, I'm thinking about
Emma, so my question will be about her." As she explained
the basics of tea-leaf reading, Defiance added two spoons of
sugar to her tea, stirred, and began to meditate on the tea and
the question.

What was Emma's danger?

She thought about Emma as she sipped the tea, sensing a heav-
iness surrounding her friend. She imagined a warrior princess
limping from a battlefield, injured but determined, wounded but
not mortally. Not in danger of dying, at least, not in this moment.

Letting her vision blur, Defiance sipped the tea and gave herself up to watching for the threat to Emma. Here was the line
between tea reading and psychic vision that Defiance's mother
so hated; the bad reputation of so-called gypsy fortune-tellers
swindling people out of money and throwing curses on those
who crossed them. Mama didn't understand, but Kizzy had
taught Defiance how to look in the shadows and delineate the
movement of life.

At last, she swirled the cup, drained it, and glanced down at
the minced leaves.

"Oh, I see a magnificent dragon." She showed the cup to Isabel.

"Actually, it looks more like an alligator to me. All teeth, no
wings."

"Both are signs of danger. There is a threat coming to
Emma, but it's still in the dark, behind a curtain. She can't see
it now."

"You're scaring me."

"Stay calm. Wisdom is knowledge." Despite her reassur-
ance to her friend, Defiance knew she would not be able to
shake her concern until she could warn Emma of the threat.
She turned the cup this way and that, waiting for other shapes
to emerge.

It was a hard cup to read. "I see a man and a woman, standing together." The shapes were rough, like the signs on restrooms. "A bride and groom?"

The wedding cake figurines in the teacup were Lydia and Graham; she was sure of it, but she didn't understand it.

"Was Lydia engaged to marry Graham Hayden?" she asked.

"She wanted to," Isabel said. "He was one of her big crushes."

"Was it his baby she was carrying?"

Isabel's eyes opened wide. "You knew?"

Defiance shrugged. "Most of my cousins and all of my sisters are married with children, and some of them needed extra space in their wedding gowns for the baby bump. A big secret, of course, but you start to see the signs." She tried to relax as she inhaled from the hookah. Walls were coming down between Isabel and her. If only they could have talked of this months ago. "I could see it in the way she walked. And the glow. Her face was like the moon. But I never talked about it with her. We never talked. Lydia believed I wasn't good enough for her."

"She was snobby to a lot of girls," Isabel said. "The only reason she was nice to me was because I found out her secret. We had a class together across campus last spring, and she was always leaving to go to the restroom. Twice I found her throwing up in there. I thought she was bulimic at first. I offered to help her, and then she told me."

"So we both knew, but never said." Defiance stared at Isabel through the dark hair that had fallen into her right eye. "We should have come clean about this earlier."

"You had just transferred here in September, and I don't like to spread rumors. I've had enough girls backstab me. I won't go there."

"But it's not a rumor if it's true," Defiance said.

"I guess. Lydia said the baby was the best thing that ever happened to her. She figured she would have to leave school after her fall term, but she didn't mind because she was getting married. She was engaged to marry Graham, but it was a secret."

"A secret, or a fantasy?" Defiance was skeptical. "Why did this never happen? He broke up with her after the baby was born? Or maybe she was making up the whole relationship. In those last days, sitting around in her bathroom, Lydia was crumbling from the inside out. I don't know what happened to her baby, but it looked like her dreams were far from coming true."

Isabel shrugged as her cell phone buzzed. "I guess we'll never know." She frowned as she scrolled down the text message. "Angie hasn't heard from her, either. She texted Rory. He's still at the mountain, not coming back until tomorrow. But they texted this afternoon, and Emma seemed fine."

"Where is she?" Defiance looked down into her empty teacup, but she couldn't see the answer in the leaves.

"We need to talk to someone about the infant's body found in the ravine," Finn told the desk officer. "Can we talk to someone working on that case?"

"Hold on a second." The cop left Finn waiting at the desk in the police precinct, while Eileen veered off to sulk in a chair in the waiting area. Goddamn her!

It had taken Finn three hours to convince her that she had to come here and retract the false information she had given to the police regarding Emma. Eileen's face and neck sparkled with some sort of makeup, as if she'd fallen in a vat of glitter, and he had to bite back commentary as he made his case. He had started arguing logic, then moved to morality and common decency. When that had failed, he had pointed out that it was against the law to lie to the police. Obstruction of justice. Did she want to go to jail? That had frightened her, though not enough to get her to the station. Finally, he had to stoop to her level. He vowed that he would not see Wiley again unless she went to the police and told them the truth.

It had taken an iron will to hold his temper down as he'd corralled Eileen and Wiley into the car, dropped the kid with Eileen's mother, and driven to the police station. The whole time Eileen had been harping about plans for Christmas. "Would you come back to us if we went to visit your family in Oklahoma?" she asked him. "It could be a healing holiday. And Wiley needs to get to know his other grandparents."

She never stopped.

He had kept silent, chanting the mantra in his head. *No, no, no.*

Now they were being directed to a desk in a large room down the hall, where a trim, fiftyish cop in uniform introduced himself as Officer Glenn Kunkel and asked them to take a seat.

"Thanks for coming in. I understand you folks have new information for me?"

"Actually, it's a retraction of information you were given." Finn introduced himself and Eileen, then explained how Eileen had called in information about the baby in the ravine that she'd thought was true at the time. "But it's false. Isn't that right?"

Eileen tilted her head at the cop, leaving a lock of blond hair dangling over one eye in a gesture she probably thought was sexy. "I thought that girl was trying to break up my family," she said. "You can understand where I was coming from."

Screw the family! Finn wanted to shout. "Just tell him the truth. She claimed to have evidence that one of my students committed a crime. Tell him."

"I never saw Emma Danelski carry a baby down into the gorge." As Eileen leaned forward, specks of glitter on her face caught the light. "I made that part up. Or maybe I dreamed it. I thought she was having an affair with my husband."

"I'm not your husband. We're not married." Finn stared at Kunkel, trying to engage him. "We never were."

Kunkel frowned as he turned back to Eileen. "So you called in a tip on this student because you were pissed off? That is against the law, Ms. Culligan. You're screwing around with our investigation." He shot a look at Finn, adding, "Against the law, and just not cool."

Thank you, Finn thought. Finally, after hours of Eileen's warped hysteria, the voice of sanity.

CHAPTER 36

Killer, killer, killer...

The word sprang from my chest in sync with my frantic heartbeat as I paced the jail cell like a caged bird. It was cold in here, but the shivers that racked my body had little to do with temperature and everything to do with the fear that shook me to the marrow of my bones. The realization that I was in this alone. The fear that I would never get out of this place.

Did they have enough to charge me with murder?

How much had Tori told Detective Taylor about Halloween night at Theta House?

My baby...she'd said the baby was mine. God, I was so stupid not to go along with that in front of Detective Taylor.

My hands balled into fists as I thought of the jabbering sisters on the Rose Council. Courtney, Tori, and Violet. They'd been quick to point the finger at me. They had made a Theta Pi promise to keep the secret—a serious oath—but in the process of protecting one sister they had thrown me to the lions.

What had Detective Taylor said? Someone had called in an anonymous tip. More like anonymous lies. That I'd hooked up with Dr. Finn? It gave a sick taint to a relationship that had nothing creepy about it. Which lovely sister had made that call?

With arms crossed against the insidious chill in my bones, I cut a path between the empty bunks and the stainless-steel toilet as I tried not to freak out about being in jail and facing murder charges. What would happen with my finals . . . the rest of the term? My student loans? In the back of my mind I remembered a counselor warning me that everything would go to shit if I got arrested. And I'd given her that bland smile, dismissing the notion as ludicrous.

I'd been a fool.

Why hadn't I gone along with the lie? If I'd told the detective that I'd been pregnant, if I'd gone along with my sisters' lies, I could have told them where the baby was. I'd been so stupid! I needed to start owning that lie, not so much to protect myself but to protect the baby. Rebecca.

Her new, hopeful life was the only bright spot in this mess. I didn't want to use her, but I needed to own that lie to protect her.

I turned toward the cell door, a thick, transparent Plexiglas barrier with bars in the middle. Detective Taylor and Officer Caldwell had tried to get me to talk, but I had closed up like a clam and asked for a lawyer. That was the last exchange we'd had, probably hours ago.

What the hell were they doing out there?

Where was the encouraging, bespectacled attorney who always showed up to defend suspects on TV shows? And what about that single phone call? They had taken away my cell phone and wallet, offering me nothing in return.

Eventually, that door would open and they'd either call in a lawyer for me or escort me to a phone.

Would I call my father and lay my troubles down on him? That was pointless. Neither he nor my brother, Joe, had the resources to pay a lawyer. G-Dan may have been a cool dude on the jazz scene, but I couldn't count on him to bail me out.

And now here I was, a twenty-year-old sophomore in college, and I had no lifeline. Granted, I had my sisters, some of them closer than others, but this wasn't like borrowing a sweater or asking for the answers to the Astronomy quiz. Bail money? Like that would ever happen.

I turned away from the scratched-up door and, breaking my resolve not to touch anything in this cell, sat on the edge of the bunk. The wooden bedframe pressed through the thin wafer of mattress. Everything in here was hard and cold, devoid of softness.

A deep breath did nothing to calm me as my heart beat sickeningly against my ribs. *Liar, liar* . . . Someday I would learn to be a better liar.

When she was in high school, a boy had accused Defiance of having ice in her veins. She had laughed, which pissed him off even more. That had been the end of that romance. Tonight, she used that innate calm to stay rational. That was why, when her friends wanted to form a search party and send all the sisters out looking for Emma, Defiance had decided to call the police first. The notion that you had to wait twenty-four hours was a myth, and she knew the police here in Pioneer Falls to be responsive to the needs of college students, their bread and butter.

"I'm calling to report a missing person," she told the cop who answered the phone. "She's not answering her phone and she missed an appointment." When she gave the name, he repeated it and told her that Emma wasn't missing after all. "Your friend is here at the downtown precinct."

He made it sound so casual, like students popped into the police station every day. "What is she doing there?"

"Well, right now she's being held for an investigation."

Trouble. Defiance had seen it coming. "You've arrested her?"

"I'm not at liberty to give information right now."

"What do we need to do to get her released?"

"The procedure is that she'll be arraigned by a judge tomorrow."

She ended the call, looking from Isabel to Patti to Angela to Darnell. "Emma needs our help."

My eyes opened when I heard the noise at the door of the jail cell. I must have dozed off at one point because now the clock on the wall said that it was 2:25. The blur on the other side of the Plexiglas door turned out to be Detective Taylor.

"Come with me," she said. Back to the interview room with its pockmarked ceiling and camera. She offered me water or soda. I wanted tea to ward off that middle-of-the-night chill. I settled for water.

Detective Taylor seemed to have softened, but then maybe that was just exhaustion fraying her concentration. "I did some checking on you," she said. "How come you're not telling me the whole truth?"

It was a complicated question, one with too many answers. I stared down at the table, wondering how much she had found out. How bad was it?

"I tried to reach your father. He's a hard man to track down. But I did get to speak with Mr. Joseph Danelski."

I let out the breath I'd been holding. Maybe it was awful . . . or not so bad at all.

"Your brother, Joe?" she prodded. "He told me that you did have a baby late Halloween night, just like your sorority sisters said. There was no documentation on the birth because everyone was afraid to go to the police or the health center. But your baby didn't die. You brought her up to Tacoma on the train and left her under their care on November first. He and his wife are in the process of legally adopting her."

My baby . . .

This time I jumped on the fabricated story. The gift of a lie that Tori and Violet and Courtney had given to me.

"That's right," I said quietly. "I had a baby in the sorority house. Lydia helped deliver it."

That day in the gorge, something wickedly creative came over me as I considered the future of the baby girl. Who would take care of her? Who would love her, not in that storybook way, but in the real day-to-day grit of kissing her grubby hands and allowing her to tumble so that she could learn to take her first steps and learn to walk? Would a clinic or police station connect her to a mother and father who would love her to the moon and back?

Maybe. But that would take time, and I couldn't let her suffer a single minute without love when I knew where to find it.

The hike out of that gorge with the weight of her on my chest had been like climbing to heaven. Difficult, yes, but exhilarating. Courtney had accidentally left her wallet in the pocket of the backpack, and I used her cash to buy diapers in town. At the school bookstore, I found an extra-small T-shirt and a Merriwether beach towel to swaddle her in. The last of the cash went to a bus ticket to Portland.

Without blinking I evolved as a criminal, from kidnapper to thief. In Portland, I used Courtney's credit card to pay for the train ticket north as well as chicken noodle soup for me. At a pharmacy near the train station I found disposable bottles already loaded with infant formula. The baby didn't seem interested in drinking, but I was glad to see a small bit of the liquid disappear. Mostly, she wanted to sleep. I got that. We napped together as the train rocked us into her future.

"Emma." Taylor's voice brought me back. "How come you didn't tell me the truth, when it would have gotten you off the hook? And don't tell me it's because of the shame involved in teen pregnancy. I get that, but would you go to jail for it?"

"I had to protect her," I said. That much was true. "The baby, Rebecca is her name. She needed an advocate."

"But you could have come to us when she was born. We would have gotten you both medical attention. I know a social worker who handles adoptions."

"I . . . I just couldn't."

"Now I know there's embarrassment about teen pregnancy. And I can't imagine the trauma of giving birth in a damned sorority house with a bunch of squealing girls. But there's no shame in what you did, Emma. No shame in bringing a baby into the world."

I closed my eyes, but that didn't stop the tears from spilling down my cheeks. If only that were true; if only things were that simple. I had not given birth to baby Rebecca. My baby had been gone before he or she was the size of a peanut. A process that had brought me tons of relief, and an ocean of regret.

She pushed a box of tissues across the table.

"While it's highly irregular to take a newborn across state lines without a birth certificate, it sounds like your brother and sister-in-law have helped you work that out."

"They have." I sniffed. "They've been great."

During the train ride north I had looked up safe haven and adoption regulations on my phone. Our situation hadn't been ideal. If I had told them that the baby girl wasn't actually mine, there was no way that Joe and Amy could have kept her. So I lied again. I said Rebecca had been born in the dorm under hellish circumstances because our student health center was so unaccommodating. I'm not sure if my brother believed me, but Amy accepted my story in a tearful hug. When we want something with all our soul, we see a clear path.

"So I was going to let you go in the morning since most of your story checked out. Then I got a call from your lawyer, and he demanded immediate release. Woo. That Laurence J. Stern? He likes to argue."

"Who?"

"Your attorney from Portland."

I balled up the damp tissue. I didn't know what she was talking about.

"He wanted to post bail, but you weren't even arraigned. I told him to calm down, that you were going home anyway."

"Okay." I nodded. It would be good to leave here. My friends were probably worried about me.

"So I do apologize for detaining you. I know you've been through a lot in the past few months. I don't have a resolution on this case or on the matter of who killed Lydia Drakos. But before you go, I want to give you one last word of warning. Your friend Lydia . . . I don't mean to scare you, but her death was no accident. It wasn't rough sex or someone spontaneously grabbing her in a rage. We haven't released all the details to the public, but she was choked by someone with strength. Someone strong enough to overcome her and crush

her larynx. The bruising on her neck was extensive. It was bru-
tal."

Her grim tone muddied the lightness I felt at being released.
"You don't think it was a Theta Pi sister," I said. "You think
the killer was male."

"I do. So what you mentioned about investigating Tori further? I don't think it would be productive. Lydia wasn't attacked by a female."

"Then why do you still have a cop following me?"

"We don't. Not since Thanksgiving."

I frowned. "A new female cop was hounding me today. No
finesse at all."

"What did she look like?"

"Blond hair and strange glittery bronzer on her face."

"Glitter Face? I met her last night. She's no cop. That's Professor Finnegan's ex-girlfriend, and I'm beginning to think that
she's as crazy as he said." She explained that Dr. Finn's former
girlfriend had been stalking him and had gotten it into her
head that Finn and I had been seeing each other. "She's the one
who told us she saw you going down into the ravine carrying a
baby. Finnegan dragged her in last night and made her confess
that she'd made it all up."

"That's creepy." I looked forward to giving Dr. Finn hell for
his poor judgment in women.

"Well, just so you know, we are not going to have anyone
tailing you in the future. Your lawyer, Mr. Stern, he insisted on
that, and it wasn't in our plans. So if you do find someone following you, be careful, and let us know."

"Can I have my phone back, please?" It was probably ex-
ploding with text messages.

"On the way to the front desk." Taylor stood and opened
the door. "Take care of yourself, Emma. Your fans await you."

I didn't know what she was talking about, but I kept moving. Signed for my key fob, wallet, and cell phone. Slipped on
my fleece jacket with a sigh of relief.

When I stepped out into the lobby and moved past the reception desk, the misery of the night fell away at the sight of

my friends. Defiance rose from the chair, strong and determined as a goddess. Isabel jumped up with a sunny smile. Angela opened her arms wide and said, "Come here, girl."

We fell together in a group hug that brought me back to
tears. "You guys, how did you know I was here?"

"We were freaking out." Isabel's hoarse voice sounded
more childlike than ever. "You disappeared from the face of
the earth last night."

"Defiance found you quickly," Angela said.

"And Angela's parents hired you a big-shot lawyer," Defiance added. "Only it seems like you won't need him."

"But he's there if you need him. Larry Stern. He's worked
with my mom for years."

"Thanks. I can't even tell you how glad I am to see you
guys." I straightened my spine, swiped at my tears, and then
wiped my hands on the thighs of my jeans. I felt like I'd traveled thousands of miles in the past twelve hours. To hell and
back.

It felt good to be back.

CHAPTER 37

None of us could sleep; we were wired with confusion and worried about the questions that remained. We didn't want to discuss any of this in Theta House, so we turned in town toward the twenty-four-hour diner, which was usually dead at this time in the morning.

As we walked, our various accounts of Lydia's pregnancy rushed out. Defiance and Isabel had known. Isabel had even talked with her about it.

"And Lydia was proud," Isabel said as we walked down Main Street, passing the closed storefronts of a hair salon and a pizza place. "She and Graham were going to get married once the baby was born. She was thrilled."

"She told Courtney the same thing," I said. "But I didn't get any of that story from Lydia. I didn't even realize she was pregnant. I thought she'd put on a few pounds, and she wore those bulky sweaters. Then, on Halloween, I caught up quickly when they locked me in her room to deliver the baby."

"*They* being the Rose Council?" Angela said. "Those bitches."

"I knew something was going on that night, Emma," Isabel said. "When you disappeared without a word, and remember? We were supposed to go party hopping together."

"That was a weird night," Angela said. "Why didn't anyone call an ambulance or get Jan when Lydia started to go into labor?"

"Because Lydia was freaking out," I said. "She didn't want anyone to know. You know how she pretended to be so proper. At the time I thought she was trying to protect her reputation. Now I realize that she wanted to keep it a secret until she could present Graham with their perfect baby. And then when the baby was stillborn, Lydia couldn't stand to be connected to it. I think she actually convinced herself the baby belonged to me. And the others went along with it because they could see how much it hurt me."

"Lydia was kind of a narcissist," Isabel said. "Her perfect baby, her perfect family, her perfect life."

"But there's more to this, girls," Angela probed. "Why did all of you keep quiet about it?"

The consensus was kindness. None of us wanted to hurt a sister.

"At least, at first, I kept her secrets out of respect. As I got to know her I realized that Lydia tried to learn about people so that she could use them. She blackmailed Tori about her nose job."

"I knew it," Isabel said.

"So she gathered secrets." Defiance held the door of Oogey's open as we filed in. "That sounds like Lydia. And she had a secret that she could use to stick it to you?"

"Pretty much. I owed her. I owed all of them."

I grew quiet as we scoped out the diner. With a few skaters seated in the window and a stoned-looking couple at a table by the door, we had our choice of tables. We took a booth in the very back, a good vantage point to see if anyone else came in.

We ordered eggs and pancakes, and then as the waitress backed off I took a long sip of water to focus. This wasn't an easy conversation, and I kicked myself for not having it with my real friends earlier.

"So Lydia and the Rose Council got their talons into me last year. It was January, and I'm sorry I ever got involved with them. It's still hard to talk about it, partly because I know it's stupid to be embarrassed about something that happens to a lot of women. Still . . ."

Keeping my voice low, I told them. I told them about the

trauma of finding out I was pregnant, the brush-off from Sam, the difficult decision. About how my skin had burned with shame and regret. About undressing at the clinic and shivering in the skimpy surgical gown. It was a terrible thing, but I didn't see any alternative. I'd been a fledgling freshman, a lost kitten, but Lydia, Courtney, and Tori had helped me through it. They'd given me money, guidance, and a ride to the private clinic in Hood River. Tori had been authoritative but organized, and I was so desperate I mistook her decisiveness for kindness. I didn't understand that there were strings attached.

"They helped me," I said. "And afterward they kept my secret, as long as I did everything they wanted."

"Like a slave," Angela hissed.

"Pretty much."

"Well." Defiance opened the seam of her tea bag and sprinkled tiny leaves into the hot water. "Those days are over. We're not taking any more shit from the Rose Council. I have half a mind to report those girls to National for being inclusive and violating sisters' rights."

"And for being asshats," Angela added.

"Total asshats," I agreed.

"I'm so sorry we weren't there for you." Isabel leaned closer to hug me.

"It's not your fault. You were always there. It was just that Lydia got to me first. She caught me buying a home pregnancy test at the pharmacy, and she wouldn't let it go."

"Bitch." Angela shook her head, the row of diamond studs in her right ear glimmering. "I don't know, girls. What do you think about splitting from Theta Pi next year and striking out on our own?"

"I'm in," Defiance said, "if we don't kill the Rose Council first."

"Or, we could stay and rebel against their evil," Isabel said. "Turn everything around. They're out of here at the end of the year. We can make Theta House a good place to be again. Full of love."

"You go, girl!" Angela high-fived her. "Our little Izzy has found her voice."

Our food came, and while we ate we joked about ridiculous ways to get back at the mean girls. I didn't realize how hungry I was until I dug into a stack of buttery pancakes dripping with blueberry syrup. We did some damage to the food, talking non-stop the whole time.

"I know this is a tangent, and don't lose your appetite, but what happened to the body of Lydia's baby?" Defiance narrowed her eyes. "It's not in the house; I would feel it stirring there, a lost soul, and things would be happening. Doors opening and closing, a rapping on the wall."

"Oh my God, that's scary as shit," Isabel said, hugging herself.

"Please, just let that go," I said. I had known this was coming, and though I longed to tell my friends the entire story, I needed to protect Rebecca. It had been different telling Dr. Finn and Kath; they weren't able to connect the dots. My loving friends meant well, but they were smart, and they already knew too much. "I promise you, Lydia's baby was handled lovingly and respectfully. And I never want to talk about it again."

In the silence that followed, Isabel squeezed my arm and Angela nodded.

Defiance studied me, trying to read between the lines. At last, she lifted her mug and held it up, as if toasting. "We will never speak of this again," she said, then took a drink. "But there are other things to discuss. The police will be back." Defiance stared down into her mug. "There is still the question of who killed Lydia."

She was right. "Can you see that in the tea leaves?" I asked.

There was a hint of a smile as Defiance put the mug aside. "Maybe. And I heard the cops talking while we were waiting. Because they are embarrassed now. All these suicides they can't stop, a murder, and now the body of a baby."

"I never paid much attention to Lydia, so I'm lost on this."

Angela nibbled on a slice of bacon. "Do we think it was the pregnancy and childbirth that put Lydia over the edge?"

"I think she suffered postpartum depression after...after she lost the baby."

"And her depression would have been worse if Graham broke up with her during that time." Isabel twirled a strand of hair around one finger as she stared across the restaurant. "Graham promised to marry her. But maybe he backed off when she lost the baby."

You promised. You promised.

The words swirled in my mind. When had Lydia said that? On the bridge.

"Oh my God, I think Graham killed Lydia."

I *so* wanted to sleep in the next day, and I probably could have gotten excused from my classes by Dean Cho. But my phone alarm went off at eight thirty and I forced myself out of bed and down to the dining room in my flannel jams and sweatshirt. I wasn't hungry for breakfast, but I was hoping to snag Tori.

Last night we had decided that I would be the one to talk to her. It made sense since I had been the one to accuse her of killing Lydia. I'd been wrong about that, I knew that now, but I didn't have high hopes about our exchange since Tori wasn't the conciliatory type.

Most of the sisters weren't morning people, so the dining room was relatively quiet as sisters served themselves from the buffet of eggs, toast, sausage patties, and fruit. I was yawning over a mug of coffee when Tori appeared. Her hair was combed into a ponytail and her pink silk pajamas were elegant, but the red in her eyes and the dry skin around a blister emerging on her lip revealed her stress. She was cracking.

"Well, if it isn't our own Theta Pi jailbird. Is orange really the new black?"

That got the girls' attention.

"Wow." I forced a smile. "You stop in at the police precinct and people start talking." I rose from the table to be eye-to-eye with Tori. "Can we talk? Privately."

"No." She spooned eggs and sausage onto a plate. When she held a coffee cup under the spout, her hand trembled.

"I'll just be in the living room when you finish eating." I went to the room next door and sat in the corner spot where Lydia and I used to talk. Poor lying Lydia. Her dysfunctions had contributed to the disease that was now gripping Theta Pi.

I didn't have to wait long. Tori came stomping in, pausing with her hands on her hips.

"What do we have to talk about? Aside from you going to jail for dumping a body."

"I told you, that body had nothing to do with me. And... do you want to sit?"

With a huff, she sat down beside me, arms folded.

"I actually wanted to apologize for what I said." I lowered my voice. "For thinking that you could've killed Lydia. It was wrong to think that about you. I know you would never do that to a sister." A major lie, but I had to make my case. "When I was talking with Detective Taylor, she shared some evidence. It's clear that Lydia was killed by someone with strength. They're pretty sure the killer was male."

"They are?" She covered her hand with her mouth, then jerked it away, I think, when she touched that sore.

"More homicides are committed by men than women." I kept my voice low. "I've thought about it a lot. I know we came up with that list of guys Lydia dated. But I keep getting stuck on one. She was in love with Graham."

"No." Tori shook her head. "She loved that Nick guy from back home."

"There was no Nick. Graham was the one she planned to marry." I was almost whispering now. "It was his baby. He promised to marry her because of the baby. But when she lost it, all bets were off. At least in his mind."

"How do you know this?" she snapped, glaring at me.

"I think she met him out on the bridge to talk. To reel him in. But instead, he got angry. Maybe she tried to blackmail him, too. He wanted to break it off, but she wouldn't listen."

She was on the verge of firing back at me, but she froze. One of those dawning moments when the tide rushes in all around you, soaking, overwhelming.

"You know Rory heard her yelling just before she died. She kept saying, 'You promised.' " I reached over and touched Tori's satin-covered knee. "She was shouting at Graham, because he was breaking his promise. His promise to marry her."

Her mouth hardened into a scowl as her gaze sank to the floor. "No, that's wrong. You're making it all up. That's not what happened."

"How do you think it happened?"

"I don't know, but it wasn't like that. Graham is heart-broken over her."

He didn't seem too upset in the car the other day when he'd been trying to get into Tori's jeans. But I held back the venom. I needed her to see the threat he posed, for her own protection.

"I don't trust him, Tori. And I'm worried about you."

"Seriously?" She turned her cold blue gaze on me. "You just want to hand the police a suspect to get you off the hook."

"I told you, they think the killer was a guy."

"Right. And you spent most of the night in the police precinct so that you could have a pillow fight with the cops?"

"I'm not a suspect. I've been cleared."

"Goody for you."

"But, Tori, you've got to be careful."

"I am not breaking up with my boyfriend because the dumb-ass cops can't get their shit together. Lydia was killed by some random guy who saw her out there blubbering. That is all."

Was that possible? Yes . . . no. Lydia's murder wasn't random. There was only one reason she would have left Theta House after days of lingering in her bathrobe.

"You need to leave me alone." She stood up and tossed her

hair in my direction. "And watch what you say. Graham's family can't have people smearing their reputation. They'll come after you."

"Tori, wait. I'm sorry, I—"

She turned back in the doorway to say, "Apology not accepted."

CHAPTER 38

Maybe it was worse because of sleep deprivation, but the image of sexy Graham with his hands around Lydia's neck was now branded into my mind. A phone call to Detective Taylor didn't help, as she told me that Graham had an alibi for the night Lydia was killed.

"Who? Where was he?" I demanded. "Because I know his Gamma Kappa brothers would lie for him. Tori would, too."

Paranoid much? I knew I sounded like a lunatic, but Taylor didn't bite. She signed off with a dismissal meant to calm me down.

Coffee with Rory was one of the few breaks from the dread of knowing a creeper was mixing with us. I jumped into his arms when I saw him, and he tried to carry me in through the Starbucks door. We would have made it if his jacket hadn't gotten caught on the doorjamb. I filled him in on the big excitement he'd missed. Well, at least the parts I wanted him to know. Some of the personal tidbits from last year were for sisters only.

Except for the aura of fear hanging over the campus, it was an ordinary day. I drilled myself on parts of the central nervous system, and somehow, despite the craziness raining down on me, the material was sticking in my brain. I kept my fingers crossed for that night's quiz.

At a task force meeting we learned that the director of the

student health center had resigned. We hoped that would open the door to positive change. Dean Cho showed us some netting that the university was considering for installation on two of the bridges, including the North Campus Bridge. She was concerned that students would complain that the netting was blocking their view of nature. We voted in favor of the netting, and she seemed relieved. Maybe her heart wasn't made entirely of stone.

The A & P test went well, and I was glad to see Rory waiting for me outside the lab. We cut through the inky dark night, carefully avoiding the topic of Lydia's killer as we cut across campus. Up in our little living room, the conversation went flying in a dozen different directions as we tried to dissect the character of Graham Hayden. Angela didn't get the attraction, and Darnell said Graham reminded him of a guy in a toothpaste commercial. Nice smile, not much more. Defiance was convinced that she'd been seeing Graham in her nightmares as a figurine on a wedding cake. The guys thought that was hysterical, but I could see that Graham was bothering her, a splinter under her skin. Rory didn't like the way Graham was being favored by the police. And dear, soulful Isabel held out the hope that we were wrong and the real killer would be caught soon.

When I finally got to bed around midnight, I dropped off to sleep quickly. The buzzing of my phone woke me up way too soon.

It was just after one. A text from Tori.

Forgiven. The one-word text helped me to breathe easier. At last, Tori was softening.

It was followed by a longer text.

Bitches like me don't deserve friends like you. Tell the sisters that I love them.

My relief at being off Tori's shit list fizzled to confusion. Tori could share the love with the sisters in person. What did she mean?

Then came a photo that shook my world. A night view of the gorge from the North Campus Bridge.

"No," I whispered. She couldn't be thinking of jumping, not rock-solid, self-absorbed Tori.

Adrenaline forced my body to a sickening state of alertness as I pushed back the covers and moved swiftly out to the living room. A jacket and Uggs were all I could manage in my rush to save my Theta Pi sister.

I ran all the way to the bridge, slowing only when I had to climb up the access stairs. My breath was roaring in my ears as I jogged along the dimly lit deck, moving steadily toward the figure of a lone woman standing at the center of the bridge, not far from the spot that Lydia had fallen from. With each breath and heartbeat, I sent her a silent message. *Hold on, hold on.*

When she turned to me, her face was cold and hard, her jaw set in a grimace that detracted from her beauty.

"I knew you'd come."

I stepped up to the handrail beside her. "I sensed desperation. I guess I was wrong."

"I'm fine. But it was lovely of you to run out here to save my life."

"Surprising, right?" I stared out over the dark river, the deep rocky slopes. Raw beauty and emptiness. "But you know what? You're worth it, Tori. That's why I went out on a limb and told you what I knew about Graham. He killed Lydia. And yeah, maybe there's no hard evidence. And I know the police have to tiptoe around him because his father is a big-deal politician. But guys like Graham don't stop hurting girls. And he's not going to elude the cops forever. He's headed for trouble, Tori. Don't go there with him."

"You are so wrong about him." Fury tainted her pretty face, a cool glimmer in her eyes. "He was trying to be nice to Lydia that night. He didn't want to meet with her, but I pushed him. I thought she might move on if she heard it right from him. I set up the meeting."

There was a beat of silence as I took it all in. "You set it up?"

"I was trying to help. Lydia was a hot mess—you saw her!

She was way too into him, thinking she would trap him into marrying her just because she had his baby. Imagine, going through that bone-crushing experience just to snag a guy. And then the baby died anyway, so the way I see it, Graham owed her nothing. I set up a meeting to calm her down and help her get the fuck over it."

"And were you here with them?"

"Only at first. I brought Lydia here, then went home so the two of them could talk. But Lydia was so out of it. She refused to let Graham go. Finally, when he couldn't reason with her, he left her here and met me back at Theta House. We don't know who attacked her, but the killer came along after Graham left."

"Really." I ran my fingertips over a chink in the railing. "That was Graham's story, and you bought it? Wow. He should go into politics like his father."

"You think you're so smart, but you don't know who killed Lydia. You don't know shit."

"I know that you'd better watch yourself with Graham. Be careful. Stay out of his way, or he'll kill you, too." I turned back toward the west bank, to the scattered lights of Greek Row. "Let's go home. If you still don't believe me, you can call the police tomorrow and tell them what you told me. If Graham is really innocent, you can help clear his name."

The sullen crease of her lips broadened into surprise as she looked at something beyond my shoulder. In the next few seconds I heard a shuffling sound behind me. Someone was there.

I started to turn back but was stopped by a sharp jolt that rippled through my body. A wild flicker of cold pain. Shock. Pain. And shock again.

My knees buckled as I lost control and collapsed forward, slamming onto the pavement.

Paralyzed, muscles seizing, I could only fight the waves of pain.

CHAPTER 39

"What the hell? What did you do to her?" Tori demanded. Her voice floated somewhere overhead, but I couldn't see her. Face to the pavement, I was trapped in paralysis.

The intense jolt of pain had subsided, but every cell in my body was still reeling.

"I shut her down." The other voice was male, low, calm. "But it'll only last a few minutes. It's a Taser gun."

"But look at her, Graham. Why did you do that?"

"Because she's turned on us. She's never going to back off. We need to take care of this. Now. Help me lift her up. It won't take much to get her over the side."

"Like . . . off the bridge? Are you crazy?"

"Sane as rain. Do you think we can let her go around and trash-talk us?"

"No, but I'm not going to throw her off the bridge like a can of Budweiser, and I won't let you do it, either."

Fear rumbled beneath the sickness raking through my body. That protective netting for the sides of this bridge couldn't come soon enough. I took a deep breath, of relief and hope and ease from pain. The shock of it was easing, but my body still felt strange and alien. I longed to slide my cell phone from my pocket, but my arms were heavy, uselessly sprawled on the cement.

"Tori. We don't have time to argue. She's going to recover and . . ."

Lights exploded in my head and my body seized. He had shot me again.

"Stop that!" she growled. "Just stop. I'm not going to help you kill her."

"You're already in this, deep in shit. You helped with Lydia. This will be the last time I ask."

"I didn't . . . you told me you didn't hurt her. That she was still on the bridge when you left."

"So I lied. Come on. Let's turn her over first. Then I'll take her shoulders and you can do the legs."

There was a gentle sobbing falling over me as I was rolled onto my back and shifted closer to the edge, propped against the half wall. I could see Tori, her face red and snotty, and Graham, his dark eyes glittering against his creamy skin. He had the look of a man possessed, a demon stockbroker determined to make a trade. My life for his greedy future.

It wouldn't be long.

Now was the time to move. Pull myself together. Kick or punch or flail.

But my body was too stricken to offer more than gentle resistance.

"Help me lift her," he ordered. "Get her legs. The good thing is that, with the stun gun, there won't be any marks. It'll look different from last time."

Cold premeditation. Fear and panic and fury were a jumbled, thorny mass in my chest, and I couldn't stop the tears that were running down my face. I was propped against the railing when Tori let out a pathetic whimper. "I can't do this. I never wanted to really hurt anyone."

I could see her now, backing away from Graham and me. He was watching her, too, watching and losing interest in me. Without any support I slid back down to my bottom.

"I'm going home," she said. "I don't want to ever see you again, and I'm just saying, you'd better stop this now."

Oh, grow a pair, Tori. I would have laughed at the ridiculousness of her protest if I weren't a few feet from being pitched over the side of the bridge.

"Bae, don't go." He took a few steps after her. "Come on. We're in this together. You can't just leave."

"Watch me!" Tori turned back dramatically and then gaped in a panic. Pointing. "Someone's coming!"

Managing to sway my head to look right, I recognized his uneven gait, his energy, his bald determination. Dr. Finn.

I had texted him that I was meeting Tori on the bridge, but I wasn't sure if he would see the message in the middle of the night or come out when he saw it.

But here he was, coming to my rescue. Of course. Thank God.

Skittish and panicked, Graham looked both ways and cursed. "Shit." He flipped up his hood. "You two, forget you ever saw me. Say one word against me, and I'll have you taken out."

I tried to mutter that he was a turd, but it came out garbled.

Graham took off running, back toward Greek Row. When Tori stepped in his way, he bumped into her, knocking her aside.

"Where the hell are you going?" she yelled.

But he was sprinting off, a black shape growing smaller and smaller in the dim corridor of bridge light. He was fast. Of course. A soccer star.

A falling star.

Dr. Finn was the perfect person to weed through the bullshit on the bridge. He read the scene properly, seeing that I was debilitated, spotting the Taser gun that Graham had abandoned, turning a deaf ear to Tori's blubbering that she hadn't done anything wrong.

When there was no sign of Graham at the Gamma Kappa house, the police widened the search and posted a bulletin for his arrest. He was found a few days later when the manager of a Pebble Beach resort recognized his license plate down in California.

With Graham in custody, I think everyone on campus slept better. But I didn't mind the habit of walking with friends, especially after dark. One night when Dr. Finn was walking me home from a task force meeting, I made him go out of the way to stop on the North Campus Bridge. Snow was coming down, giving the evening a festive feel, and with Lydia's killer behind bars and just one final exam left, I was beginning to feel truly liberated.

The wind blew fine snowflakes through the air as we started across the bridge.

"I'll feel better when they get the netting up on this bridge." Dr. Finn gestured toward the view. "It's too gorgeous to be a suicide destination."

"And cameras are a good idea, too," I said.

"In the future, when the budget allows. Right now I'm more focused on getting the health center in line. For both women's health and mental health."

"Speaking of mental health, how's your crazy girlfriend?"

"Ex-girlfriend. Please. Thank you for asking, but I'm trying to maintain professionalism and keep her out of my work. After two tours in Afghanistan and eight years in college, it's not going to be a crazy ex-girlfriend that takes me down."

I smiled. He had apologized for her bad behavior a dozen times. Eileen Culligan had also called the administration to deliver lies about Dr. Finn getting romantically involved with students. He'd had a lot of explaining to do with Dean Cho, but he'd straightened things out.

We paused at the center of the bridge, and I opened my arms wide to catch snowflakes. "We live in a magical place."

"I want you to know, I think about your miracle baby nearly every day. When things go wrong, when the shit hits the fan, I can turn it off for a minute and think that there's a life out there because you did the right thing."

"You give me credit I don't deserve."

"Nonsense. You're my hero." He braced his forearms on the rail and leaned down. "You showed me something that was right under my nose. I'd been neglecting my son, hoping he would go away with Eileen. I've been self-absorbed. A navel gazer. You opened my eyes to things I can do to effect positive change."

"Wow. I'd take a bow, but really, you did all that yourself."

"The synthesis possible in human interaction."

"Um . . . big words mean little nothings?"

"You know what I'm saying."

"I do. I'm still on the fence about Theta Pi, rethinking what it means to me. A lot of good has come out of my involvement with the sorority, but there've been disappointments and moments of cruelty, too."

"True, but you've weeded out a few bad apples."

Although Tori's charges of aiding and abetting a murder were probably going to be reduced because she was testifying against Graham, she had been put on probation from the sorority and the university. I knew she wouldn't be back. The unofficial word was that she was planning to finish her degree at a small private women's college in San Francisco once her case was decided. Without her, Courtney was a lost lamb looking for someone else to follow. Violet didn't seem so cold and evil when she was operating on her own, but I wondered about the morality of someone who involved themselves with Tori.

And wasn't I guilty of that, too? I'd been her sister. I had tolerated her cruelty.

"I just know that I'm done with mean girls. Moving forward, my friends and I are committed to making Theta Pi a group of girls who operate from a place of kindness and who support one another's strengths. If that doesn't work, we're out of there."

"I hope you can make it work out."

As we looked out over the snowy ravine, I wondered if my brother was holding Rebecca right then. Or maybe she was in Amy's arms, working on a bottle while Amy sang softly or told her a story. I imagined Rebecca in a cozy romper, stretched out in her crib, blissfully asleep. Babies needed a lot of sleep; I had learned that quickly on the train ride north.

That strange morning in the gorge when Rebecca had come alive, I had searched my mind for anyone who understood babies, anyone who would be a good mother. I'd recalled my sister-in-law's tearful report of another failure with in vitro fertilization. "We can't afford another round, and it'll be a few years before we can save enough to adopt," Amy had told me last year. At the time I had felt her pain, but she'd been such a stranger to me and the problem had seemed too personal to discuss.

But that morning in the ravine, Amy's words came back to me. So I brought Lydia's baby to them and swore that she was my newborn. After that, I left it up to my brother to deal with the paperwork and legal matters of getting a birth certificate and adopting. Amy and Joe had been shocked but thrilled, and from their phone calls it was clear that the joy had not worn off.

Standing at the rail, Dr. Finn and I looked down into the dark ravine, a beautiful abyss beneath the dancing snowflakes. We had both come a long way since the night we met on this bridge. He'd been wrapped up with the crazy girlfriend, and I had been trying to make my peace with a death I couldn't understand. I had thought my stars were burned out and fading, but I'd been wrong. Today, tonight, we were just beginning to shine.

CHAPTER 40

Finn followed Wiley over to the colorful mural at the center of Pioneer Courthouse Square. The kid would run for three or four steps, then look back and howl in laughter when he saw Finn following him. Every time Wiley laughed, it was like he'd just heard the most hysterical joke in the world.

Bright, genuine laughter. Finn couldn't get enough of that.

Finn paused in tandem with his son, waiting as the boy turned back and roared with laughter. Good times.

At first, Eileen didn't want Finn to take Wiley for visits. She had seen Finn's involvement with the boy as a way to weasel her way into his life again. But Finn had asserted himself through his attorney, and Eileen had backed off. Within two "visits," Finn had realized that he didn't resent the boy when his mother wasn't around, harping on Finn.

He chased Wiley through the square for a good half hour, skirting around a musician, a homeless man with an enormous backpack, and a few other children who had come into the city to see the lights of the towering Christmas tree. On days like this he was grateful for the technology that allowed him to scamper around the square, playing with his son. When Wiley began to slow down, Finn swept him into his arms, blew some raspberries onto his neck, and carried him over to the curved steps where their new friend waited.

"Want some pretzel? It's still warm." Sydney Cho broke off a small piece and handed it to Wiley, who put it in his mouth and started dancing as he chewed. Eileen wouldn't have liked the idea of Sydney or any other woman spending time with her son, but it was just another reality of life she would have to get used to.

"Mm. Finn hungry." He tore into the pretzel and broke off a large section.

"You don't have to play Neanderthal to get my attention."

"That was my best Brendan Fraser."

"Not necessary. Scott Finnegan is enough for me." She smiled, and something inside him warmed. In her blue jeans, nubby sweater, and sunglasses, Sydney Cho was urban chic and adorable at the same time. He wanted to kiss her here in the sunny square, in front of the world, but he wasn't sure she was ready for that level of exposure. He contented himself with moving his hand to her knee. "Thanks for coming into town with us."

"No problem. I needed to get some hiking gear." In the same movement she gave Wiley another piece of pretzel with one hand and sank her fingers into Finn's hair, just above his ear. With a movement that sent shivers over his scalp, she stroked his hair back, leaned down, and kissed him. She made it seem simple, organic.

And she made it clear that they were on the same page.

She was just what he needed in his life: an economy of motion and drama.

When I arrived in Tacoma a week before Christmas, the station was trimmed with greenery, shiny ornaments, and starry white lights. It was the first time in my college career that I had my own place to go for a holiday, and the sight of lit candles in the windows of the row houses near the station brought tears to my eyes. In colonial times, those candles were a sign of welcome to family and travelers. Welcome home.

The sun was setting, but it was just light enough to make out the parking lot. Joe was waiting there, leaning against the fender of his truck. He waved me over, gave me a bear hug, and stowed my luggage in the back.

"This is going to be the best Christmas ever." He waited for me to get my seat belt on, and then backed the truck out of its spot. "Wait until you see Rebecca. She's hit all the two-month milestones," he said proudly. "She can hold her head steady, and she'll try to grab at that duck you gave her. It's like she's just discovering that her arms can work for her. She's amazing."

"I knew she'd love that duck." It was a ridiculous thing to say since Rebecca was just seven weeks old and how could an infant have a like or dislike in the toy world? Still, I beamed with pride.

"She'll suck her fingers," Joe said. "That's a two-month marker, too. And she really loves her pacifier. Amy is worried about her getting too attached to it, so we're doing some research on it. The pediatrician thinks it's okay, so I'm inclined to let her have it." Joe shot me a glance. "When you find something in life that takes you to your happy place, I think you need to go for it."

"Unless it's drugs and alcohol," I said.

"For sure! Hell, yeah. But it's going so well, and I'm glad you're here to spend Christmas with us."

"Me, too." I had avoided coming here for Thanksgiving. Back in November, I had kept my calls and texts to Joe and Amy to a minimum, afraid that someone would overhear and make the connection to Rebecca's birth mother. I'd lied to Joe and Amy about that, but I figured it was a lie for their protection. As everyone here in Washington believed I was the mother, there hadn't been a problem getting a birth certificate and giving custody of Rebecca to my brother and his wife. If the authorities knew she wasn't my baby, she would have been sent to child services and adopted by a family on the waiting list. Nope, nope, nope. I wasn't going to let that happen.

"See the boats out there?" Joe pointed toward the Sound, on my side of the car. "That's the holiday parade." The water of the Sound was black, almost invisible in the night, but small boats festooned with multicolored lights moved along in a line in the distance as we drove along the rim road. There was a boat with a pink flamingo and flashing palm trees. Another had a giant Santa face and Santa's sled full of toys.

"Very cool."

"We'll take Rebecca to see the parade when she's old enough. Maybe even next year. She'll be walking by then. Can you believe it? Most kids start walking at around twelve months."

"You've been doing your research," I said. "Good job, Daddy."

"Well, I had to hit it fast. Having a kid seemed like mission impossible for us until you turned it all around. I'm grateful, Em. I know it was really hard for you, and I don't want it ever to be awkward between us."

"And this is the last time we're going to talk about that part, okay?" I needed to move on from the past, and I didn't want Rebecca's roots coming up when Rory or my friends came to visit after Christmas. "You and Amy are Rebecca's parents now, and I think that makes her the luckiest kid in the world."

"Thanks," he said. "Auntie Em."

I smacked his arm. Brothers.

The porch of their tiny Victorian cottage was strung with blinking Christmas lights and a wreath was hung on the door, which opened as we pulled into the driveway. Amy stood in the doorway holding Rebecca, the two of them silhouetted by amber light.

My new family. I was *so* ready to be an aunt, a sister, a friend.

I ran inside to a big round of hugs. Amy offered to make me a latte with her new coffeemaker, and as she worked in the kitchen I stood at the counter and entertained Rebecca, who was strapped into her infant seat.

Sometimes her blue eyes were so enormous, so impossibly large for her little head. And her downy soft hair was pale and golden as a summer beach. That was one of the surprises of Rebecca. Right now she looked nothing like Lydia or Graham, who both had ebony hair and mahogany eyes. Ironically, she looked a lot like me. I suspected that Lydia had lied about the baby's paternity, too, and I hoped the baby's biological father possessed more of a moral center than the young man currently awaiting trial for murder.

But none of that mattered. She was now Rebecca Danelski, daughter of Amy and Joe.

"You are such a lucky little girl," I said. "Lucky ducky." I dangled the ducky above her, and her little face lit up with joy. Gaping mouth, bright eyes, pudgy hands. She was a bundle of wonder as she reached for the fluffy yellow toy.

"Are we having fun yet?" I asked, giddy with love. "Are we having fun?"

She chortled and kicked her little legs. I took that as a yes.

PRETTY, NASTY, LOVELY

Rosalind Noonan

ABOUT THIS GUIDE

The suggested questions are included to enhance
your group's reading of Rosalind Noonan's
Pretty, Nasty, Lovely!

DISCUSSION QUESTIONS

1. Every character in the novel possesses some sort of secret: something tender from their past that they don't mention, or something that they hold dear and reverent like their sorority ritual. Do you think that most people have secrets? What circumstances would justify revealing a secret?

2. Upon learning that someone jumped from the bridge, Emma sees sorrow ahead. "Even the suicide of a total stranger was going to be upsetting; I knew the ripple effects of a tragedy, the mothers, fathers, sisters, and friends who ached in grief as they fumbled through a world of loss. I'd been twelve when my mom and sister Delilah had been killed in a car crash that left me unscathed; I understood how the tragedy of a few seconds could impact the rest of your life." Can you pinpoint a moment or event in your life that changed your path or your perspective?

3. What did Lydia's secret life entail? What do you think drove her to create the mythology of a Greek business tycoon's granddaughter?

4. Suicide is one of the leading causes of death among college students in the United States. In what way does the Merriwether University campus lend itself to suicides? Discuss ways that college administrators might address this issue.

5. An old saying advises, "Keep your friends close and your enemies closer." How does that apply in Emma's relationship with "frenemies" like Tori and Courtney?

6. Emma's yearning for sisterhood was heightened by the loss of her mother and sister. What unfinished business

with the women in her family might have driven her to pledge a sorority? What details of her sister's death pushed Emma to research suicide?

7. When a female student gives birth in a college dorm, the event is often cloaked in denial and lack of medical care. Although there is sometimes a stigma attached to the student mother, some universities provide special housing for student mothers and families. Should a university make special accommodations for student mothers? What sort of policy should a sorority like Theta Pi have for unwed student mothers?

8. How does Dr. Sydney Cho grow through the course of the novel?

9. Before college, Emma is adrift, estranged from her father and brother. How does sorority life fulfill her need to have a family?

10. By the end of the novel, Emma has experienced the benefits and hazards of sisterhood in a sorority. What are the pros and cons of pledging a sorority like Theta Pi?

11. What kind of father will Finn turn out to be? How about Emma's brother, Joe? Do you think Emma's father, Gary, has the potential to connect with his daughter in the future?

12. What do you think the bridges in the novel symbolize?

Connect with Us

Visit us online at
KensingtonBooks.com
to read more from your favorite authors, see books
by series, view reading group guides, and more.

for sneak peeks, chances to win books and prize packs,
and to share your thoughts with other readers.

facebook.com/kensingtonpublishing
twitter.com/kensingtonbooks

Tell us what you think!

To share your thoughts, submit a review,
or sign up for our eNewsletters, please visit:
KensingtonBooks.com/TellUs.